The Tombstone Conspiracy

A Western Story

Other Five Star Titles
by Tim Champlin:

The Last Campaign
The Survivor
Deadly Season
Swift Thunder
Lincoln's Ransom

The Tombstone Conspiracy

A Western Story

TIM CHAMPLIN

Five Star
Unity, Maine

Five Star Western
Published in conjunction with Golden West Literary Agency.

Cover photograph by Johnny D. Boggs.

September 1999

Standard Print Hardcover Edition.

First Edition

Five Star Standard Print Western Series.

The text of this edition is unabridged.

Set in 11 pt. Plantin by Minnie B. Raven.

Printed in the United States on permanent paper.

Library of Congress Cataloging-in-Publication Data

Champlin, Tim, 1937–
    Tombstone conspiracy : a western story / by Tim Champlin.
— 1st ed.
        p. cm.
    "Five Star western"—T.p. verso.
    ISBN 0-7862-0998-4 (hc : alk. paper)
    I. Title.
PS3553.H265T66   1999
  813'.54—dc21   99-35659

For my son, Kenneth, and his wife, Jennifer,
with all good wishes for their future happiness

CHAPTER ONE

March 7, 1863
Northern Virginia

Brady Cox Brandau jerked upright in his chair, startled out of a doze by a sharp rap at the door of his hotel room. Instantly alert, with drawn gun, he listened for a second knock. It came. Then, after a pause, a third.

He exhaled with relief at the familiar code and shoved the long-barreled Colt back into its holster. He moved to open the door. A hooded figure slipped through the narrow aperture.

"I was expecting you earlier," Brandau said, twisting the key in the lock.

"Brand, the general wanted to party," the young woman answered, throwing back the hood of her heavy cloak to reveal lustrous, black, shoulder-length hair. "I couldn't get away until after midnight. Never saw a man who had such a capacity for champagne. Must have something to do with his upbringing," she added.

"He didn't suspect anything, then?"

She looked pained. "Of course not. The younger they are, the easier they are to fool," she added, with a touch of professional pride.

Brandau thought of Brigadier General Edwin Stoughton. At twenty-seven, the handsome Stoughton, who came from a well-connected Vermont family, was the youngest man in the Union Army to carry such a high rank. If rumor could be trusted, Stoughton was more interested in revelry than in fighting. A paper general who attracted women with the uniform, Brandau assumed. He himself was a captain at twenty-four, but he'd automatically gained that rank by raising and equipping his own company of mounted volunteers from his native Mississippi. After numerous battles, he brought them east to become part of Captain John Singleton Mosby's Partisan Rangers who were conducting guerrilla warfare on the Union forces in the Shenandoah Valley of Virginia and in the vicinity of Washington. They had become known for making lightning raids on marching columns of infantry, disrupting communications by cutting telegraph wires, and derailing and destroying supply trains and bridges.

"What about Colonel Wyndham?" Brandau inquired.

"He's in Fairfax now, but he'll be leaving at daybreak for Washington, Stoughton said."

"Too bad. Mosby would love to get his hands on that Britisher."

She looked her question at him.

"Personal grudge," he explained. "Wyndham's been lambasting Mosby in the newspapers. Called him 'a common horse thief' for one thing." Brandau pictured the out-size mustache and goatee Colonel Percy Wyndham affected and thought of a few things Mosby might call the Englishman, if it got down to personal insults. The English adventurer had served with Garibaldi and was now a commander of Union cavalry.

"There's a gap in the federal picket line around Fairfax County Courthouse," she said. "I can pinpoint it for you," she added, turning away and unfastening the hook of the cape at her throat.

"Allow me, my dear," he said in his soft Mississippi dialect, moving to take her cloak and toss it across the bed.

"It's chilly in here," she remarked, wrapping her arms around herself as she stepped toward the glowing coals in the grate. She took the poker and stirred the dying embers, then added two sticks from the wood box.

"Maybe this will help," Brandau said, coming up and wrapping his arms around her from behind, drawing her close.

"Ah . . . better," she purred.

They were silent for several seconds, watching the fire blaze up.

"Ann, this information might be what Captain Mosby needs. If he can snatch General Stoughton right from his hotel in a Yankee town, J. E. B. Stuart will almost have to cut Mosby loose with his own command of partisan rangers."

"How will this help win the war?" she asked.

"It'll demoralize the Yankees. If we can use the element of surprise and audacity and ride right into town during the night and kidnap that general out of his bed, along with any other officers we see . . . and maybe a few horses and guns into the bargain . . . it'll tell the Yankees they're not safe anywhere."

"What makes you think you can pull off a raid like that?"

"He's not guarded, is he?"

"No. Just an aide-de-camp and an orderly."

He nodded. "Just so. Mosby's banking on the fact that the Confederate forces are miles away, and Fairfax is so near Washington City and surrounded by federals, that they think they're perfectly safe." He smiled grimly. "They haven't yet felt the whipping that Captain Mosby and Captain Brandau can put on their pride." He turned her around to face him. "That's what being a guerrilla ranger is all about . . . hitting the enemy when and where he least expects it . . . striking the rattlesnake in his own den."

"This is just a game for boys," she sniffed. "I tell you where the other gang is hiding and how to get to them, then you go capture their leaders. I like it better when I can report troop movements so you can set a trap and wipe them out!"

He noted the gleam of her dark eyes in the firelight. Here was an eighteen-year-old girl who loved living on the raw edge of danger. If she were caught spying for the Confederacy, she would be hanged, regardless of her sex.

He'd been in love with her since they'd first met a year ago. But one thing needled the back of his consciousness and made him uneasy—her tendency to enjoy bloodshed. Nothing seemed to excite her like slaughter, especially when she could supply the intelligence that caused it. Her hatred of the Yankee invaders almost matched his own. Maybe that, in addition to her physical attributes, was what attracted him to her. He could understand her hatred, since she'd lost both parents and an older brother early in the war.

He wanted to ask if the handsome General Stoughton had put his hands on her, but somehow the question stuck in his throat. Maybe he didn't really want to know. He didn't want to think about what she had done, and would do, to coax information out of her victims. Knowing her hatred of Yankees, that could be just about anything.

"It'll be dawn in about four hours," he said. "Why don't you stay here and get some rest." He knew she had no permanent home, but only ghosted from place to place, offering her services to various Confederate commands, supplying intelligence information for a price. All the while she maintained a chameleon-like existence, wearing wigs and various disguises as she mingled with the high society of Washington's elite, attending dinner parties and balls, often on the arm of some desk-bound officer who had knowledge of troop movements in the field. Brandau wasn't even sure of her real name, although he'd always known her as Ann Gilcrease. And she had always called him Brand, whether from his surname, or a shortening of his nickname, Firebrand, an appellation hung on him by the men of his Mississippi company early in the war.

"Would I really get any sleep if I stayed here?" she asked, sliding a sidelong look at him from under her black lashes.

"Some," he hedged, smiling in spite of himself.

CHAPTER TWO

At ten o'clock the next night Brandau was still having trouble keeping his mind off Ann Gilcrease and on his business as he kneed his mount closer to hear what Captain Mosby was saying.

He felt, rather than saw, the group of two dozen horsemen around him in the dark. Thanks to Ann, the diminutive Mosby knew exactly where the gap existed in the wide, triangular picket line around the village of Fairfax County Courthouse.

"Keep closed up and no talking," the leader was saying. "Follow me and ride like you had business in Fairfax. If any of the pickets see us in the dark, they'll just assume we're a federal patrol. We should get there sometime after midnight, and I'll instruct you from there. Any questions?"

There was none.

"All right, then, let's move out. And remember, the success of this operation depends on surprise. If we're discovered, scatter and meet at the usual place Thursday night at ten."

The ride into Fairfax was a nerve-racking one for Brandau. The night was overcast and chilly, with mud and patches of leftover snow underfoot. The soft earth helped muffle the thudding of their horses' hoofs.

Among the raiders was a sergeant who had recently defected from the Fifth New York Cavalry and had intimate knowledge of the roads around the village. When the column was twice challenged by pickets, this sergeant replied, in his best Brooklyn dialect, that they were the Fifth New York Cavalry.

Because of Ann Gilcrease's accurate description and directions, Brandau was able to direct Mosby, who was riding beside him. They detoured off the turnpike and passed unobserved through the picket line about midway between a cavalry post at Chantilly and the town of Centreville. They reached Warrenton turnpike and proceeded to ride unmolested into the town of Fairfax County Courthouse where they arrived at the town square just as the clock in the tower was striking two. The few sentries stationed outside the hotel that served now as a hospital and the men guarding General Stoughton's hotel were quickly and quietly captured and disarmed. The corporal asleep in the telegraph office was taken into custody and the wire cut.

Captain Mosby reined up, dismounted, and rapped on the door of the hotel that Ann had informed them was Stoughton's headquarters.

"Who's there?" came the sleepy inquiry from an upper window.

"Fifth New York Cavalry with a dispatch for General Stoughton."

A minute or so later the door was opened by a man wearing only a shirt and drawers. Brandau grabbed him by the collar and in a hoarse whisper, said: "This is Captain John Mosby. Take us to General Stoughton's room."

The man suddenly looked wide awake and led them up the stairs without a word. He opened a door off the hallway, holding up the lighted lamp he was carrying. "There."

A man lay, face down, in the rumpled bed, snoring softly.

"General Stoughton!" Mosby said sharply.

The man didn't stir. Brandau saw two empty champagne bottles on the far side of the bed.

Mosby lifted the tail of the man's nightshirt. A sharp smack on the sleeper's bare buttocks brought the man quickly awake. "Get up and come with me, General!"

The befuddled man looked up with puffy eyes, "What is this?" he snapped. "Do you know who I am, sir?"

"I reckon I do, General. Did you ever hear of Mosby?"

"Yes, have you caught him?"

"No, but he's caught you."

The rest of the operation that night went as smooth as anything in which Brandau had ever been involved. When the outfit known as Mosby's Rangers rode out of town less than an hour later, it was in possession of one brigadier general, two captains, thirty enlisted men, with all their arms and equipment, and fifty-eight horses. They passed through the gap in the picket line as before and were safely beyond effective pursuit by the time dawn broke.

As a result of this coup, Mosby was promoted to major by J. E. B. Stuart, with authority to raise his own battalion.

Brandau was given the job of paying Ann Gilcrease with gold and a fine chestnut mare for the information that had enabled the raid to be so successful.

General Edwin Stoughton was imprisoned for four months, at which time he was released during a prisoner exchange. In disgrace and humiliation, he promptly resigned his commission and went back to civilian life.

During the last weeks of the war, Brandau saw Ann Gilcrease several times, noting that her murderous zeal for the Confederate cause only seemed to grow more intense as the chances for victory slipped away. She seemed to have an inborn instinct for the duplicity required to be a good spy. The ease with which she could slip from one identity to another, changing her name, her appearance, and even her dialect to become numerous different people, prevented the federal authorities from discovering that she was one and the same person.

Brandau continued to ride with Mosby who was seriously wounded three times before the war ended, and recovered completely from all of them, and wound up with the rank of colonel. When Lee surrendered, Mosby gathered his men and thanked them for their service. He did not surrender his command; rather, they simply disbanded and scattered into the hills and valleys from whence they had come.

After Appomatox, Brandau looked in vain for Ann Gilcrease—for that was the name by which he would always know her. But, with the cessation of hostilities, he was unable to locate her. After several days, he gave up the search and started by horseback on the long ride to his plantation eighty miles south of Memphis. He had the name and address of her aunt in Kentucky and resolved to pursue Ann once he had settled things at home.

During the three weeks it took him to ride from Virginia to his family home, he received the news of Lincoln's assassination. He had no love for Lincoln, but he did respect the man's adherence to principles. He saw the tall president's death as the breaking of a fence that held the wild dogs of Northern revenge in check. The enemies of the more moderate Lincoln would now come down on the prostrate South, he feared, with all the weight of a mace, exceeding anything that had taken place on the battlefield.

As he made his slow, sorrowful way south, through Tennessee and into Mississippi, scrounging food for himself and his horse, he saw the poverty and desolation of the countryside, both farms and villages. His own home place lay three miles back from the Mississippi River on a rise of land that was safe from any flood waters.

A soft, May mist was falling the morning he rode up the long carriage drive toward the columned mansion. He had not had word from his parents or his young brother and sister for months, but this was hardly surprising, given the disruptions of wartime communications and his own constant moving around.

As if in grim expectation of what he would find, he drew rein while still a quarter mile from the house and looked around. The grounds were completely deserted, the spreading cotton fields fallow. Spring growth was already greening the uncut undergrowth of past years beneath the maples and oaks. One magnificent magnolia still stood not far from the house. Of all in his view, it alone seemed unchanged. A corner of the upstairs verandah was collapsed, he suspected from cannon fire rather than neglect.

He clucked to his horse and moved closer, the chill of the gloomy, wet day penetrating not only his wool uniform, but his soul as well. He looked up from under his wide hat brim. The windows of the upper floor stood gaping, their sashes broken out along with their glass. The magnificent old house of his boyhood and youth stared out at him with vacant eyes.

Dismounting stiffly, he looped the reins of his tired mount around one of the porch supports. The brass knocker was missing, and paint was flaking off the front door that stood ajar. He pushed it open and went into the entrance hall. Bird droppings punctuated the layer of dust that coated everything. The huge, cut-glass chandelier lay in thousands of shattered fragments on the wooden floor. The banister was missing from the curving staircase.

With a sick feeling in the pit of his stomach, he turned

right and went into the library. About half the bookshelves were empty. Many volumes lay scattered on the floor near the brick fireplace where leaves had been ripped out to start fires. Half-burned spindles and splintered chair legs lay on the andirons. Numbly, he ran his fingers along the elegant leather bindings of Gibbons's DECLINE AND FALL OF THE ROMAN EMPIRE that still rested on a shelf. The irony seemed to flow out of them. "It's happened again," he muttered. "The barbarians have sacked our civilization."

The rest of the house was in a similar vandalized state. He wondered if he would find the graves of his family in the small burial plot a hundred yards behind the house. Before he even looked, he would have bet his horse and revolver that their bodies were not there. And he would have won that bet. The Brandau family plot held only the bodies of his great-grandparents and grandparents and a sister who had died in infancy, all the stone markers overgrown with weeds and creepers. He dreaded to think what could have happened to his family. He hoped they might have fled north to Memphis, or taken refuge with a neighbor—maybe the Newtons on the next plantation. He counted back and realized he had not had a letter dated since the siege of Vicksburg. He hoped with all his heart they had not gone there to be with his aunt and uncle and been caught in the futile starvation of that months-long siege. But, somehow, maybe they were still alive. The odds were against it, however. He knew it was unlikely he would ever see any of them again in this world.

As he walked back to the house, a glance and sniff at the well told him some dead animal had polluted it beyond immediate use. He would have to camp out tonight, obtaining water from the river. He could not even get a change of clothes from his own house since all the closets had been stripped bare. Maybe his family had taken the blankets and clothes when they fled, he thought.

In search of grain for his horse, he found only one sack of sprouting barley in the barn, and it had been ripped open by rodents. A few rusty, broken tools were scattered around in the dusty straw. A piece of rotted harness hung on a nail. Even the manure appeared to have been there a long time. The invading troops had either killed his family and ransacked the house, or his family had fled at the approach of the enemy. But, in either case, the lovely old mansion, built by his great-grandfather, had been ruined. At least, it had not been burned down like so many others he had passed on his way home, their blackened chimneys mute testimony to the hatred and destructiveness of war. But he had no money to rebuild and repair the place, even if he could prove that his family owned it. All he possessed were his horse, his Colt .44 revolver, the filthy, gray uniform he wore, and one five-dollar gold piece in his pocket he'd been hoarding for emergencies. He'd already heard rumors of Northern businessmen coming south to claim title to abandoned properties as prizes of war—claims that would no doubt be upheld by newly appointed judges that would soon be sitting in the courthouses of the region.

Too depressed even to reënter the house, he walked around, gathered some fallen, dead branches, and built a fire in the circular drive in front of the house. As dusk came on, he unsaddled his horse and picketed him to graze. Then he sat cross-legged on his saddle blanket, staring into the fire and listening to his stomach growl as he sipped water from his canteen. As the damp, warm night drew on and the crickets began their serenade, he heaped more dead limbs on the fire until he had a roaring blaze from which he had to back up several feet. The wet boots and wool socks were set a safe distance away to dry. The familiar odors of damp wool and woodsmoke enveloped him. But these things were far from his conscious mind as he drew his Colt and wiped the moisture from it, then checked his spare powder in the saddlebags. A deep, abiding hatred of all that was Yankee and Northern and arrogant began to fill his soul. He had not been the cause of this war, but he had fought in it, and against what he saw as the tyranny of those in the industrial states who were envious of his way of life—those who could not leave other people alone to live as they wished. It was the same with religious intolerance, he thought.

The more he pondered his situation, and that of many thousands of others he had seen, he resolved that he would not let it die here. He knew that harder times were coming. Many thousands had been killed and wounded on the Northern side as well, and the non-combatant politicians and businessmen of the North would blame the Confederacy. Greed and revenge would now be on the minds of those who had won. They would be overflowing the South like a Biblical plague. He didn't yet know how, but he would be ready for them. They would feel the sting of his fury. He would not be an unwilling victim. He would gather others around him who felt the same. They would resist; they would go underground. He had plenty of experience as a guerrilla fighter. *His* war had not been lost. This was only a temporary setback. He took a deep breath, seeing in the dancing flames the future for himself and those like him.

CHAPTER THREE

June 12, 1881
Mojave Desert, Arizona Territory

Lieutenant Ben Arnold was hot and tired. And he knew he was going to get a lot hotter and more fatigued before his escort detail of eight troopers saw these heavily loaded wagons to Fort Yuma, California.

He squinted at his men, riding the point and both flanks. The dusty hat brim was no longer protecting his face from the westering sun. He pulled off a gauntlet and scrubbed a hand across his wind-burned face. His unshaven cheeks felt like dry sandpaper. Would this desert never end? He was a year out of the Academy and had so far spent his entire military career in the Arizona Territory. Here on the frontier, where a month of experience was worth at least a year at some Eastern post, he considered himself a veteran of the ongoing campaign to subdue the Apaches. Therefore, he felt it his due to be selected to command this squad of recruits on the long trek from Fort Huachuca to Fort Yuma, California, just across the Colorado River from Yuma, Arizona Territory. He was especially proud because his superiors had entrusted to his care a load of ordnance consisting of a disassembled Gatling gun and several spare magazines, along with fifty-thousand rounds of ammunition. But most of the wagons carried a total of one-hundred and ninety-two seven-shot Spencer carbines, nestled in thirty-two wooden cases, thumb-screwed shut and government sealed. In addition, other cases in the wagons contained ten thousand rounds of .56-50 caliber rimfire cartridges for these repeaters which loaded through the butt plate with a cartridge tube. The M1865 carbines, made for the government by the Burnside Rifle Company, were long out of date, made obsolete by the fast-firing, Winchester lever actions. But they were still equal to the firepower of a battalion of regular infantry, who were presently equipped with the .45-70 single-shot Springfield trapdoor rifles. But Lieutenant Arnold had long since accepted the fact that the military minds of high-ranking officers were almost invariably conservative. This was especially true of those officers who held the purse strings and made decisions about "these new fangled jim-crack rifles."

But what was in the wagons was not his concern. Getting them to Fort Yuma was. They were nearly four-fifths of the way from Fort Huachuca to Yuma, he estimated. Even though he'd never been across this part of the god-forsaken Mojave Desert before, he'd been briefed about what to expect. And as the eight six-mule wagons labored up the rise to the pass in the Mohawk Mountains, some sixty miles east of Yuma, he rode up to the man in charge of the contract wagons. "Crocker, better pull up here and let the mules blow a little while my men and I ride on ahead and check out the spring."

The leathery teamster boss nodded and kneed his horse toward the lead wagon to signal the driver.

Arnold's hand-drawn map indicated there was a spring of good water in this low pass, next to the broken rock walls of an old, burned-out Butterfield stage station. The problem was, in this vast, arid country, everyone—Apache, soldier, and travelers—had to use the same life-saving water holes, so it was best to be sure no enemy was presently occupying the place.

He led his eight troopers at a trot up the sandy road past the wagons. Just as they topped the rise and came in sight of the ruins of the swing station, the westering sun flashed directly into his eyes, temporarily blinding him. Instantly, the pass was filled with the roar of gunfire, and Ben Arnold felt his mount pitch forward. The next moment, he was rolling on the ground, snatching at his holstered Colt. He yelled for his men to take cover and return fire, as he dashed for the cover of a mesquite bush several yards away, bullets kicking up dust behind him. As he slid to a stop on his belly, the Colt jumping in his fist, he saw rifle barrels belching smoke and flame from behind the broken rock walls. From the volume of fire, he guessed there were at least seven or eight men with repeaters. The blasts racketed back and forth from the sides of the pass, blending into one continuous roar. Ambush was a favorite Apache trick, and he'd led his detail right into it without taking proper precautions.

He had no time for more than a quick taste of bitter regret as he wormed his way into a slight depression in the hard soil and looked quickly around for his men. Most of them had been cut down in the first volley. He counted six bodies lying inert. Only two troopers were still returning fire from behind scant cover. Even as he looked, these last two pitched forward and lay still. He cursed vigorously under his breath and took aim at the top of a head that just protruded above the barricade. It was not an Apache. He drew a fine bead and squeezed the trigger. The hammer fell with a dull click on an empty shell. With the swiftness born of desperation, he punched out the empties and reloaded from the cartridge loops in his belt. In the minute it took him to do this, the rifle fire died. He lay still, hoping they thought he was dead. He'd lost his hat and was covered with dust as he lay squinting through the bush toward the stage station. He had no idea who these men were, or what they wanted. It had to be the rifles and the Gatling gun in the wagons. He hoped Crocker and his teamsters were crouched behind their wagons, awaiting the attack that was sure to come now that his protective escort had been eliminated. But he doubted their resistance would amount to much, given the concentrated firepower of those rifles.

He turned his head to look back down the road. It was nearly a fatal mistake. A rifle cracked, and he felt something hot burn the side of his face and sear the surface of his back like a hot iron. He gasped at the sudden pain and dropped his head on his arm. After a second or two, he realized the wound was superficial, but he could feel the blood soaking into the back of his uniform. He lay very still with his eyes closed, his breathing shallow and slow—he hoped imperceptible—to anyone who might be looking. Playing dead was his only chance.

He could hear men moving around now and some low voices. "Catch those damned horses, or shoot 'em!" a man's voice said.

Arnold heard hoofbeats and shots in the direction of the wagon train behind him. He held his breath as thudding footsteps approached. He sensed someone standing over him, and was aware of a man's harsh breathing. Then he felt something hard jar his ribs as if he'd been prodded with a rifle butt. He willed himself to be completely limp. He was still holding his loaded pistol, but would use it only as a last resort. For all he knew, the man might be aiming a shot at the back of his head right now as the *coup de grâce*. Any second might be his last. He prayed that the amount of blood he felt soaking his back would be enough to fool the rifleman into thinking he was already dead.

Just then he heard the rattle of trace chains and the grinding of heavy wagons.

"Charley, get on down the hill and bring up our horses," a voice commanded. He heard a grunt and the soft padding of feet jogging away from him.

"C'mon, hurry it up! Get these mules unharnessed and watered."

Arnold lay still for a long time, ignoring the burning where the bullet had cut along the surface of his back and buttocks. He heard men moving about, the shuffling of animals, the splashing of water kegs being filled from the well, snatches of conversation. It seemed an eternity. Flies began buzzing around the drying blood on his dusty cheek, but he gritted his teeth and ignored the tickling irritation. To move now would be to die.

Finally, he heard a whip crack, and a single wagon began to rumble away, followed by the sounds of many mules and horses receding down the hill. He didn't move until all sounds had died away, and then waited what he estimated was another ten minutes. He smelled woodsmoke and coal oil. Then he moved his head a few inches so he could look out from under the bush. The sun was down, and the pale sky was flushed pink and gold. Nothing but the wind rustled through the dry brush, and flames crackled as he counted seven wagons blazing where they had been halted on the approach to the low pass.

He got to his knees, feeling the stiffness in his back. Then he stood and went to the well, where he pulled up a bucket and sloshed some water over his head. Wiping a sleeve across his face, he turned and looked down the hill. One wagon and all the mule teams were gone. Apparently, the cases of guns and ammunition had all been packed on the backs of the mules, and one wagon used to haul the casks of water. Flaming wagons were lighting up the twilight, illuminating the scattered heaps that were the bodies of Crocker and his teamsters. Being careful not to silhouette himself against the firelight, he looked west and could see the wagon, the mule train, and the horsemen trailing a light plume of dust more than a mile away and heading southwest. Apparently they were not afraid of being pursued into the vast sweep of that burning hell that was the *Gran Desierto* in summer. As far as they knew, they'd left all witnesses dead.

He was puzzled by the direction the killers were taking as he watched them grow smaller in the distance. There was nothing in that direction but miles and miles of the worst desert on the continent—all the way to the Gulf of California and the whole peninsula of Baja California. It appeared the raiders were headed for Mexico across the worst wasteland he'd ever seen. If they made it, it would be a long, grueling trip. He had no idea who these men were or what they planned to do with the guns—probably sell them to some revolutionary faction in Mexico, who were always on the lookout to buy weapons and ammunition from north of the border to fight for one cause or other.

"Shit!" he exploded in frustration, staring after them. It had been a very smooth, professional operation. A ruthless operation, carried out by men who killed without compunction to accomplish their goal of capturing this shipment of weapons. Men as hard as this desert.

But the deed was done, and he reminded himself that he should be grateful he had escaped with his life. But he didn't know how long that life would last when he suddenly realized he was stranded afoot many miles from anywhere. Two horses had been killed in the hail of gunfire, and their bodies lay, stripped of their gear, thirty yards away where the buzzards were already circling, apparently wary of the creature that still walked upright nearby.

Arnold had neither the strength nor the tools to bury his soldiers, so they would have to lie where they'd fallen. He felt a little light-headed, probably from loss of blood, rather than the heat, he guessed. He stripped off his blue shirt, cringing as the cloth stuck to the clotting wound. At least, there was an unlimited supply of fresh water, he thought as he washed the wound as best he could. Then he washed out his shirt and trousers and put them on wet, amazed at how quickly they began to dry in the heated air. He had to have nourishment, and the only food available was the flesh of the two dead cavalry horses. He took his knife and sliced several chunks of meat from the hindquarters of each animal. He was not by nature a squeamish individual, but the warm flesh, and the heat and the flies around the fresh blood began to make him nauseous. He carried a block of matches in his saddlebags for starting campfires, but now all his gear was gone, and he had no means of starting a fire, so the meat would have to be consumed raw before it began to spoil.

"By God, if the Apaches can do it, so can I," he muttered grimly, as he sliced off a hunk of the juicy red meat and popped it into his mouth. "Hmm . . . not bad. Like rare steak," he said, trying to ignore the stinging sensation that was probably sweat trickling into the raw groove of the bullet wound on his back.

He ate his fill of the meat and then cached the rest under some rocks and had a long drink of water before he sat down to rest, his back against the ruined rock wall of the stage station. He doubted if there were any wolves in the vicinity, but the always voracious coyote would be at the carcasses before the buzzards took charge by morning light. He could subsist on raw meat and water for a time, and his superficial back wound would begin to heal. But how long would he have to stay here with his dead comrades and the teamsters? It was many miles to anywhere from here—sure death this time of year without water, and he had no containers to carry water. As long as he stayed put, he was relatively safe. And he could stay hidden and watch the approaches to the spring. He had his Colt and about sixty rounds of ammunition to defend himself, if it came to that. He might even be able to kill a rattlesnake or something else edible, if he really got desperate. It would be days before anyone came searching. He would sleep some distance away from the spring in the shelter of rocks and brush and take his chances with scorpions, tarantulas, and rattlers; they were less dangerous than the human predators he was likely to encounter.

It was nearly dark now, and he suddenly remembered to check the bodies for weapons or ammunition. The sidearms and carbines had been taken, but he collected another fifty-six rounds of .45 cartridges the raiders, in their haste, had overlooked. Feeling more secure, he moved off down the hill about a hundred yards and found a spot for himself to spend the night behind a thick clump of mesquite where he still had a clear view of the road leading up to the pass. If he had the strength in the morning, he promised himself, he'd drag the bodies off the road and pile some rocks over them. It might keep the buzzards off.

The pain and stiffening in his back and the turmoil in his mind kept him awake for hours. If he survived, he'd no doubt face a board of inquiry—maybe even a court-martial. At the very least, he expected a reduction in rank. He would never again be trusted with any great responsibility. But survival was the main issue at the moment. He put all future problems from his thoughts. *Don't shake hands with the devil until you meet him in the road,* his Irish mother used to say. He smiled at the memory. "Hell, I've survived this long," he muttered. "I'll make it the rest of the way."

Finally, sometime in the blackness of the pre-dawn hours, he slept from sheer exhaustion.

When he opened his eyes, the sun was just tipping the eastern horizon. He rolled over with a groan and sat up, feeling the soreness in every muscle.

A slight movement caught the corner of his eye, and he jerked back, reaching for his holstered gun. A saddled cavalry horse was browsing on the leaves of a nearby bush. One of the mounts from his detail had somehow eluded the bushwhackers! What a godsend! He held his breath and moved slowly. If he could catch him, his troubles were over. As he slowly moved toward the horse, the animal sidestepped, and Arnold noticed he was tied to a mesquite by a long tether. Before he could digest the significance of this, his eyes fell on the brown figure of an Indian hunkered motionless a few yards away.

Arnold sprang back, his heart pounding, and leveled his Colt at the Indian—an Apache by the look of him. He glanced quickly left and right, but there was no sign of any others. He knew, if they didn't want to be seen, their naked, brown bodies could fade into the landscape better than a desert lizard.

The Apache made no move, but remained squatting, arms hanging limply over his knees, staring impassively at Arnold. The silence dragged out until Arnold expected to hear the crack of doom. Finally, he could stand it no longer. "Who are you?" he asked, just to break the terrible tension.

It was almost as if the Indian had been waiting for him to ask.

"Rabbit," he replied, touching his breast lightly.

"Rabbit?" Arnold was confused. "Where?"

"Me, Rabbit," the Indian repeated.

Damned funny name for an Apache, Arnold thought. Maybe it was just some Indian word that sounded like the name of the long-eared rodent. More likely it was a nickname hung on him by some white men.

"Where'd you come from? What are you doing here? Are you alone?" Arnold rushed on, hoping that somehow this man could speak English as well as understand it.

"Find horse loose. Army horse."

"Yes. Yes. He's mine," Arnold nodded emphatically. "Where did you come from? Are there more Apaches around here?" He had not lowered his gun, but he was past his first heart-stopping fright and was noticing details of the man's dress. He was wearing a mélange of white and Indian clothing. Above the moccasins, he sported a ragged pair of blue pants with the crotch cut out and a breechclout hanging over the aperture. Two muscular arms protruded from a vest that was his only upper garment. A blue cloth headband held the straight black hair in place—hair that was chopped off more or less even with his jawline.

The Indian didn't reply at first. "Me live there," he said, sweeping an arm at the vast desert behind him.

"How did you get here?" Arnold asked, assuming he'd caught the cavalry horse miles away and ridden his back trail to this spring.

"Run."

"On foot?" He must have come from nearby. It seemed inconceivable to Arnold that a man would be afoot in this desert in June, even an Apache. He carried no container for water. Only a wicked-looking knife at his belt.

"You Apache?"

The man who called himself Rabbit nodded. "Rabbit bring horse. You have whiskey?"

So that was it. He was a reservation Indian who was addicted to white man's liquor.

"No whiskey." Arnold shrugged, then wondered if he should have been so hasty. If he had no reward for Rabbit, then Arnold probably had no horse. "We both ride to Fort Yuma," Arnold suggested, raising his pistol.

"No. That way." Rabbit pointed back in the direction from which Arnold and his wagon train had come.

"Too far. We have nothing to carry water in," Arnold demurred, feeling more at ease with this aborigine. Maybe the Apache *was* alone. Arnold didn't understand, but he was willing to accept the transportation fate had provided.

As he watched and wondered, Rabbit was busy gutting both of the dead horses that were swarming with flies. The buzzards were circling in the morning sky, awaiting breakfast. The Indian cut out several feet of large intestine from each horse, washed them indifferently in a bucket of water from the well, looped a knot in the end of each one, and, after hacking off the spikes of a nearby cactus, jammed them through the knot to keep the viscous gut from sliding open. Then he filled each one with several gallons of water. When he finished, he tied off the ends and draped one makeshift canteen over the horse's neck and the other over the withers.

He proceeded to take a very long drink from the bucket, then held it up for Arnold to do likewise. *Stoking up for the trail*, Arnold thought, tipping up the bucket and swallowing as much water as he could possibly hold. Then he led Rabbit to the cached meat from the night before, but the

Apache declined to eat. Instead, he watered the horse. "We go," he said, pointing east.

Arnold didn't argue. Perhaps Rabbit knew of hostile Apaches in the direction of Fort Yuma. He mounted up. "We'll ride double," he said, sliding over the cantle of the saddle and indicating the Indian should sit in front of him.

The Indian just shook his head and started off at a jog. Arnold kicked his mount into motion and followed. He kept his Colt in one hand, still wary of this good fortune. Maybe Rabbit was leading him into an ambush by several of his tribesmen and that was why he didn't want to ride double. There was no reason he could see that Rabbit should help him, except maybe for whiskey. He had a fleeting thought of just riding off with the water and leaving this self-sufficient Apache to his own devices. But he had to respect a half-naked man who could cross this desert on foot with no water, and somehow live off the land and survive.

As it turned out, the only reward the Apache wanted was a jug of whiskey which Arnold gladly purchased at the sutler's when they reached Fort Huachuca two nights later. The Indian refused to show his face in the vicinity of the fort, so Arnold rode back out a mile into the desert and handed the Apache the liquor. The Indian took a swig to test the contents, grunted, and disappeared into the desert night.

CHAPTER FOUR

Fort Bowie
Arizona Territory

Alexander Thorne realized his gray suit, white shirt, and cravat were entirely out of place in the heat of the Arizona desert mountains. And he could read those same thoughts in the face of General George Crook whose faded blue shirt, brown pants, and flat-heeled boots were anything but military. He wore no insignia of his rank, but the forked beard and hawk-like nose advertised the man's well-deserved reputation as an Indian fighter.

"Well, Thorne, what do you think you can do about this?" Crook demanded peremptorily, regarding the other with steady gray eyes.

Thorne found himself looking away from the face of the general in order to collect his thoughts. "Well, General, I've got a contact in Tombstone . . . an undercover operative for Wells Fargo. His company's gold and silver shipments are being hit, too. There may be a connection," Thorne replied.

"Did you bring any men with you from San Francisco?" Crook asked, striding around the living room of the commanding officer's house. He had not invited Thorne to sit down.

"No, sir. I operate better alone, and don't attract any undue attention."

"Humph! I suppose you've been briefed on all this?"

"Yes, sir. But I'd like your slant on it."

"You can talk to Lieutenant Arnold, of course, but the long and short of it is a band of about nine or ten men hit a contract wagon train loaded with Spencer repeating carbines and ammunition and one Gatling gun, killed all the teamsters and all the soldiers escorting it, except one. Lieutenant Arnold was wounded but escaped death by some miracle and, through an odd set of circumstances, managed to get back across miles of desert to Fort Huachuca to report what happened. If he hadn't survived, we'd likely be blaming the Apaches, since the hoofprints found were all from unshod ponies and mules, and the tracks were made by moccasins."

"Are there any gangs operating in the area that . . . ?"

"Gangs? Hell, yes there are gangs!" the general exploded. "The whole southern part of the territory, including that silver camp at Tombstone, is crawling with gangs. When they aren't preying on the stagecoaches and innocent citizens, or stealing cattle from the Mexicans, they're killing each other."

Thorne waited patiently for the tirade of the obviously frustrated general to subside. "What I meant was . . . are there any *particular* outlaw gangs who would be more apt to pull this kind of job and take on the military? Any that might have a market for those guns in Mexico?"

Crook shook his head. "None that I know of. Could have been anybody. They don't seem to specialize . . . just take whatever thievery comes handiest." He strode to a sideboard and decanted a small glass of amber-colored liquid and held it up with a questioning look.

Even though he didn't want it, Thorne accepted the brandy with a nod. Crook replaced the glass stopper without taking one himself. "Those guns might be in the hands of some Mexican revolutionaries by now," he continued.

"What revolutionaries?" Thorne asked.

"Hell, I don't know! Isn't there always some kind of revolution going on down there?"

Thorne let that go without comment.

"I invited you up here to the house . . . away from that office . . . so we can talk in complete privacy," Crook went on. "I think you know I'm a very straightforward type. Deviousness does not come naturally to me. I can deal with the Apache mind and use their own kind to help me break them down. But this is different. I'll have to leave it to your department. I have neither the time nor the patience to pursue these robbers and killers. Besides that wagon train, they've intercepted two government payrolls in the past two months. We're pretty sure it's the same men. They shoot all the witnesses and try to make it appear it was the work of Indians."

"I'll do what I can, General," Thorne responded, beginning to sweat in the close atmosphere. He set the glass down and shrugged out of his coat and loosened the cravat, then moved toward an open window where a breeze was stirring the curtains.

"Now you look more human," the general remarked with a smile, as he resumed his pacing. "You're one of Allan Pinkerton's men, I'm told . . . at least you started out with him during the war. Then you stayed on when the National Detective Police became the Federal Secret Service."

"That's right, sir. Served under Colonel Lafayette Baker in the beginning."

"So you've had plenty of experience."

Thorne nodded.

"Well, to each his own, I guess. That's why I'm here

trying to force Geronimo's followers onto the reservation for keeps."

Thorne had not expected to be interviewed by Crook, the commander of all the troops in Arizona Territory, but the general just happened to be passing through here, while the commandant of Fort Bowie was at Fort Apache for a few days.

"That's all, Thorne." Crook waved a hand of dismissal. "I just had to blow off a little steam. There's nothing more frustrating than an enemy you can't confront. But I should be used to that by now with the hit-and-run tactics of the Apaches."

"I think I'll have a talk with Lieutenant Arnold."

"You'll likely find him in the officers' quarters. He still on limited duty while he recovers from that wound. I presume you'll keep us posted on any developments?"

"Yes, sir," Thorne nodded, picking up his coat and letting himself out the front door.

As it turned out, Arnold provided little more information about the ambush beyond what Thorne already knew, other than to describe the setting and the direction the robbers had taken. One thing Thorne found curious was the lone Apache who'd shown up a few hours after the attack. Was it just happenstance that a half-civilized Indian, who spoke and understood a little English, had come out of nowhere with a cavalry horse he'd presumably found wandering in the desert and saved Arnold's life? There didn't seem to be any connection between the robbery and the rescue, but Thorne filed away this information in the back of his mind for later reference.

Before departing Fort Bowie for Tombstone, Thorne packed away his suit in his saddlebags and outfitted himself from the sutler's store in a pair of comfortable canvas jeans and cotton shirt. As he rode a borrowed horse and cavalry saddle down the slope away from the adobe buildings and toward the wagon road through Apache Pass, he wore one of his .45 Colts on his belt, instead of in a shoulder holster, while the other remained in his saddlebags. He carried nothing to identify himself as a Secret Service agent. As a cover for the horse's U.S. brand and the McClellan saddle, Crook had ordered a bill of sale made up for him. Reluctantly, the general had also provided Thorne with a false discharge certificate, stating that Alexander Thorne, Sergeant, age thirty-nine, was being honorably discharged from the United States Army. If he were somehow backed into a corner, this would at least provide him with a background he could document. His thought was to pass himself off as a newly discharged soldier, eager to speculate in mining properties or some other business venture in Tombstone. This would give him a reason to ask a lot of questions and do some snooping.

The Occidental Saloon never closed, but was experiencing its only lull of the day, just before the supper hour, when Alex Thorne walked through the batwing doors from the shaded wooden boardwalk. He saw four customers leaning over their drinks at the far end of a long bar. An aging swamper was tilting chairs against the round tables and preparing to sweep a liberal scattering of dirt and fine sand from the wooden floor. The walls and the front of the bar were painted white, giving the place a light, airy appearance, even without sunlight or the use of the coal-oil chandeliers.

Thorne had ridden the train and then the stage from San

Francisco all the way to Fort Bowie, and so was not used to the long day he had just spent in the saddle, coming down from Fort Bowie to Tombstone. As he stepped to the bar, he could already feel the soreness on the insides of his muscular thighs. He removed his hat and set it on the bar.

"Be right with you," the bartender said over his shoulder, as he leaned over a washtub behind the bar. A few seconds later, his head bobbed up, and he shook the water from his hands and grabbed a towel as he turned around. "Only slack time I've had all day to wash up some of these dishes and glasses," he said, wiping his hands and massive, hairy forearms. "What'll it be?" He looked up, and Thorne saw instant recognition in the eyes.

"Beer."

"Beer it is," the bartender replied, reaching for a glass on the backbar and placing it under one of the taps.

"How've you been, Paddy?" Thorne asked in a low tone.

"Workin' me backside off, and finding out very little," the big man growled under his thick, black mustache. "And yourself, Alex?" he asked, sliding the foaming glass toward him.

"Couldn't be better," Thorne said, tipping up the glass and draining it. "Another," he gasped.

"Man you've got a thirst I could hang me hat on," Paddy Burnett said, refilling the glass.

Thorne drank half of it before coming up for air.

"It's the climate," Burnett opined. "Sucks a man dry as a buffalo chip. That's why all the saloons in this town are doing a boomin' business."

"Good to see you again," Thorne said quietly. "Is there a place we can talk?"

"This is as good as any for now," Burnett said, glancing down the bar at the only four customers still in the Occidental. "We'll be gettin' busy shortly, though. You just get in?"

Thorne nodded, then quickly briefed him on his trip and his stop at Fort Bowie. "Any ideas who might have pulled that job on those Army guns?"

"Strangely enough, I haven't. And this is probably the best place in town to catch all the gossip. Even what gets leaked in the other saloons, like the Crystal Palace or the Oriental, usually finds its way here, too. I just keep me mouth shut and me ears open and ask a leading question now and again to set some drunk to talking. But, so far, nothing solid."

"Maybe some outside gang that doesn't frequent Tombstone?"

"Frequent . . . I like that," Burnett said, squinting toward the ceiling as if holding the word up for inspection. "That's one thing I like about you, Alex. You always had a great flair for the mother tongue."

Sometimes Burnett could be aggravatingly casual and joking when there was business to take care of, but Thorne just took another swallow of his beer and heaved a sigh. He knew the big man could get the job done in a hurry, when the time came. But along the way, the fun-loving Irishman wasn't about to take anything too seriously. *Maybe I could take a lesson from that, myself,* Thorne thought.

". . . Wells Fargo has taken some big losses, too," Burnett was saying. "In the past six months, the Grand Central Mining Company has filed claims for losses with Wells Fargo of just over a million dollars. That was, by far, the largest amount by any one company."

Thorne whistled softly. "Did they get *any* of their bullion through to the railroad?"

"Oh, yes. The Grand Central is headquartered in

Youngstown, Ohio. Its owners control not only the Grand Central, but the Leviathan, the Naumkeag, the South Extension, the Emerald, the Moonlight, and the Grand Dipper, along with many other smaller mines. They ship an enormous amount of bullion every month."

"Then it's logical they'd have the biggest claims."

"What are you saying?"

"A company that size is probably owned by several wealthy investors. Just trying to figure if maybe they're looking to increase their income by hiring some outlaws to rob the company's insured shipments and then splitting the take with them."

Burnett shrugged. "Possible. But how could you prove it?"

Thorne picked up a crumbling piece of cheese from the free lunch and let his eyes wander to a color poster on the far wall advertising **Cyrus Noble Whiskey,** and depicting a group of men bucking the tiger at a faro table. But his mind was not on the painting. Even if someone inside the company was setting up the robberies, that wouldn't explain the ambush of the ordnance wagons or the robberies of the military payrolls.

"I've been working here four months now," Burnett was saying, "and J. J. Valentine . . . me top boss in San Francisco . . . is beginning to get a little itchy for some action, or results, or information. I get the feeling he thinks I'm just enjoying meself here."

"What's the local law doing about the situation?"

"Well, not much, I'm afraid. Helluva mixed up political situation around here. Sheriff Johnny Behan has a couple of deputies I wouldn't trust to clean out m' cuspidors. He gets up a posse and goes out every time there's a robbery, but . . . he always comes back empty-handed, with some excuse or other. There're folks hereabouts who're thinkin' maybe he knows more about these stage hold-ups than he lets on. And I've about concluded they're right. Another one who thinks so is John Clum, editor of *The Tombstone Epitaph*. He and the editor of *The Nugget* have been going at each other in print. *The Nugget* supports the sheriff."

"What about these Earp brothers I've heard about? Isn't one of them deputy U.S. Marshal here?"

"You're thinking of Wyatt. He's been here since last year with three of his four brothers . . . Virgil, Morgan, and James. Morgan's the youngest, and a hothead. Virgil's steady . . . a good man, I'm thinkin'. James takes no part in politics or law enforcement. Virgil was appointed temporary city marshal since Marshal Fred White was killed by Curly Bill Brocius. And Wyatt was appointed Deputy U.S. Marshal by Rawley Dake, the marshal in Tucson, based on his earlier reputation as a lawman in Kansas. Wyatt also owns a part interest in the Alhambra. Runs a faro game there."

"You've got a lot of information on the Earps," Thorne commented.

"Well, they took a shine to me right off. They were meetin' the stage, when I came to town. Expectin' to see Morgan. They say I look enough like him to be his brother. Except for me build, of course. But that's how I got to know them. If you're thinkin' of askin' for their help, I'd recommend against it. I believe the fewer people who know about the two of us . . . me workin' for Wells Fargo, and you bein' a government man . . . the better. Besides, Virgil is the only one I'd put complete trust in. He's rock solid, in my opinion. But those brothers are a clannish bunch. If one knows about us, they all will. Next thing you know, we might as well advertise in the newspaper."

"I get you," Thorne said, draining his beer. "One more."

Burnett refilled the glass.

"Have the Earps got any backing?"

"Those who've had time to pay any attention are choosin' up sides. If it goes as far as gun play, there's a dentist named John Holliday who's a friend of theirs. Mean as a snake with the piles when he's drinkin', which is most of the time since he can't practice dentistry on account of his consumption. There was some rumor about him being mixed up in a stage robbery, so I'm really not sure which side of the law he's on. That's why I think it's best to steer clear of the Earps, since they've got associates like that."

"What's the other side look like?"

"From where I'm standin', a lot worse. A bunch of ne'er-do-wells who run with the Clantons. They call themselves 'The Cowboys.' Old man Clanton has five sons and three daughters. They have a ranch a few miles from town on the San Pedro River. The old man and three of the boys ride with the likes of the two McLaury brothers, Pete Spence, Frank Stilwell, Johnny Ringo, Curly Bill Brocius, and a few others. The names wouldn't mean anything to you now, I'm sure. Most of them have no visible means of support. The word is they've taken up stage robbin' because it's easier and safer than ridin' across the border and rustling Mexican beef to sell to the Army. But there's no proof, you understand."

"You think they're being tipped about which stages to hit?"

"Hard to say. One stage, each way, everyday between here and Tucson and one south to Bisbee three times a week. And damn' near every stage going or coming carries gold coin, greenbacks, or bullion, so they could pretty well take their pick and get *something*."

"Like bears in a salmon run," Thorne agreed. "With the

fighting of these two factions, I guess you and I can't count on much help from the local law."

"Ah . . . the truth, if I've ever heard it spoken," Burnett agreed. "Hell, I haven't told you the half of it. There's a lot more goin' on . . . from speculating on city lots to who controls the gambling and the collection of fines, to Wyatt and Sheriff Behan competing for the same woman. It gets complicated and very nasty. But, roughly, that's how it all stacks up." Burnett looked past Thorne to address the swamper who was still cleaning the floor. "Billy, when you get through there, wipe down the tables and light the lamps."

The last customers finished their drinks and walked out through the batwing doors.

"There is one thing that most of these robberies have in common," Burnett continued quietly. "But, for the life o' me, I can't figure out what it means, if anything at all."

"What's that?"

"At most of these stage hold-ups, the robbers have left behind one o' these." He reached into his vest pocket and pulled out a flat, wooden disk about the size of a silver dollar. Burned into one side of the disk was a circle, divided into quadrants by two crossed lines. In each of these quadrants was a tiny star. "Ever seen anything like that?"

Thorne shook his head, turning the disk over in his fingers. "It's not the brand of any ranch around here, is it?"

"Nope. That's the first thing the Earps checked out. No registered brand. *The Tombstone Epitaph* even ran a drawing of that design and asked if anyone recognized it. That was ten days ago, and nobody's come forward yet."

"Not the symbol of some fraternal or civic organization, either, I suppose?"

"Not that anybody knows about."

"Well, at least it's a start. Sounds as if it's the sign of

some organized gang who want to be known for their daring exploits. Many outlaws want to be given credit, even in some mysterious way."

"Just like Black Bart in California."

"Exactly. Leaves his calling card at every stage hold-up . . . usually a little poetry suitable to the occasion."

"Black Bart works alone and acts like a gentleman. I'm afraid we have a much more brutal bunch to deal with here," Burnett said grimly.

"Well, I've got to concentrate on the robberies of the government guns and payrolls," Thorne said. "But, it's possible they're all being pulled by the same gang." He finished his beer. "I've got to go get some supper and a room for the night. First thing in the morning, I'm leaving for the Mohawk Mountains. Maybe by starting at the scene of this ambush, I can pick up a trail."

Burnett whistled softly. "That's one helluva long way across the Mojave Desert. You goin' alone?"

Thorne nodded.

"The Army's already sent a patrol out to bury what was left o' their bodies. They tramped all around that area and didn't find much of anything. But, if I was you, I'd be more afraid of the weather than the Apaches this time o' year."

"You're not me. I'll take plenty of water."

"Can't carry enough for your horse, too."

"I've got some good military maps that show where the water holes are. You forget, I've operated in the southern California deserts before," he added at Burnett's skeptical look.

"Likely most o' them water tanks are dried up in midsummer," he muttered.

"Got any better ideas?"

"No. But I just hate to lose one of my best friends.

You've been living in San Francisco where it's always cool and damp. I'm tellin' ya, it's murder out in that desert."

Thorne had to grin at the genial Irishman's sudden seriousness. "I'm tougher than I look. Did you know I used to be nicknamed The Lizard?"

"Shit!"

Thorne flipped a silver dollar on the bar for his beer. "I'll be in touch as soon as I get back. Better give me about two weeks." Just as he turned away, he caught a glimpse of a lean, brown, half-naked figure that darted out of the rear gaming room to the far end of the bar. Thorne stared.

"Get the hell outta here!" Burnett said, seeing the furtive figure at the same time. "I told you about coming in here!" he growled in an irritated tone. He waved a big arm at the Indian who glided back into the gaming room toward the back door.

But Thorne saw the bartender grab a full bottle of whiskey by the neck as he followed the Indian out. *An expensive club,* Thorne thought. He didn't wait to see more as he pushed out the batwing doors and started for his horse.

CHAPTER FIVE

In spite of his casual attitude toward Burnett's concerns, Thorne took him very seriously when it came to challenging the desert. He still recalled with pain the trek into the southern California desert in pursuit of a major counterfeiter. Thorne had lost the fugitive and nearly his own life in the process. That had been five years ago, and he had taken his lesson to heart.

The horse he'd obtained at Fort Bowie was a long-legged dun that seemed to have plenty of stamina. As far as his own conditioning was concerned, he didn't smoke, drank only sparingly of nothing stronger than beer, and kept his weight to a lean one-hundred-and-seventy pounds on a frame of bone and muscle that was an inch under six feet. He was approaching forty, but felt he was probably in the best condition of his life. Married in his mid-twenties, he and his wife had not been blessed with children before her early death from typhoid fever five years later. He often wondered what direction his life would have taken had she lived. Unable to continue his job of tracking phony money in Washington after her death, he had requested a transfer to the West for a complete change of scene, and had been working out of the San Francisco office for the past eight years.

The next morning, he boarded the stage for Benson and through to Tucson, trailing his horse behind the coach.

He'd have plenty of time in the saddle, he thought. No sense starting any sooner than necessary.

Six days later, Thorne dismounted at the ambush site near the ruins of the stage station. The first thing he did was to water his horse from the well bucket. Then he took a long drink himself, amazed at how thirsty he was. The desert sun had sucked him dry without his even realizing it. Then he hobbled his horse and let him graze on some clumps of sun-cured grass while he sat down on a low portion of the stone wall and rested. It was shortly after midday by the sun, and what little breeze was blowing up the pass was like a wind from an open door of hell. From where he sat, he could see four of the seven wagons that had been burned and several mounds of dirt and rocks where the Army burial detail from Fort Huachuca had buried all the bodies, side by side.

After resting several minutes, he got up and made a thorough inspection of the site, pocketing a few of the empty shell casings he found inside the broken enclosure. They appeared to be from a .44-40 Winchester, a common enough weapon on the frontier. From the number of shells scattered around, the bushwhackers must have delivered a withering fire that quickly cut down the unsuspecting travelers. The ground was hard caliche, but scuffed up by the many hoof marks and boots of the burial detail. In a couple of sandy areas, he saw the prints of moccasins. If he didn't already know these were white men, the toed-out prints of their stride would have told him.

As he was poking through the blackened ruins of a wagon to see if the raiders might have missed anything, his eye fell on what appeared to be a coin on the ground nearby. He picked it up, and his heart skipped a beat as he saw it was the twin to the wooden disk Burnett had shown him—the mysterious symbol of the circle with the cross and the four stars. He doubted it'd been dropped by one of the dead teamsters. What, then? He could only conclude it had been deliberately left by one of the robbers. Thorne crouched on his heels and turned the disk over in his fingers. It was not scorched, so it probably hadn't fallen from the burning wagon. *The human mind was a strange thing,* he reflected. If one of the attackers had left this behind on the chance that someone would find it, what did the person hope to achieve?—recognition?—identification as part of a particular gang? They had gone to some trouble to leave Indian sign. What good was this symbol, if only members of the gang knew what it meant? Perhaps, after a time and a number of robberies, they would reveal its meaning, even if the individuals behind it remained anonymous.

He stood up and pocketed the disk. There was apparently nothing else left here to see. He would pick up the tracks of the mules and the single water wagon and follow them as long as he could. About three weeks had passed since the robbery—many days of wind and dust devils that very likely had scoured away most, if not all, of the tracks the marauders might have left. But this bunch was brazen. They would have taken no pains to hide their trail, daring anyone to follow where they led into the waterless reaches of the summer inferno.

He retightened the saddle cinch, removed the hobbles, and mounted, hoping that his four full two-quart canteens would see him through to the next water, wherever that might be.

It was three days and eighty weary miles later that he found himself on the vast reaches of the *Gran Desierto de*

Alter of Sonora, some forty miles below the Arizona-Mexico border. *Traveling at night would be preferable,* Thorne thought, squatting in the shade of his horse, but trailing at night was impossible. *Even the very devil would burn his feet in this place,* he reflected, squinting off across the flats where shimmering waves of heat rose from the baked earth and scrub growth. As he suspected, the raiders had taken no trouble about erasing their tracks. So it was no problem at first to follow their trail, even for an indifferent tracker such as himself. Long stretches had been erased by the wind where the tracks in the soft sand that overlay the hard caliche soil had been obliterated. But, by patient persistence, he had picked it up again, and then was as happy as someone working a puzzle, when he finds the right piece.

Only now did he realize the error of his eagerness. He had been sucked into a trap like a fly in a bottle. Once in, he could not find his way out. He had a pocket compass and his map, but now he was so far into this chase, it was too far to return, and probably fatal to go on.

He was in the *Gran Desierto.* Only one of his four blanket-sided canteens held any water—about a quart of the nauseous ooze he had strained through his bandanna. It was all that remained of the two quarts he'd managed to salvage from the bottom of the nearly dry Tule Tank yesterday some four or five miles due northeast across the Arizona border. He had easily followed the trail to the Tule Tank where the eighth wagon had been abandoned, and, apparently, the water kegs strapped to the mules. The tracks of many men, horses, and mules had ringed the natural rock tank that held only scummy liquid mud, alive with wigglers. The raiders had plenty of good water from the well in Mohawk Pass, but appeared to have stopped here to let the animals drink what they could of the remaining viscous fluid before moving on. He hoped they had not felt it necessary to poison the remaining water, but he couldn't be sure, considering how his dun horse had been acting. Of course, it was probably fatigue, heat, and thirst. The animal was about finished. He stood sprawled-legged, his head hanging. Thorne had not drunk any of the water he'd strained into his canteen, but had poured a quart of it into his hat for the dun about twenty miles back. The horse had been sinking fast ever since. Thorne knew he would be afoot soon, even though the dun carried a relatively light load. The Army McClellan saddle weighed only about a third of an ordinary saddle, and Thorne had been walking for the last thirty miles to save the beast as much as possible.

Still, squatting in the shade of his horse, he mentally drew a circle around his present position. Then he bisected this circle with a line north to south and another from east to west. Thinking of each of these quadrants in turn, he tried to determine in which direction was the nearest water and of his chances for reaching it. In the northeast quadrant about thirty miles away on the Arizona side were the Tinajas Altas Mountains, where there was very likely water still cupped in the hollows of several rock tanks. In the southeast quadrant was nothing but more burning desert. The southwest quadrant of his imaginary circle almost touched the Colorado River, and still farther south was the ocean waters of the Gulf of California.

He squinted his eyes against the maddening glare and looked to the southwest through shimmering waves of heat. He had a hard choice to make, and it had to be made now. The dun would never be able to carry him another step. Thorne had to make up his mind if he were still going to continue toward the southwest in hope of picking up the trail he'd lost somewhere eight miles back. The tracks had simply vanished beneath the blowing sand, but he had continued, hoping to pick them up later. If he gave up, waited for night, and made a forced march back, he could probably cover the thirty miles or so to Tinajas Altas and its life-giving water. From there, with full canteens and traveling at night, he could probably work his way back from water to water and on to safety. Even if he picked up the raiders' trail now, what could he do against several heavily-armed men with only his handguns and in his weakened condition? Walk up and ask them for a drink?

He smiled ruefully. Burnett had been right. It was a foolish venture from the start. Only his pride had gotten in the way. That, and the fact that neither he nor Burnett had the slightest clue of where to start looking for these robbers and killers. At least, Thorne had been on their trail for more than eighty miles. That beat sitting in town, waiting for something to happen. Since the trail was many days old, he felt sure the robbers had reached their destination and had cached the rifles or disposed of them by now. To continue on an old trail that he'd seemed to have lost, with no water, seemed suicidal. His thirst was—how had Burnett put it?—*something he could hang his hat on.* His stocky friend didn't know the half of it. His throat had become a burning, tortured thing, his mouth so dry no saliva had formed for a long time. His crusty lips were cracked. A sheen of sweat covered his face, but it was drying before it had a chance to drip off his nose. The resulting salt made him feel as if he were covered with sand. It was fluid he could ill-afford to lose.

How he wanted to go on! But he had reached the end of his tether. Yet, even as he looked through the shimmering heat waves that rose from the baking surface, his half-closed eyes picked up a series of dots, like widely spaced beads on a string. He felt his pulse quicken. Tracks. They seemed to vanish. He glanced away, then back, and there they were again, trending off to the west through the scattered creosote and scrub mesquite toward the lip of a sand dune in the distance. The Sirens were leading him on.

He took a deep breath and stood up. Maybe just a little farther, he rationalized, focusing on the tracks, and ignoring all else, especially his terrible thirst. His horse, with strings of saliva coiling from his mouth, gave a groan and collapsed on the ground.

"It's time, old boy," Thorne said aloud, drawing his Colt. He stripped off his damp shirt and wrapped it around the short barrel of the pistol to smother the muzzle blast. When he put the animal down, he was sure the sound of the muffled shot didn't travel more than a quarter mile.

Slinging two canteens over each shoulder, he started once again. He carried no rifle, but had packed a short-handled camp spade. The surface heat burned through the soles of his flat-heeled boots as if he were walking on live coals. As he trudged away from his dead horse in pursuit of his elusive quarry, he still held one ace up his sleeve. In this direction, about a dozen miles farther, was Laguna Seca, a dry lake bed that held water for a short time after rare cloudbursts or when an occasional tropical storm blew in from the Pacific. It was possible he could dig for water there. But a voice in the back of his mind kept reminding him that no water existed there most of the year, especially now during the hottest months. *That's why it's called seca—dry*—the voice insisted. It was almost like the voice of conscience. *This is not the rainy season,* the voice persisted.

He was glad he'd had the foresight to pack the spade. Did he anticipate digging for treasure? Or did he know, in the back of his mind, that he would be desperately digging a *pozito*—a small well—in the bottom of a dry lake bed, trying to find water to save his life? It mattered not to his fevered brain that was being broiled under his hat by the afternoon sun. The tracks he followed were leading in the direction of Laguna Seca, anyway.

Once, when about a half mile from his dead horse, he looked back. Black dots already circled in the pale, cloudless sky. The news of fresh meat traveled fast to nature's clean-up squad. He turned and plodded onward, one foot ahead of the other, numbly keeping the tracks of the heavily laden mules before him.

The sun finally slanted down in a welter of red and gold, with one last blast of fiery heat before sliding over the rim of the world. Thorne sat down to rest as darkness closed down quickly. He would preserve his precious remaining strength until the moon rose.

Some time later, the soft moonlight was lighting his way from a clear sky. The heavy blanket of heat had not dissipated, but the temperature had probably dropped twenty degrees, and the darkness gave the illusion of coolness.

He finally reached the pale dune that had looked so close earlier and started to climb, plowing ankle-deep in the soft sand. The deep mule tracks, sharply etched in shadow, angled away up the slope. When he reached the lip of the dune and started down the concave side, the tracks disappeared, covered by the blowing sand. He paused to catch his breath from the heavy exertion and was vaguely irritated that his strength was beginning to fail him. He was puffing like an eighty year-old climbing a flight of stairs. He leaned on the short spade, gasping, his heart pounding. By squinting his eyes and cocking his head to one side, he was able to pick up the black specks again, some eighty yards or more away where the land leveled out and the desert shrubs had not yet been smothered by the giant dune. He plunged down the steep side of the dune and picked up the line of tracks once more. After several yards, he paused and got down on one knee to examine them closer. Even where the layer of sand was still thick, the tracks were not as deeply depressed. He stood up, wondering. The mules had apparently been relieved of their loads. He turned and looked back at the light-colored dune that bulged thirty feet above the desert floor.

Temporarily unmindful of his thirst and fatigue, he retraced his steps and started up the steep side of the dune, using his spade as a walking stick, thrusting the blade deeply into the sand here and there at random as he went.

The spade thudded against something solid. He paused, his heart racing, and jabbed the blade in at several spots. Something solid lay buried less than a foot under the surface. He began digging and scraping away the sand until he had exposed part of a canvas tarpaulin. Working his way down to an edge, he brushed it clean and pulled the corner of the tarp back.

"Damn!" The moonlight revealed several wooden cases with the words **Property of the U.S. Government** burned into them. Using the blade of the spade, he snapped the metal bands around one of the boxes, then unfastened the thumbscrews. Lifting the lid, he saw three Spencer carbines resting in their individual cradles, and three more beneath them. He lifted one out, breathing heavily. The thick cosmolene coating glistened in the moonlight. He plowed around until he was certain that all the cases were there, including the ammunition boxes. He even uncovered one box containing part of the disassembled Gatling gun. He had found the stolen guns, but who had taken them, and why?

That question remained unanswered.

He replaced the carbine, screwed down the lid, flipped the tarp back over the boxes, and shoveled the sand back over it all, smoothing out all the markings with his hat as he backed away. Now that he had found the stolen weapons, was he to die in this place, unable to get back to report his discovery? The odds were certainly long against him, he thought as he went on down the dune and started once again in the general direction of Laguna Seca.

About three hours later, the wide, shallow depression, with its cracked mud surface loomed up ahead of him. The dry lake bed. He stumbled down into it, surprised at the weakness of his legs. He skirted the edge of the dusty bowl, seeking what seemed to be the lowest level. The moon was nearly gone now. He paused at a deeper depression where some dusty, desert tamarisks grew just above him, near the lip of the depression. These plants still clung to life, their roots thrusting deep into the dry soil for moisture. *It would have to be this spot or none at all,* he thought as he jabbed the spade deeply into the sandy earth. For several minutes no sound was heard, but the soft slurring of the metal spade against sand and loose soil and his own harsh breathing. The hole went down a foot, then two feet. He paused, sweat dripping from his face, his chest heaving. He climbed up the bank to determine whether he could feel a breeze. There was none. The heat lay like a dark blanket over the moonless landscape.

Suddenly, somewhere off in the middle distance, he thought he saw a spark of light. Then it was gone. Had he really seen something or was it his imagination? If he'd been in a more humid Eastern climate, he would have taken it for a firefly, but there was no such thing here. The moon was down, so it could not have been its light reflecting off a piece of mica. No. It had to be man-made. He watched for two or three more minutes, while his breathing steadied, but did not see it again.

He climbed back down and resumed his digging. The hole was down to more than three feet now, and he had to widen it to keep the sand from collapsing back and filling in to what he had just scooped out. He began to fear that this was a futile exercise, but it was the only hope he had. He sat down on the edge of the hole and considered drinking the last quart of smelly water that remained from the Tule Tank. He unscrewed the canteen and tipped it to his lips. The water was so vile that he could only take one small swallow. His raging thirst commanded him to gulp the rest of it, but he resisted. Even if he could get this stuff down, his stomach would likely reject it. He set the canteen aside and resumed his digging, thinking that, maybe, he was excavating his own grave.

The consistency of the sand in the bottom of the hole seemed to change slightly. He squatted and thrust his fingers into it. Did it feel damp? Maybe it was just cooler. He dug out several more spadefuls. He felt again with his hands. There was a slight seepage, and then the sand dissolved into precious water as the liquid quickly began to fill the bottom of the hole around his boots. He breathed a prayer of thanks, grabbed an empty canteen, and submerged it in the water that was now several inches deep. Yanking off his bandanna he rinsed it in the water, then placed it over the mouth of a second canteen and began to strain water into it.

He had filled one container, capped it, and was reaching for the second, when the sound of a voice chilled him to his toes.

"Ah, *señor*, a hot job, this digging. No?"

A darker blackness loomed above the hole where he squatted. He could smell woodsmoke and sweat from the man who spoke. He had been so intent on the water, he had not heard the footfalls in the soft, sandy soil.

"Is it treasure you look for, away out here in the desert?" the oily voice asked, then chuckled.

Thorne stood up slowly. He dared not reach for his holstered Colt, or its twin in the leather-lined side pocket of his jeans. He was reasonably certain that the speaker had a gun pointed at him, probably less than three feet away.

"What do you call yourself?" a second voice asked in Spanish from several yards to one side. A match flared and the farther man lighted a *cigarillo*. In the brief glare Thorne saw the lean, dark face of a Mexican.

"How about a drink of water?" Thorne asked, leaning his buttocks against the side of the hole. He noted the outline of the figure above him was barely discernible as the sky began to pale slightly with the coming dawn.

"Ah, you are thirsty? We have water and you can have a drink . . . as soon as you tell us who you are, and who sent you here." The voice was hard-edged now, no longer mocking.

"It was such a beautiful night, I thought I'd take a moonlight ride," Thorne replied.

"Don't play the fool with me, *señor!*" the unseen man snapped. "We found your horse dead several miles back and have been following you."

So the spot of light Thorne had seen had been perhaps one of the men lighting a smoke in the distance.

"Get out of that hole. You won't find any water in that *pozito*," the voice said. "Paco, get his gun."

"But of course, Carlos," the second man said, sliding up behind Thorne and reaching down to slip his ivory-handled

Colt from its holster. Thorne was thankful he'd had a tailor in Tombstone sew on the extra heavy pocket to carry the twin of that revolver on the left side.

"I will ask you only once more . . . what are you doing out here on the *Gran Desierto* this time of year?"

"Riding south to San Ignacio," Thorne lied, thinking suddenly of the name of a village to the southwest that was a haven for outlaws and killers of all kinds.

"That is on the Colorado River. Why didn't you take a riverboat? No man crosses this desert in summer."

"I had no money. Besides, you are here," he bluffed.

"We have business. What is yours?"

Thorne had conveniently ignored the order to climb out of the hole. The slowly pearling sky began to silhouette the figure standing above him. Thorne saw no reason for evasion. These men intended to kill him, no matter what he answered.

"You came here looking for something, perhaps?" The Mexican was beginning to lose patience. "I want an answer quickly, and I want it honest!" he snapped.

"Yes, I came looking for something," Thorne answered. "And I found it. Are you *hombres Rurales* or *Federales?*"

A harsh laugh was his answer. "You tell me who sent you, and I kill you quickly. If not . . . the Apaches have taught us many tricks of keeping a man alive for hours . . . screaming."

In the distance, Thorne saw a speck of light. The faint stirring of a dawn breeze brought the flutter of hoofbeats. He was expecting no help. It was likely more men like these. He had to make a move quickly. "I found the cache of rifles and ammunition," Thorne said, shifting his position to get both hands on the spade he still held.

"And who sent you to find them?"

"They are worth a lot of money to certain groups here in Mexico."

"Who sent you after them?"

"I came alone."

"You didn't expect to carry them back on your one horse we found shot back there. Who were you reporting to?"

Thorne took a deep breath. The sounds of the riders were closer. He saw eight or nine horsemen ride over the lip of the Laguna Seca, less than a half mile away. One of the riders yelled something in Spanish. The man above the hole instinctively turned his head toward the sound. In that instant of inattention, the spade came up in one swift motion, its blade chopping the underside of the gun arm. The pistol flew out of his grasp as the man yelled in surprise and pain.

Thorne crouched and spun in the hole, drawing his other Colt from the leather-lined pocket with his left hand. A shot exploded from Paco, and a slug burned across the back of his left hand. Paco never got off another shot since Thorne dropped him with a bullet in the chest. He whirled and fired a second shot into the closer man. The body swayed and fell forward across the hole.

Thorne shoved him out of the way and scrambled up, retrieving his other gun from the dead Paco's hand. The riders had heard the shots, seen the flashes, and were riding hard toward him. He ran to his attackers' two horses, some thirty yards away, and yanked their reins loose from some scrub bushes. He leapt into the saddle, holding the reins of the second horse, and kicked his mount into motion.

Shots and yells sounded behind him. He galloped straight north, firing back over his shoulder until one revolver was empty. Then he holstered it and leaned over his horse's neck, concentrating on outrunning his pursuers. A clear day was dawning.

By the time it was fully light, the horsemen were far back on the desert. And, when the sun tipped the horizon, they had given up the chase and were nothing but black specks in the distance.

Thorne pulled up, switched to the led horse, uncapped one of the big canteens that hung from the pie-shaped saddle horn, and had himself a long drink. And then another.

"Heaven couldn't be much better than this," he murmured aloud, as he kicked his horse into a trot and rode toward the border.

CHAPTER SIX

Alex Thorne cut into the fried steak the waiter at the Shoo-Fly Restaurant had just set before him and grinned across the table at Paddy Burnett.

"Alex, m'lad, you look god-awful!" Burnett blurted out.

Thorne managed a weak grin through cracked lips. "You know how to cheer a man up. Actually, I'm feeling a lot better than when I hit town. It's amazing what a good night's sleep in a real bed will do for a man's outlook on life."

"You look like you've lost at least fifteen pounds."

To Burnett, a man's general health could be gauged by the poundage he carried. If a man didn't stay beefed up, he'd have no reserves to fall back on when he got sick.

"Probably have. But I'll be back to normal in a few days."

"You're damned lucky to be here at all," Burnett said with no trace of humor.

"Absolutely," Thorne agreed around a mouthful of food. "But a man has to make his own luck now and again. If I'd turned back, when I ran out of water or my horse gave out, I'd never have stumbled onto those guns."

Burnett nodded. "Well, I warned you about that desert in summer," he said, sliding his chair back and crossing his legs. He held up his empty coffee cup to signal the waiter. "What did General Crook think of your report?"

Thorne had ridden straight to Fort Huachuca where he'd found the general in consultation with the post commander, and had turned in the two captured Mexican horses and saddles for another cavalry mount.

"He couldn't have been happier . . . at first. He had no idea I'd run 'em down this quick." He paused to butter a piece of bread. "Problem is, the guns have probably been moved by now, since I got away to report their whereabouts. The general knows he can't send a company of troops down there with wagons to retrieve them, anyway, without the permission of the Mexican government. Since we don't have any idea who stole them, he can't even lodge a protest with the Mexican officials. Besides that, the Mexican government will deny responsibility for every gang of *bandidos,* both Anglos and Mexicans, who are raiding and murdering on both sides of the border with little opposition."

"So you nearly got yourself killed for nothing," Burnett said.

"About the size of it." Thorne took a bite of mashed potatoes and gravy. "You heard anything here?"

"The stage coming down from Benson was robbed four days ago."

Thorne looked up sharply.

"Got the payroll for the Toughnut and Contention Mines. Several thousand dollars."

"How did they know?"

"It was pretty much common knowledge around town."

"Anybody hurt?"

"Shotgun guard was cut down, first thing. But it wasn't the real guard. It was Bud Philpot, the driver, who had a bellyache and had switched places with the guard a couple miles this side of Benson. It's caused an uproar in this town. It's one thing to steal money . . . even money that was to pay

61

these hard-working miners. But to gun down Philpot. . . . He was one of the most popular men in these parts. There've been a lot of accusations flying back and forth in the newspapers. The *Nugget* editor accuses Doc Holliday and the Earps of having some hand in it, and John Clum at the *Epitaph* accuses the Clantons and the cowboys who ride with them."

"But no proof either way?"

Burnett shook his head.

"Didn't find one of these at the scene?" Thorne asked, tossing the wooden disk with its cryptic symbol onto the table.

"Nope. Either they didn't leave one, or it's a different bunch."

Thorne wiped his mouth with a napkin and pushed back from the table.

"You're not going to finish that steak?"

"Stomach's shrunk, I guess," Thorne replied.

"Do you mind?"

"Go ahead."

Burnett pulled the plate toward him and speared a small piece of meat with a knife. Wasting food, to him, was as serious a sin as robbing the poor, Thorne thought.

A few minutes later they were outside on Allen Street.

"Well, where do we go from here?" Burnett asked as they moved down the boardwalk. "Damn, I hate to go to work. I'm getting mighty sick of taking orders from loud-mouthed drunks, just on the chance of picking up some information. It hasn't worked so far. Think maybe I'll take a couple days off and ride down to Charleston, about ten miles from here. A lot of the cowboys hang out at J. B. Ayers's saloon there. Most o' those lads know me, so I won't attract any attention. Might pick up some loose talk there that could help us."

"I think I'll rest up another day, and, then, see if I can figure out my next move," Thorne said.

"Julie!" Burnett called suddenly, his whole demeanor changing. He waved to a woman across the street. "Come here." He turned to Thorne and said: "I want you to meet someone."

Before they could move, the woman crossed the wide, dusty street toward them, carrying a parasol in one hand and daintily lifting her skirts away from the piles of manure with the other.

Burnett was beaming as she approached. "Julie Ann Martin, I'd like you to meet a friend of mine, Alex Thorne."

Thorne touched his hat. "It's a pleasure." He nodded.

"Mister Thorne," she acknowledged, dropping her eyes coyly. Her wavy dark hair fell, unbound, around her face.

"Julie works as a faro dealer at the Crystal Palace," Burnett said. "She and I rode into town on the same stage a few months ago," he explained. "We've been seeing each other," he added.

"You might say that," she cooed in a soft drawl, giving Burnett a look that implied much more than she said. "Paddy, dear, I've got the evening off. Why don't you take me over to the melodrama at the Mining Exchange Club. Eddie Foy is playing."

"I'd really like to, Julie, but I've got to work tonight. Our third bartender has come down with a bad case of the grippe. . . ."

"Well, all right, if that's the way you feel about it," she pouted, staring off down the street.

Thorne thought she was reacting like a temperamental school girl.

"Maybe I could see you later tonight," Burnett suggested hopefully.

"No. You don't get free until after two in the morning. I'll be in bed asleep by then." She turned to Thorne. "Perhaps your friend, Mister Thorne, could take me."

"Well. . . ." Thorne looked at his friend. "If Paddy doesn't mind." He couldn't think quickly enough to sidestep this situation.

"My big bear of a man doesn't care. Do you, dearest?" She patted his ample midsection.

Burnett managed a sickly grin. "No, go right ahead. You got anything to do, Alex?"

Thorne shook his head. There was no escaping the invitation. "Be glad to escort so beautiful a lady. What time is the show?"

"Seven-thirty," she said. "Why don't you pick me up at the Crystal Palace about seven?"

"Seven it is," Thorne said, smiling.

She slanted her gray eyes at both men, then glided away down the sidewalk.

"I have to go on duty in ten minutes. Come on and have a beer before you go," Burnett said.

The Occidental was not as crowded and smoky, Thorne noted with satisfaction. Three men were playing faro in the game room, while two others looked on. A three-handed poker game was quietly in progress at one of the tables. He knew things would be picking up in an hour or so.

Burnett tied on his apron, dipped two fingers into a jar of wax, and smoothed his walrus mustache in the backbar mirror. "I'm here, Swain," he nodded to the other bartender he was relieving.

Thorne, who was leaning on the bar, had just taken the first swallow of his beer, when the batwing doors flew open and three men clumped in, spurs jingling.

"Gaw-damn, that was a hot, dirty ride. I need something

64

to cut the trail dust out of my throat!" one of them almost shouted. "Whiskey! And draw me a beer chaser."

The three men bellied up to the bar near Thorne, ignoring him.

"Get your fat ass over here and give us some service!" a second man ordered, when Burnett didn't move fast enough to suit him.

Thorne saw Burnett's jaw muscles working as he moved to comply, saying nothing. He set down three shot glasses, but, as he started to pour, the first man snatched the bottle out of his hand and sloshed the three glasses full, spilling whiskey on the polished surface of the bar. As they knocked back their drinks, Burnett was drawing off three beers from a tap.

Thorne took them in at a glance. They were all dressed as wranglers, two of them wearing leather chaps over their canvas jeans. All wore vests and light blue or white shirts and sweat-stained, dusty hats, which two of them had thrown down on the bar.

The leader grabbed the beer and downed it in three or four long gulps.

"*Whew!*" He banged down the foam-streaked glass. "I needed that!" He drew a sleeve across a sweating, sunburned face and turned to view the room. His dilated, bloodshot eyes indicated The Occidental was not his first stop.

"We just sold a herd in Benson for top dollar," he announced. "Drinks are on me! Everybody!" He pulled a deerskin pouch from his pants pocket and several gold coins rang on the bar.

There was a general hubbub as the six men, including the dealer, deserted the faro table and crowded up with back slaps and congratulations as they ordered their drinks.

Another round was ordered. Even two of the three men at the poker table got up to take advantage of the free drink offer.

Thorne edged away unobtrusively, eyeing the three cowboys. Burnett was kept busy for a couple of minutes, pouring drinks and drawing beers. When he got a break, he moved toward Thorne.

"The curly-haired one with the goatee," he whispered through his heavy mustache, "that's Ike Clanton, the old man's eldest. The one to this side, with the mustache and thinning topknot, is Pete Spence, and the young fella on the far side with the black hair is Frank Stilwell."

"Are they actually in cattle ranching?"

"Yeah. But I think they're also into changing a few brands and writing up their own bills of sale as proof of ownership."

"Hmm. . . ."

"Let me put it this way . . . several of the ranchers in northern Sonora don't have to worry about what to do with any extra stock that might be roaming their ranges."

"So an honest day's work isn't really on their schedule."

"Right. Whatever profit comes easiest to hand. They're not too particular."

Thorne looked toward the poker table at the only man in the room who was still seated. From across a space of twenty feet, Thorne felt the man's piercing glare that was directed toward the group at the bar. Even sitting down, the man at the table appeared somewhat short and slight of build under the dark suit. With dark hair, mustache, and regular features, he was rather handsome, but Thorne could almost feel the taut, fierce energy radiating from him. The pallor of his face indicated too many hours indoors, common among professional gamblers.

Thorne looked his question at Burnett.

"That's Doc Holliday," he replied quietly.

Then Thorne noticed the telltale marks, as if someone had rubbed a faint spot of rouge on each of the lean cheeks. Consumption.

Holliday folded the cards in his hands and laid them, face down, on the table.

"You interrupted my game," Holliday said in a surprisingly forceful voice.

The men at the bar continued their animated conversations.

"You interrupted my game," Holliday said again, cutting through the babble of voices. "And I'm holding the best hand I've had today."

The men gradually stopped talking and turned to look at him. Ike Clanton leaned his back against the bar and hooked a boot heel over the brass rail. "Now isn't that too damned bad," he said belligerently. "It's not my fault, if your friends would rather drink free than play poker with you."

Stilwell and Spence chuckled.

"You son-of-a-bitch, you've been pushing me for a long time," Doc said in a deadly even tone, his hands sliding down off the table.

"Don't call me any names, you damned lunger," Clanton replied, his weathered face getting redder.

"You talk pretty big for a man who's not heeled," Doc replied.

Clanton spread his vest to show that he was, indeed, unarmed. "If you didn't have a gun under that table, I'd wipe this floor up with you," he said.

"Then, let your two friends have a go at me," Doc replied.

Spence and Stilwell, who both wore holstered weapons at their hips, made no move.

Several seconds of tense silence followed. Thorne was aware that Burnett's hand slid down under the bar.

"Your argument's not with them, Doc," Ike Clanton finally said in a less abusive tone.

"It's with all of you damned cowboys," Doc retorted.

Anticipating fireworks, the men at the bar began sidling away from the three cowboys.

Out of the corner of his eye, Thorne saw someone appear behind the batwing doors, then disappear without entering.

"You and those gaw-damn Earps think you run this town," Ike said, heating up again. "But I've got news for you. This was a cowboy town before any of you showed up, and it's gonna stay that way."

"Don't bring my friends into this, when they're not here," Doc said, putting his right hand on the table once more, this time gripping a .38 nickel-plated Colt Lightning.

Using Thorne to shield his movement, Burnett brought the double-barreled shotgun to bear across the bar.

"That's enough, Doc," the bartender said, thumbing back both hammers. The clicking was loud in the silence. "There's not going to be any more trouble in here today. Put it away. Have a drink and cool off."

Holliday glared at Burnett, and then back at Clanton. Nobody moved. Thorne found himself holding his breath, ready to dive for the floor in an instant.

"I'm not fooling, Doc," Burnett said. "You or anybody else who starts anything is gonna get both barrels."

Doc stood up slowly, still holding his gun. "I assume you gentlemen have thrown in your hands," he addressed the poker players. "So I'll claim the pot." He shoved the ivory-handled pistol back into the crossdraw holster at his belt.

Then he took his hat from a nearby chair and, in one sweeping move, raked the small pile of bills and coins into it, scattering wooden chips on the floor. He backed toward the door. "If you gentlemen will excuse me, I think I'll do my drinking at the Alhambra. Something stinks in here." He shouldered his way out the swinging doors and was gone.

Thorne let out a long breath. The tension was broken, and the murmur of voices started again. Burnett let down the hammers of the shotgun and stashed it below the bar.

"That was a near thing," Thorne muttered to Burnett.

"It's happened before," Burnett shrugged. "And it will probably happen again, until there's nobody around to stop it."

Just then a tall figure blocked the fading light from the doorway, and the town marshal, Virgil Earp, came in, hand on his holstered gun. "What's going on in here?"

"It's over now," Thorne said.

Burnett saw him and came back to the end of the bar. "Doc and Ike almost got into it," he said. "But I got 'em calmed down. Doc took off, headed for the Alhambra."

Ike and Pete Spence glanced at Virgil, but did not address him. Spence turned to Clanton and said something under his breath, and the two of them laughed.

"There's going to be trouble with that bunch before it's over," Virgil said, leaning on the end of the bar and accepting the cup of hot coffee Burnett shoved toward him.

"Let's go, boys," Ike said a few minutes later. "I think we've had all the fun we can have here for now." He set down his empty glass and started toward the door, followed by Spence and Stilwell. He paused, drunkenly, in front of Virgil Earp. "You better keep a tighter rein on your friend, Holliday," he said. "Or it won't be consumption that does for him."

"Doc does what he wants to," Virgil said evenly.

"You're right about that," Stilwell replied. "Holliday is definitely a horse of a different color."

The men brushed past Virgil and went out the door.

Burnett turned to Thorne. "Alex, let me introduce you to Town Marshal Virgil Earp. Alex Thorne, fresh out of the Army and looking to speculate in some mining properties."

The two men shook hands. Thorne noted the firm handshake, the steady eyes in the round face. The lawman, with a sweeping mustache, was dressed in a black suit and white shirt. His hair was carefully slicked down. The marshal's star was pinned to his coat lapel, and he wore a heavy six-gun strapped around his waist under the suit coat.

"I'd better be on my way," Thorne said, glancing at the Regulator clock on the wall at the back of the room. "I have to pick up our mutual friend for the theater."

"Take care of her," Burnett said, steeling himself not to think about it.

"Which way you headed?" Earp asked.

"The Crystal Palace."

"That's the way I'm going."

The two men walked out together, and Burnett turned to wait on two customers who'd just entered.

If the daytime Tombstone was a hive of activity, the night was even more so, Thorne observed as he and Virgil Earp strode down the boardwalk. Allen Street was alive with men. He could only guess what had drawn all these people to Tombstone. On foot, horseback, and wagon the human throng flowed back and forth—miners in rough clothes, better dressed men who might be merchants, tradesmen, or speculators. A few women with small children in tow appeared here and there in the flow of foot traffic. Teamsters, gamblers, blacksmiths, saloon-keepers, carpenters, barbers, hotel clerks, whores—the rush of everyone going about personal or public business rivaled the hum of activity in a city the size of San Francisco.

"What kind of mines are you interested in?" Earp asked suddenly. "My brothers and I own some mining interests we might be willing to sell, if the price is right."

"I just mustered out of the Army," Thorne said. "Looking to get in on the ground floor of some new discoveries. Risky business investing in new mines that haven't proved up yet. A lot cheaper, though."

"Well, the newspapers are full of ads for mining stock. But you'd best be wary of most of that."

"Thought I'd take the stage down to Bisbee, and see if I can pick up something there," Thorne said, trying to sound convincing.

"You say you're just out of the Army?

"Retired sergeant."

"If you're interested, you might be able to earn yourself a little money on the way to Bisbee," Virgil said.

"How's that?"

"Ride shotgun on the stage going there day after tomorrow. My brother, Wyatt, was scheduled to do it, but he's out with a posse, trying to pick up a trail on those men who got the Toughnut payroll the other day." He snorted. "Doing Johnny Behan's job for him!"

"I'll take it," Thorne said.

"It's just the night run down, and then back the next day. Should be pretty routine. The robbers have been hitting the Benson stage lately. Report to the Wells Fargo office before six in the evening. I'll tell Williams you're substituting. He'll have a shotgun and any instructions you need. The stage leaves from in front of the Cosmopolitan Hotel."

The two men stepped back against the front wall of a store to let a group of men pass.

"You hear that?" Earp asked, looking down the broad, dusty thoroughfare.

"What?"

"A night in Tombstone. This town hasn't slowed down since I got here. At least in Dodge City we had a little slack, when the herds weren't in. But this place is wide open all the time."

Thorne was suddenly conscious of the noise emanating from the open doors of several dozen saloons and dance halls—the tinkling of pianos, raucous laughter, and shouted curses. A gunshot exploded somewhere down the block, muffled by the walls of a building. Glass crashed, and he saw two men stagger into the street, swinging drunkenly at each other, one with a broken bottle.

"And it's not even dark yet," Earp said, a note of wonder in his voice. "When the miners get off work at ten and finish setting their charges by midnight, most of them will come trooping down here."

From the outlying desert and low hills came the continuous thumping of the steam-powered stamp mills. Thorne was surprised how quickly he'd gotten used to this noise. The never-ending rumble of the ore-crushing mills formed a background for every other noise.

"Unless I'm way off the mark," Virgil Earp continued, "the coroner will have at least one or two dead men to deal with over breakfast." He removed his hat and wiped a sleeve across his forehead, gazing out on the burgeoning night life of Tombstone. "Reminds me of what a newspaper once wrote about Ellsworth, Kansas."

Thorne looked curiously at him.

" 'Hell is still in session. . . .' "

CHAPTER SEVEN

"I think we're all wasting our time," Milton Joyce, the big, red-haired owner of The Oriental saloon said, disgustedly stubbing out his cigar in a brass ashtray. "We've had meetings like this before, and they've come to nothing. Just a lot of talk."

It was the next evening, and a group of eight men had gathered at the comfortable adobe house of John P. Clum, former Indian agent and founder and editor of *The Tombstone Epitaph*.

"Don't get all riled up," Richard Gird said, leaning back, crossing his legs, and hooking his thumbs into his vest pockets. "Taking the law into our hands as a citizens' committee of vigilance is a decision that requires a lot of thought and discussion. We don't want to go off half-cocked."

Thorne looked around the room at the gathering which included some of the town's influential citizens. Burnett, who was there representing the owner of The Occidental, had invited Thorne as his guest, as he put it—"To see what's about to happen in this town, if we don't break up this gang of robbers and killers."

Besides Clum, Gird, and Joyce, the group included Ellis Bigelow who operated the bowling alley, Ed Spangenberg, gun shop owner, and George Parson, prospector and land speculator.

"Why, hell, what more is there to talk about?" Milt Joyce

continued. "Look at this piece in today's edition of your own paper, John. You quote part of Doctor Goodfellow's coroner's report on a man found murdered in an alley last week. Here, let me read part of it in case some of you haven't seen it." He folded open the paper and ran his finger down the page until he found the item he wanted. "Doctor Goodfellow says that he 'performed assessment work' and found the body 'rich in lead, but too badly punctured to hold whiskey'." He looked up at Clum who was barely suppressing a smile. "Now, I ask you, is that the attitude of a professional? Things have come to a sorry pass, when the coroner starts joking about murder victims!"

The young, bald-headed Clum broke into a chuckle in spite of himself. "Now, don't go gettin' on Doc. Milt, you know him as well as anybody. He's a very good physician, but he just likes to have a little fun. Doesn't take anything too seriously."

"Yeah," George Parsons agreed. "Like when he snuffed the lamp in his office the other night with a blast from his Forty-Five just for pure devilment. About five hundred people came running to see if someone had shot him."

"I agree with Milt," Richard Gird, the influential mine owner said. "Why should law-abiding folk have to put up with letting these outlaws run wild, killing and robbing?"

"Don't you think we should let the law take care of it?" Ed Spangenberg ventured. "After all, we elected Sheriff Behan, and the U.S. marshal, Rawley Dake, over in Tucson, appointed Wyatt Earp as deputy marshal."

"Well, for one reason," Clum said, "Behan has appointed known outlaws to serve as his deputies at various times. As for Marshal Dake, he's being investigated by Washington for embezzlement and dereliction of duty."

"You can see for yourself the men in these offices haven't

been able or willing to handle the criminals," the stocky, bearded Gird persisted. "The situation is getting worse all the time. And now the so-called *law,* here in town, is splitting into two warring factions." He shook his head. "And I'm not so sure either side is out to protect the rest of us."

"What do you suggest?" Burnett asked.

"I believe we should form a citizens' safety committee," Gird said firmly. "As a group, our power would be great. We could sure put the fear of God into some of these rustlers and stage robbers, lot jumpers, and bunco artists."

"Call it whatever you will, but it's still a vigilance committee," Ellis Bigelow said derisively. "What're you planning to do . . . pick out two or three you suspect and just hang 'em?"

"If it's necessary, and we have the proof," Richard Gird affirmed. "But we'll post handbills first, warning any and all of these characters to get out of Tombstone, or else."

There was silence for several moments as the assembled men entertained their own thoughts.

"There's plenty of precedence for this action," Clum put in. "San Francisco in the 'Fifties and Montana in the 'Sixties. It worked then, and it'll work now. It's only a temporary measure until some real law is established."

"I don't know about this, John," Bigelow said. "A vigilante committee is a pretty drastic step. It's almost like a mutiny at sea. We'd be overthrowing established authority."

"That's just the point," Richard Gird said, his voice rising as he leaned forward. "We have no established authority. They're all fighting among themselves for the power to rob the public treasury and are consorting with known criminals. The system just isn't working."

Bigelow sat back in his armchair, his fist to his mouth, and said nothing, clearly bothered by the whole idea.

"Gentlemen, whether we form a vigilance committee or not, something must be done, or Acting Territorial Governor Gosper will intervene," John Clum said with gravity. His previous experience as a respected Indian agent at San Carlos and his influential position as an editor lent weight to his words, in spite of his relative youth. Yet, his bald head and heavy mustache did add an air of maturity, Thorne thought.

"The reputation of Tombstone as a lawless community has even attracted the attention of the President of the United States," Burnett said. "He's considering invoking martial law and sending troops in to keep order."

"The governor has hinted to me that he would condone citizen action, if that's what it takes," Clum said. "And I've prepared the people of this town for it by a couple articles that will run in the *Epitaph* tomorrow." He riffled through a sheaf of papers. "Here's part of what they will say . . . 'Men are shot in the streets and the killers are turned loose because no evidence is brought before the Grand Jury to indict them; men are found dead in various places and a newspaper item is all that is known of the matter; indictments are found and no witnesses are at hand to convict'." He slipped out another paper from the stack. "And here's where I lay it out straight . . . 'Lynch law is very effective at times. The body of a miner found shot in an alley two days ago is a case in point. If caught, these assassins may be taken care of by vigilantes'."

"Good."

"Well done."

There was a general nodding of assent in the room.

"Maybe just the threat of vigilante action will be enough," Bigelow said.

"I'd like to think so, but I'm not naïve enough to really

believe that newspaper threats alone will do it," Clum answered.

"There are many other men in this town who will join us, if we quit talking and really do something," Milton Joyce said.

"You're right. There won't be any trouble rallying support, once we start," Spangenberg agreed.

Thorne kept his mouth shut and listened, alarmed at what he was hearing, but understanding the frustration of these law-abiding men.

"Anybody for coffee?" Clum asked, standing up and striding through the low archway into the next room of his two-room, bachelor home.

"Not for me," Bigelow said. "It bothers my sleep."

"Huh! What bothers my sleep is the gunfire into the wee hours every night," George Parsons said.

Clum returned with a blue enameled coffee pot and set it on the circular table with several matching cups.

"Help yourselves, gents."

Burnett, Thorne, Joyce, and Parsons availed themselves of the black brew.

"Most of you are aware, I'm sure, that the territorial legislature is preparing to split Pima County and form another county approximately eighty miles by eighty miles in size. It'll be named Cochise, and Tombstone will be the county seat," Clum remarked after a short break. "That will certainly benefit this town and facilitate the collection of taxes. But, more to the point of this meeting, I believe it will cause even more friction and competition for public offices . . . positions that will provide opportunities for graft, from the county sheriff to the justices of the peace and judges."

"So, you're saying the formation of a new county means

we have even more reason to take the law into our own hands?" Bigelow asked.

"Exactly. We've got to show the governor that we can quickly make this new county a law-abiding one, come hell or high water," Clum said.

"We've already got the hell, but I don't see any signs of the mines flooding yet," Gird said with a wry smile.

The discussion continued for another thirty minutes, but finally broke up, having come to no firm decision. They agreed to feel out some of the other businessmen in town and then meet again three days hence.

"I thought you oughta be part of that," Burnett said to Thorne as the two of them walked toward The Occidental.

"Vigilance committees are a chancy business, all right," Thorne said. "Sometimes I agree with them, and sometimes not. It depends on the circumstances."

"It's hard to keep this sort of movement under wraps. If Behan and the Earps don't already know about it, I'm sure they will shortly."

"The force of the law is on the side of the badge," Burnett said, "regardless of how good or bad the man wearing it."

"As an undercover agent, I need to work with whomever I can to get to the bottom of these robberies before this town explodes in open warfare. And I don't think we have much time," Thorne said.

Burnett paused on the sidewalk to fish a match from his vest pocket. "There're some basic differences that underlie this situation," he said, raking the match into flame against the rough board wall of a store front.

"What's that?"

He didn't answer immediately as he puffed a fresh cigar to life. Satisfied that his smoke was properly aglow, he resumed walking. "The ranchers and cowboys around these parts are nearly all Democrats and generally from Texas or other Southern states," he said. "The townsfolk and the Earps, on the other hand, are mostly Republicans and hail from places north of the Mason-Dixon line. There are exceptions, of course. Doc Holliday, for one."

"Doc may be from Georgia, but he doesn't give a damn about politics, one way or another," Thorne remarked.

"True enough, but generally that's the way the division falls. The cowboys and ranchers, both the honest and the outlaws, are a bunch of independent cusses. They resent the federal authorities telling them what to do, or having *any* restrictions put on them, especially by any U.S. deputy marshals."

"All of which makes for a natural animosity before anything else happens," Thorne agreed.

"The national administration is Republican, so the political appointees are going to be the same. But there is one notable exception . . . Johnny Behan is a Democrat, but was appointed because his family has high Republican connections."

"Which adds another point of contention with the Earps," Thorne said.

"Now you're getting the picture," Burnett said, puffing on his cigar. "I have to go to work. You coming over for a beer?"

"Not tonight. Think I'll just go back to my hotel, have some supper, and relax."

Two hours later, Thorne was startled by a knock at his door. He put down the newspaper he was reading, swung his legs off the bed, and slipped the Colt from its holster on the bedpost. Who, besides Burnett, knew where he was staying? He stepped softly to the door. "Who is it?"

"A friend," came the muffled reply of a female voice.

He opened the door a crack, and a rush of pleasure swept over him at the sight of Julie Ann Martin. "Well . . . come in."

He closed the door behind her and took the wrap from her shoulders. "Nice!" He nodded at the sight of her bare shoulders and the cleavage at the top of the dark blue dress. "You must be on your way to work. No wonder men gamble at your faro table."

She smiled. "The men who gamble at my layout are men who would gamble if I were a bearded miner," she said. "They've got eyes and minds only for the gold. Most of them are completely obsessed with any kind of gambling, any game of chance. I'm just window dressing. I'm there to provide atmosphere and, if possible, to prevent men from going to other saloons and gambling houses."

Thorne grinned, pointing out the only chair in the room as he lounged back on the bed. "If I were a cowboy or a miner with a few dollars in my pocket, I'd be attracted to your table before I'd sit in a poker game with a bunch of men," he said.

He was curious about the reason for her visit, but wasn't about to ask. He would just enjoy the pleasure of her company for the moment.

"I came by to thank you for a most enjoyable evening the other night," she said lightly. "I can't remember when I've had such fun."

"Likewise," Thorne said. He paused, then plunged ahead. "Are you and Burnett seeing each other on a regular basis?" he asked.

"Oh, Paddy and I are good friends, but he has no claim on me," she said.

He'd heard that good friend thing before. The kiss of death for any kind of serious relationship. Her inference was obvious. The eyes, the inflection, the words, her very presence here, made it clear that she wanted Thorne to make a play for her.

He hesitated, thinking of Burnett. When he didn't reply right away, she continued: "I took the night off, so I don't have to go to work. I thought maybe we could have a drink."

Was that the only reason she was dressed this way? "I don't really think that would be a good idea," he heard himself saying. Inside, he was calling himself a fool. Agitated, he stood and paced to the window.

"You know, we never did talk much about you the other night," she said in a conversational tone, not pressing him. "Did you spend twenty years in the cavalry? You must have had some exciting times."

"Actually, except for the war, most of it was pretty dull," he said, his back to her. "After the war, I was stationed at several posts back East and around Washington City. Mostly drill, guard duty, and ceremonies."

"My . . . right near the seat of the government and all the powerful men in this country."

"I was just a lowly Army sergeant . . . had no actual part in it."

"Somehow, I don't really believe that," she whispered almost in his ear.

He turned, and she was standing close to him. Her arms went around his neck, and they locked in an embrace. Thorne's knees began to feel weak as they kissed.

The next three hours were as blissful as any Thorne had ever experienced. By the time she dressed, kissed him good bye, and left, he could hardly remember his own name, much less anything else he might have said to her during or after their lovemaking. He felt ashamed of his own weakness, especially for having betrayed his old friend, Paddy Burnett. Even though he planned to say nothing, he was certain that word of this tryst would somehow get back to Burnett and possibly ruin their friendship. At the very least it could only damage their working relationship. Was she intentionally trying to play them against each other? To what purpose?

He strode to the window and stood looking out onto the lights along Allen Street. But he neither saw nor heard the humming revelry of Tombstone below him.

He was disgusted and irritated with himself. Yet, such was the mystery and eternal fascination of women—this woman in particular—that he found himself already thinking ahead to his next meeting with her.

CHAPTER EIGHT

Sandy Bob Crouch was an easy-going, affable man who loved his job. It was almost as though he existed for no other purpose than to drive four, six, and sometimes, eight horse hitches. If there was ever a man born to the whip, Burnett had told Thorne, it was Charles Robert Crouch. His nickname, Sandy Bob, Thorne guessed, must have derived from the tawny mane that flowed out from under his broad-brimmed hat.

The long shadows were stretching down Allen Street, when the stage rolled out the next evening with four passengers, the Wells Fargo chest, and Thorne and Crouch riding on the box. Thorne braced himself against the footboard and settled into the rhythm of the rocking coach, the loaded shotgun cradled in the crook of his left arm.

Crouch laced the reins between his fingers, subtly signaling the leaders as they pulled up the long grade to the northwest, swung wide around the weathering headboards of Boothill cemetery, and started back down the road, away from the sun, toward Bisbee. Driving was so effortless for Crouch that he kept up a running conversation as Tombstone was left behind and darkness gradually enveloped the landscape.

But Thorne responded only in grunts and single words as his mind was distracted by memories of the night before and the lovely Julie Ann Martin. Not since his wife had he been so charmed by a woman. Crouch's talk became a droning monologue in the background as Thorne tried to pinpoint what it was about her that had so infatuated him. Perhaps it was her complete interest in every word he said. Maybe it was the whole ensemble, rather than any one thing, that left such a pleasant aura in his memory. He could see why Burnett was so stricken with her, and he vaguely wished he'd met her first. She was a mature woman in her late thirties, and her dialect indicated a Virginia origin, which she had confirmed. The last two nights with her had totally captivated him. She was a woman who saw what she wanted and went after it. Everything had been perfect, yet there was a grain of sand in the soothing ointment. Experience told him he was seeing only the surface of this beautiful, personable woman, only experiencing the outer mask she had decided to show, as though she were an actress putting on a charming performance for his benefit. But, then, some women were naturally devious. Perhaps she was only holding something of herself in reserve, until she'd known him longer. From all indications, she and Burnett were very close, possibly even lovers. He still felt that he had somehow betrayed his old friend's confidence in him. He was certainly attracted to her and, under any other circumstances, would have pursued her. Even though he felt all was fair in love and war, he resolved not to see her again as long as he was working with Burnett. Their efforts to stop the robberies had to come first. Perhaps they were both fools. She could be a high-class prostitute, for all he knew. Her past was a mystery to him. A woman as attractive as Julie Ann Martin was normally not single by her mid-thirties. Maybe she was widowed or divorced. There was no telling. Maybe Burnett knew more about her. But for now, Thorne would withhold judgment.

While these things were churning through his mind, Crouch was keeping up his friendly chatter, telling stories of people he knew and places he'd been. Alternately trotting and walking the six-horse team, Crouch had the desert miles rolling smoothly under them as the road wound southeastward toward the mining town of Bisbee. Although Thorne had never been there, he knew the booming town of Bisbee was tucked into the steep folds of the Mule Mountains, just north of the Mexican border. The road to Bisbee passed through the small mining community of Hereford. A gibbous moon was silvering the landscape by the time they were a mile or so beyond Hereford.

Then the flashing roar of several guns lit up the night. Crouch reacted instantly, cracking his whip over the backs of the team. The horses lunged into a gallop.

Another fusillade came from both sides, but Thorne could see nothing in the blackness but the muzzle flashes. Just as he raised the shotgun to his shoulder, the stage bounced into a dip, and he had to grab for a handhold to keep from being pitched off the high seat. A bullet *whanged* off the iron rail next to his fingers. He slid down into the boot and braced the shotgun, loosing the charge in both barrels at the flashes. Next he had out one of his Colts and was firing at the moonlit figures on horseback that were closing on the stage. He had the satisfaction of seeing the closest rider tumble from his mount. Then something hit his back. Crouch had been hit and had slipped from the seat.

"My shoulder!" the driver gasped. "Take the lines. I can't hold them."

Thorne eased the man down into the boot, took the leather reins from his fingers, and struggled over Crouch to obtain the seat, hardly conscious of the gunfire coming from both sides of the coach. Now both his hands were occupied, and he couldn't respond. But he heard shots from below him and realized the passengers were firing out the windows.

In the few seconds since Crouch had fallen, the team, frightened by the shots and sensing no one at the lines, was running full speed, out of control. The coach rocked and bounced, and he braced his boots wide on the footboard, getting a grip on the reins. The wind had whipped his hat off so that it hung by its cord on his back. He was vaguely aware of shouts and answering pistol fire from the coach, but all his attention was on the horses. He got a good grip on the lines, set himself, and eased back with a slow, steady force, trying to restrain the several tons of panicked animals that were thundering into the night ahead of him. But the horses were having none of it. Thorne could only hang on and try to hold them to a straight course as the tall stage pitched and swerved dangerously on the rutted, uneven road. As long as he had the lines, there was a chance he could keep the runaway team from upsetting the two-thousand-pound coach and crushing them all in a pile of splinters.

The gunfire slackened, and he cast a quick glance to his right and left. A great cloud of dust was boiling out behind them from the hoofs and wheels, and the robbers seemed to have fallen back. *Maybe not outrun, but discouraged by the return fire,* Thorne thought.

How far they careened along on the ragged edge of disaster, he didn't know. But finally the horses began to slow. He gradually drew them down to a walk, and then to a snorting, panting stop.

"Whew!" He lifted his foot from the brake and whipped the lines in three quick turns around the brake handle.

Then he yanked his Colt and clambered back onto the roof of the coach, all ears and eyes, his heart still pounding. When the dust drifted away from them, he saw nothing on the moonlit, desert landscape. The attackers had vanished.

A door of the coach burst open, and the passengers tumbled out, all talking at once. But Thorne ignored them, as he holstered his gun and slid down into the front boot, fumbling for the wounded Crouch. The driver groaned when Thorne started to lift him. "Easy," Crouch cautioned. "I think the bullet clipped my collar bone."

Thorne got the canteen and gave him a drink. "I'm sure I hit one of 'em," Thorne said, as he took off his vest and fashioned a makeshift sling to hold the driver's arm and shoulder in place. "Can you make it to Bisbee?"

"Hell, I'll have to," Crouch said. Throne was glad to hear some of the old fire in his voice. "You take us on in. You've done a good job so far." He glanced over the side of the coach. "Better check on the passengers."

The passengers were shaken. Milton Ruskin, a red-haired cigar and liquor drummer, had caught a few shotgun pellets in the side of his face and neck, but insisted he was fine. He'd already stanched the flow of blood with his bandanna. Bones Brannon, a Tombstone gambler, was profuse in his thanks to Thorne and Crouch for saving the $600 in cash he was carrying. The third male passenger, a mine foreman, was unhurt, also, and had been the one doing most of the shooting to help drive off the attackers. "I'm getting damned tired of these guys robbing our mine payrolls and bullion shipments," the foreman growled. "Hope I did them some damage."

"Well, the four of you saved this coach," Thorne said. "After the driver was hit, I was too busy to do any shooting."

"Is Crouch hurt badly?" Brannon asked.

"He'll do until we can get him to a doctor in Bisbee."

A silver, pocket flask reflected the moonlight as Milton Ruskin tipped back a drink. "Here, let me borrow a little of that," Thorne said, reaching for it.

"Steadies the nerves," the drummer said, handing it over.

Thorne poured some of the liquor onto his bandanna, then handed the flask back.

"What're you wasting it for?"

"Crouch needs it on his wound," Thorne answered shortly.

No one seemed much concerned about the woman passenger. Thorne recognized her as a young Tombstone prostitute, whose pockmarked face detracted from her soft, gray eyes. She was somewhat distraught, but got herself together, and nodded affirmatively when he inquired about her condition. "I'm fine," she said, placing a hand on his arm. "Don't worry about me. I've been through a lot worse than this." He saw the moonlight glint briefly from the nickel-plated barrel of a Derringer, as she slipped it back into her handbag and turned to reënter the stage. Thorne automatically gave her a hand up, catching a faint scent of lilac.

The rest of the trip to Bisbee was uneventful, Thorne handling the team with growing confidence. Crouch hung on, grimacing, gasping out an instruction now and then, as the moon waned and they threaded their way through the black cañons of the Mule Mountains, finally pulling the bullet-riddled stage safely to a stop at the stage station near the foot of Brewery Gulch.

CHAPTER NINE

"I'll see you later tonight." Julie Ann Martin put her fingers to her lips and touched Burnett's mustache, giving him what Thorne saw as a very private smile. She slipped away from their table at the Can-Can Restaurant and disappeared out the door in a swish of skirts.

Thorne wondered again about Burnett's relationship with this woman, but decided tact was the better part of curiosity and kept his mouth shut. Thorne was still attracted to her, but now began to see her as a clinging type—not really to his taste at all. And her flirtations seemed more appropriate to a young girl. He shook his head to clear the thoughts and silently attacked the wedge of apple pie before him.

Burnett was quiet for several seconds, staring after Julie's departed figure. "Ah, a fine woman, that one . . . ," he mused softly, automatically smoothing the ends of his mustache.

It was late the next afternoon, and Thorne had just returned on the stage with a new driver. A doctor in Bisbee had removed the bullet, set Crouch's broken clavicle, and put him to bed with a sedative.

"Damned lucky we got away without losing the Wells Fargo box or getting somebody killed," Thorne said between bites. "Crouch will be out of action for a few weeks, but he'll recover." He took a sip of coffee. "I don't know how much we were carrying in that treasure box, but somebody was mighty anxious to get their hands on it."

"Thirty thousand in gold coin for two banks in Bisbee," Burnett said softly.

"Ah, no wonder. . . . Did anybody else besides you and the Wells Fargo agent, Williams, know about it?"

Burnett shook his head thoughtfully. "Hard to keep something like that from leaking out, though."

Thorne wondered how many bank employees might have known as well. "Maybe the company should tighten up a little," he said, "try shipping at odd times, or some way other than by stage."

"Several years ago, up in Dakota Territory, the bosses came up with the idea of melting a bullion shipment into one big, four-hundred pound ingot."

"What happened?"

"The robbers somehow got wind of it and showed up with a stout wagon and team, along with eight men to haul it off. So Wells Fargo tried an even bigger lump of gold, and hauled it out in a wagon with guards. The wagon hit a bump, and the weight broke an axle."

Thorne chuckled grimly. "It's almost like a chess game . . . one side makes a move, and the other counters."

"Yeah," Burnett said dryly. "Too bad it's not as harmless as chess. Posse's still out after the ones who got that Toughnut payroll several days ago," he went on. "A lot of the saloons and the cribs in this town are going to be hurting for business until those miners get their wages."

As they paid their bill and walked out into the late afternoon sunlight, Thorne asked: "You overhear anything at J. B. Ayers's Saloon in Charleston that might help us?"

"Nary a thing. Either the cowboys who hang out down there don't know anything, or they're really close-mouthed, even when they're drinkin' . . . not really like them. Most of those boys like to blow, if they think they've done something big and bold."

As they crossed Fourth Street, Thorne saw Virgil Earp's lean figure striding toward them.

"What's up, Virge?" Burnett asked.

"One of Clanton's boys just rode in with a dead body across his saddle."

"What?"

"Yeah. Billy Clanton claims he was riding into town this morning and came across the body lying under a mesquite bush with a bullet in it."

"Who is it?"

"I never saw him before. No identification on him. That's why I came looking for you, Thorne. Billy's got the body down at the Wells Fargo office, trying to collect the company's standing reward of three hundred dollars gold for any dead hold-up man. Thought I'd look you up, and see if you could identify him as one of the men who attacked the Bisbee stage. This man hasn't been dead more than a day."

"I'll take a look, but I never really got a view of their faces. Just a few dark forms and some muzzle flashes."

As they talked, the three men fell into step, walking in the street toward the Wells Fargo office.

"By God, I'm glad you're back, Virgil," said Rufus Williams, the balding Wells Fargo agent, jumping up nervously as they entered the office. "Tell Billy to get this body out of here. I'm not the damned undertaker."

"Not until I get my three hundred dollar reward," the young cowboy demanded, putting one booted foot on a wooden chair and leaning one elbow on his knee.

"You don't have any *proof* that this man was trying to rob

Wells Fargo," Williams said slowly, as if trying to explain something very basic to a child.

"Take a look," Virgil directed Thorne, pointing at a body lying on its back on the floor.

Thorne squatted down and examined the face. The man had dark hair and a stylish, thick mustache. He appeared to be no more than thirty years old. He was dressed in canvas pants, suspenders, a collarless striped shirt, and a leather vest. A watch chain was attached to a buttonhole of the vest, the other end of the chain disappearing into the left vest pocket. Connected to the chain was a coin-shaped fob with a device worked into it—the now-familiar symbol of an X with four stars, one between each of the cross pieces. The open-faced, silver-plated watch contained no inscription.

The middle of his shirt was stained with dried blood around a ragged hole. Thorne patted the man's pockets and felt lumpy articles that he guessed were coins and possibly a pocket knife. Apparently the man hadn't been robbed, he thought, as he rolled the body over. Near the center of the vest was a small bullet hole. An irregular pattern of dried blood stained the leather. A large-caliber slug had evidently passed through the victim, either striking or passing very near the heart. But the detail that struck him was the small, blackened circle around the bullet hole. Powder burns. Thorne rolled the body back over.

"Well, do you recognize him?" Virgil demanded.

"No. Never saw this man before."

"Could he have been one of the robbers?" Virgil asked.

"You'd have to question the passengers who were shooting to find out what they saw. But it was really dark. I can tell you that this man was not shot by anyone on the stage."

"How do you know?" Virgil snapped.

"Powder burns. This man was shot in the back, close-up."

"Get that body down to Doc Goodfellow's," Virgil ordered Billy Clanton.

"What about my reward?" Billy whined.

"Get out of here before I arrest you on suspicion of murder," Virgil gritted.

"You're trying to cheat me out of my rightful reward. You're all in this together." He glared at them before stooping and grasping the body under the arms and heaving it over his shoulder. Nobody offered to help as he fumbled with the door handle, staggered outside with his burden, and wrestled the body across the pommel of his saddle.

Thorne noted that the body wore a gun belt with an empty holster.

Rufus Williams followed them to the door, looking very relieved.

Billy Clanton mounted with difficulty and started slowly down the street.

"Johnny Behan brought his posse in yesterday . . . empty-handed," Virgil said, watching Billy Clanton ride around the corner and out of sight. "But that's no surprise. Think I'll go see what Doc Goodfellow says about that body."

Doctor George Goodfellow was a short, muscular man who was blunt-talking and afraid of nothing. He was liked and respected by every faction and every person in Tombstone for three reasons, Burnett had told Thorne—he was neutral and was very careful to stay that way; he was a good physician; and he was a sociable sporting man, willing to bet on everything from a wrestling match to a poker game.

Doc habitually wore a high-crowned white Stetson and permanently sported a bushy, tapered mustache that hid his mouth.

Just now the hat was put aside, and he was in his shirt-sleeves as he stripped the clothes from the unidentified body on an examining table in the back room of his office.

Billy Clanton had left the body and departed, still acting offended and disgusted that he would receive no reward for his effort in delivering the corpse.

"How long has he been dead, Doc?" Thorne asked, after watching for several minutes.

"Hard to say, exactly," Goodfellow replied, carefully moving the man's arms and legs and bending low to examine the penetrating wound.

"*Rigor mortis* has come and gone, so it's been at least fifteen hours. Then, too, if he was really lying in the desert, he wasn't there long enough for the vultures and coyotes to find him and begin their work. I'd say he departed this life roughly fifteen to twenty hours ago as a result of a large-caliber slug that penetrated from back to front, near or through the heart."

"Billy Clanton claims he found the body in the desert this morning," Virgil said.

"Virge, do me a favor and take a look through his pockets," the doctor said, motioning toward a pile of clothes on a chair. "Maybe it'll give us a clue to his identity."

Virgil emptied the pockets, placing the contents on a side table. Thorne watched over his shoulder.

"One watch and chain . . . no inscription, one Barlow knife, one pocket comb, and a silver dollar and thirty-seven cents in change," Earp intoned. "No billfold. Nothing to identify him."

"Are you familiar with this symbol?" Thorne asked, holding up the chain with the fob.

"Same symbol we found on those wooden disks left at some of the robberies," Virgil answered. "Know what it is, Doc?"

"No . . . could be anything. Some kind of fraternal or civic organization, maybe." He turned back to the body. "Virge, go ahead and take custody of his personal effects. I'll have the undertaker fix him up and put him in a glass-topped coffin in the window of the hardware. Could be somebody will know him. If not, Camillus Fly will take his photo, and we'll bury him in Boothill. Won't be the first unknown man buried there, and I'd wager not the last, either."

Virgil piled the dead man's pocket articles onto a large blue bandanna, and tied up the corners.

"Well, I'll be reporting to the coroner's jury this afternoon," Doc said, looking up with a twinkle in his eye. "Provided I can get them to convene in the Eagle Brewery Saloon."

Thorne accompanied Burnett to The Occidental, when the big man went on duty at six o'clock. He stood nursing a beer, while Burnett set up the backbar for the evening's rush.

"I haven't seen anything of Doc Holliday the past few days," Burnett remarked, glancing around at the few patrons. "And I won't be the poorer for it, if he never shows his face in here again," he added. "Dealing with that man is like walking around a keg of black powder with a lighted cigar. He's got a fatal lung disease, and I'm betting he'd rather go out with a bullet than a gasp."

"A man who has no fear of being killed can be mighty dangerous," Thorne agreed. He tipped up his beer just as two men entered. Thorne was startled at the resemblance of one of them to the bartender.

Burnett waved at the pair as they headed toward the billiard table near the back of the room. "Morgan Earp," Burnett said, indicating his look-alike. "That was me twenty years and sixty pounds ago."

"You sure your last name isn't Earp?" Thorne asked.

Burnett came closer and leaned on the bar. "Morgan's done his best to keep from getting sucked into this Earp-Clanton scuffle," he said in a low voice. "He'd rather shoot pool, drink beer, and chase women than fight. But, I'd have to say, he can be riled pretty easily. Not long on patience, like Virgil. More impulsive, if you know what I mean."

Thorne nodded, fingering his beer glass.

Suddenly, he jerked back, startled, at what he saw—the head of an Indian hardly five feet from him. The long black hair, secured by a red headband, swung from side to side as the Indian quickly scanned the barroom. He was standing in the open doorway to the gaming room, dressed in a white man's dirty, striped shirt and leggings made from a pair of blue cavalry pants.

Then the Indian looked around and spotted Burnett with his back to him. He tapped the big man on the shoulder. "Food," he grunted, rubbing his stomach. "Hungry."

Burnett reacted as though he had been expecting this visitor. "Thorne, take him out back. I'll be along in a minute as soon as I can scare up something for him to eat." He looked at the Indian. "Rabbit, go with him. I will come." There was an unusual gentleness in his voice.

Thorne took Rabbit by the arm and guided him through the gaming room, past the faro layout, to the back door, feeling the stares and hearing the muttered comments of several men.

They stepped out into the dusky light and walked away from the saloon. Before Thorne's eyes adjusted to the dusk, he caught a faint whiff of the privy and stopped. The Indian stopped uncomfortably close to him, and Thorne couldn't decide which smell was worse—the outhouse or the odoriferous aborigine.

It seemed like more than several minutes before the door opened and Burnett's big frame blocked the door frame.

"Here ya go, Rabbit," he said, coming up and handing the Indian a cloth sack. "This oughta hold you for two or three days. Where you staying now? Maybe I could get you a ham or a side of beef, or maybe even a deer, if you could dry it and smoke it."

Rabbit's only answer was a grunt of satisfaction as he hefted the sack. "You good man, Burnett," he said in a rough, gravelly voice. "I pay you back."

"No need," Burnett replied. "Go on with ya. And try to stay outta the whiskey for a while. That stuff will kill you."

The Indian grunted again and started to move away. Then he stopped and turned back. "You good man, Burnett," he said again. "I give you gold."

"Yeah, yeah. That's OK. All I want is for you to take care of yourself and stay out of trouble."

"You no believe me? I take you to gold in the hills."

"Thanks, Rabbit. Maybe later. The only reward I want is to watch you race at the next holiday or festival. Right now, you better go feed yourself." He slapped the Indian gently on the shoulder, and the beggar turned and jogged away into the darkness with his sack of food.

The two men returned to the saloon. They went to one end of the bar, off by themselves, and Burnett drew Thorne a fresh beer.

"Rabbit's kind of a pet project of mine," Burnett said in answer to Thorne's questioning look. "Actually, I just feel sorry for the man. He's a Mescalero Apache, from New Mexico. I think his mother was a captured Tarahumara from the Sierra Madre Mountains of Sonora. They're legendary long-distance runners, which might explain some of his stamina. As near as anybody can get the story, he's something of an outcast from his tribe. Don't know why. Nobody knows where he stays. Just a loner who lives a nomadic existence in the desert and mountains, but he appears in towns long enough to beg for food. He may have been self-sufficient at one time, but he's got one great weakness that undermines everything else."

"His addiction to whiskey?"

"Right. Anytime there's a Fourth of July celebration, or any kind of festival where there are parades and horse races and foot races for prizes, he appears and outruns all competitors. Can't get a bet on him any more, even with huge odds, he's become so well known. Up to about a thousand yards, I've never seen anyone faster. He's an amazing athlete."

"I always heard that Apaches had terrific endurance as long-distance runners," Thorne said, sipping his beer.

Burnett nodded. "That's usually the case. But he's an exception. He's a sprinter. Lightning reflexes. It's a damn' shame that he's ruining it with alcohol. If he keeps up that heavy drinking, it won't be long before he'll destroy his health. Probably die drunk in the hills or the desert. Some prospector will find his bones."

"You called him Rabbit?"

"That's what he goes by. The men who first saw him run hung Jack Rabbit on him. I've heard his Apache name, but it's nothing I could ever get me tongue around."

"He was the Indian who saved Lieutenant Arnold after the ordnance wagons were ambushed?"

"One and the same," Burnett nodded.

"What was that business about giving you gold?"

Burnett chuckled. "He's been telling me that for months. I think it's just his way of trying to save face. Doesn't want to admit he's begging."

"I can understand that. If he had really found some gold,

he'd be using it for himself and wouldn't have to beg."

"He may be down and out, but he's still got some pride. If there's anything at all to that offer of gold, I figure maybe he's found a trace of color in some slag heap at one of the mines around here. Or, he could be referring to something like the Adams diggings."

"The what?"

Burnett glanced at him as though he were surprised that Thorne would question something that was common knowledge. "Another of those lost mine stories," he explained. "People been searching for it for at least thirty years. This one apparently has some basis in fact. Briefly, the story goes that a renegade Indian led a man named Adams and a few of his friends to a rich mine in the mountains north and east of here somewhere. God knows why he would've done 'em such a favor. But anyway, hostile Apaches ran 'em off, and they were lucky to escape with their lives. When the Adams party went back later, they weren't able to find it again. Sound familiar? But some reputable men swear they saw Adams with some rich samples from the first trip. So men have been searching for years for this mine all the way from the White Mountains clear over into New Mexico and West Texas." He chuckled. "I doubt if Rabbit's found the Adams diggings, but I go along with him and just pretend to believe whatever he says."

"Why don't you question him about it?"

"Most of the white men he's had dealings with were very greedy and gold-hungry," Burnett replied slowly. "I don't want him to think he has to reward me for helping him."

"Somebody needs to help him to a bath."

"When he's sober, he keeps himself clean. But he's been goin' downhill."

CHAPTER TEN

Two days later, the posse rode into town about mid-afternoon with a prisoner.

Thorne had just emerged from The Oriental saloon where he had been watching Doc Holliday gamble with Ike Clanton, Tom McLaury, Pete Spence, and a man he recognized as a foreman at the Contention Mine. Thorne thought it odd that Doc would gamble with cowboys, but apparently where money or business or gambling were concerned, feuds were put aside for the time.

Thorne squinted at the lean Wyatt Earp, who was leading the horse of an obviously wounded prisoner up Allen Street. Bringing up the rear was the big, stocky figure of deputy Bill Breakenridge, riding beside Deputy Dave Neagle.

Morgan Earp came out of the Crystal Palace and went to meet his brother, talking and walking beside the horses until they reined up in front of the sheriff's office and wearily dismounted. Breakenridge reached up for the wounded man who half fell out of the saddle. As Thorne came up, he could see that a bandage made from a torn, white shirt was wound around the man's chest under a blood-stained plaid shirt that was merely draped over his shoulders.

Johnny Behan came out to meet them with a look of something other than pleasure on his face. He and Thorne followed the lawmen and the prisoner inside the office.

"It's Bill Heard. Works on a ranch over in the San Simon Valley!" Behan exclaimed. "What'd you have to shoot him for?" he demanded, as Breakenridge eased the wounded man into a wooden armchair.

"We didn't," Wyatt snapped. "Somebody else did. The stage guard . . . did that for us. That's what slowed him up. His good friends left him behind, when we got hot on their heels. We think Curly Bill and Pony Deal were two of the others, but we couldn't catch up to them. Looked like they may have changed horses at the Clanton Ranch."

"I know this man. I can't believe he's an outlaw. I've never known him to do anything worse than get drunk on a Saturday night," Behan said.

Wyatt snorted a derisive laugh.

Behan's face reddened, but he turned to the man in the chair. "He needs medical attention. Somebody get Doc Goodfellow."

"Bullet went clean through his left side," Neagle said. "Don't know if it hit anything vital. It's pretty much stopped bleeding. But all that jarring on horseback probably didn't help him none."

"By all means, get Doc Goodfellow," Wyatt said. "We want this one to get better, so he can tell us all the friends he's working with, including Frank Stilwell."

"Better get him into a cell on a bunk," Morgan added.

"I'll go get Judge Spicer to set bail," Behan said to the prisoner, who seemed only about half conscious. "Don't you worry."

"Don't get in a rush, Johnny. In his condition, he's not going anywhere right away," Wyatt said, his steel-gray eyes narrowing. "And I'll be right here, so if some of his buddies spring him on bail, I'll just arrest him again on a federal charge of robbing the U.S. Mail."

"You have no proof!" Behan was controlling his temper with an obvious effort.

"We'll see about that," Neagle said. "When we found him, he was riding a horse with a narrow, left hind shoe. Same as the tracks we found at another robbery site."

"That proof ought to do for starters," Wyatt said, rubbing a hand over the three-day growth of stubble on his jaw. "Morg, stay here and be sure nothing happens to our prisoner, while I run over to the hotel for a bath and a change of clothes. Then I'll come back and relieve you."

"Sure thing, Wyatt," his younger brother answered.

Thorne drifted into a corner out of the way to watch the proceedings. Wyatt left, and Doc Goodfellow arrived with his medical bag in hand, less than ten minutes later.

Thorne was standing by the open cell door as the doctor deftly removed the makeshift bandage to reveal an angry-looking bullet hole just above the lower edge of the rib cage. Goodfellow used a stethoscope to listen to Heard's chest in two or three places. Then he knelt by the cot and gently eased the man over onto his stomach. What appeared to be a larger hole, clotted and smeared with blood, marked Heard's back, higher up. The doctor probed gently around the wound, and then ran his hands over the rib cage.

Heard was lying still, unconscious.

"Will he make it, Doc?" Behan inquired, leaning against the barred door.

"Hard to say. Bullet went through, but it clipped a rib, and I think it caught the lower lobe of his lung. He's lost a lot of blood." He flipped the stethoscope from his neck and replaced it in his bag, then took a wad of cotton and a bottle of strong carbolic and began to clean the wound carefully.

As the doctor worked, Thorne glanced down at the dried blood that stained the man's belt and pants the color of burnt umber. He wondered if a bullet from his own gun had done this. He had been in gun battles before, but shot only as a matter of desperate necessity, to save his own life or someone else's. The devastating effects of lead slugs on the human body never failed to appall him. He was just dragging his eyes away from the sight, when his gaze was arrested by a mark on the wide leather belt. Sweat and blood had stained the belt, but burned into the leather, as if by a branding iron the size of a silver dollar, was a circle with a cross bisecting it. And between each of the four arms of the cross was a tiny star. It was the same enigmatic device that was on the watch fob of the unidentified body found in the desert and buried two days earlier.

Thorne leaned closer for a better look, until Doc Goodfellow glanced up to see what he was about.

"Sorry, Doc." He backed away, not wishing to say anything in front of Behan. He hoped Bill Heard would live and be able to talk, because he not only had information about his fellow robbers, but about the insignia which was definitely a connecting link in all these robberies.

Still unconscious, Bill Heard was transferred from the county jail to the back room of Doc Goodfellow's office so that he could be more easily treated and watched over by the town's physician. Town Marshal Virgil Earp deputized his brother, Morgan, to stand guard over the prisoner. Morgan would be relieved periodically by Breakenridge or Neagle.

When it became obvious that Heard was in a deep state of unconsciousness from which he showed no signs of immediate recovery, Thorne retired to his second home—The Occidental—to think and confer with his Wells Fargo counterpart. Doc Goodfellow could give no idea if or when Heard might wake up or be able to speak. "He could slide into a deep coma and die. We'll just have to wait and see."—was the way he had put it when Sheriff Behan and Thorne and Dave Neagle, the deputy, had left the prisoner lying on the clean sheets of the bedstead in his back room.

Thorne knew that the survival of this prisoner was critical, if they were to get any information that might break this chain of robberies—provided they were unable to catch one of the other highwaymen in the act. And the chances of that were slim. These men were good at their trade.

These disturbing thoughts were running through Thorne's mind as he sat morosely sipping a beer at a table in The Occidental, while Burnett waited on a steady flow of customers. In case Heard did not survive, Thorne decided he would have to concoct some scheme that would trap the hold-up men on their next attempt.

Still deep in thought, Thorne went out the back door across the alleyway to the outhouse. When he came out, he found Burnett in the alley, smoking a cigar.

"I once knew a stage driver who took care of his own shipments without the use of a guard," Burnett said and chuckled, after they'd discussed the hold-ups a minute or two. "Coming out of the Black Hills, there are plenty of places where a stage or a wagon can be stopped. This driver put a loaded double-barrel shotgun down inside his right pants leg and wired the triggers up under his shirt to his hand. When he was stopped, he'd raise his right leg like he was going to step on the brake lever. But he'd just aim his foot at the robber, raise his hands, and pull the wire. A double load of buckshot in the face will sure make a man lose interest in stage robbing." He laughed. "This worked for a while, until the word got around. Then they began coming up on the stage from behind, or started shooting first."

"Well, I know they've tried welding iron strongboxes inside the coach, and even plating the outside with armor," Thorne said thoughtfully, "but hold-up men just took to hauling black powder with them and blowing the stages to pieces. That got even more expensive than losing the bullion."

"Well, the Southern Pacific extended their line east, past Benson, a few weeks ago," Burnett said. "It won't be long before it's in full operation. Then the stages will only have to run as far as Benson, and the bullion can be put on a train for Tucson and San Francisco."

"That'll be some safer," Thorne conceded. "But, somehow, we've got to catch these robbers and recover whatever hasn't already been spent. I'm convinced nearly all these jobs . . . even the robberies of the military rifles and the payrolls . . . are being done by the same gang, and that symbol is their badge. Somehow they're getting inside information."

"If I don't come up with something soon, Wells Fargo may just cut me loose," Burnett said. He took a deep breath. "Any ideas what to try next?"

Thorne thought for a few moments. "Maybe load a coach with passengers who are actually undercover lawmen, and well-armed. Let the word out that an extra heavy shipment of gold and silver is going out, then gun down anybody who makes a try for it." He shook his head. "That's risky, though. So far, there haven't been too many men killed in these hold-ups. But the driver and guard could easily get shot in that situation. Or it could result in a Mexican stand-off. Another problem with contriving such a trap is that it's almost impossible to keep a secret like that in this town."

"There's got to be some way . . . ," Burnett mused.

"There is. When Heard wakes up, threaten him with a hemp tie, unless he tells everything he knows about who's in this with him and where they're hiding out."

"Heard may never wake up."

"We'll just have to wait and see." Thorne straightened up from the hogshead he'd been leaning on, as a figure walked down the alley toward them. The late afternoon sun was behind the man, and all Thorne could make out was a silhouette. He stepped back and shaded his eyes.

The pair stopped talking until the man passed. But he didn't pass. He walked up to them with the easy, graceful gait of a natural athlete. It was Burnett's Apache friend, Rabbit. And, from what Thorne could see and smell, he was sober and clean.

"Well, hello, Rabbit. Good to see you," Burnett greeted him, shaking his hand. "You've met my friend, Alex Thorne."

The Indian acknowledged Thorne with a curt nod of his head and an extended hand, white man fashion. The Apache was dressed in faded Levi overalls, with the crotch cut out and covered with a loin cloth. He was wearing a heavy, tan cotton shirt and a leather vest. His black, straight hair had been cut so that it barely covered his ears, and a blue bandanna functioned as a headband. Thorne noted he was also carrying a large Bowie knife in a sheath at his belt, although he did not appear to have a gun.

"Are you hungry?" Burnett was asking him.

"I have eaten," the Indian replied in a low voice.

Burnett said nothing, waiting for Rabbit to continue. Thorne hoped Burnett would not offer him whiskey.

"You look well," Burnett finally continued. "Do you have money?"

"I have no need of money," the Indian replied. "But I

know where there is much gold. You come with me, and I will give it to you."

"Gold to a white man is like whiskey to an Indian," Burnett replied in a grave tone. "A man cannot take just a little of it. And too much of it will eat out his insides and kill him. And then what has he gained, if he is dead?"

Thorne realized that the big bartender was just humoring the Apache, and kept quiet, content to observe the strange friendship.

The Indian did not reply as he absorbed this bit of wisdom, and the silence stretched out for probably a minute or more. The sounds of laughter and voices drifted to them from the saloon as a man opened the back door and crossed the alley to the privy.

Rabbit hunkered down with his back against the saloon wall.

"Smoke?" Burnett asked, offering him a slim cigar from his vest pocket. The Indian took it without a word, and Burnett struck a match to light it for him. Rabbit puffed silently and contentedly for some time, appearing to savor the fragrant smoke of the rum-soaked cheroot. For a man who had a reputation for being the fastest in the territory, Rabbit was in no hurry now as he smoked and stared into the distance, ignoring the two white men. It made Thorne's legs ache just to watch the Indian runner remain squatted next to the wall for long minutes at a stretch.

Finally Rabbit rose, knocked the fire off his cigar against the board wall, and carefully tucked the stub into his vest pocket for future use.

"You come with me tonight, and I will take you where there is much gold," he said to Burnett.

It was the first time Thorne had seen the big man obviously discomfited.

"I can't go. I must go back to work," he said, looking at the impassive face of the Indian. Thorne thought his tone actually sounded sincere.

"You not understand," Rabbit said. "There is much gold." He held his hands apart, indicating the great amount. "You never have to work again. You, too," he added, looking at Thorne.

Burnett appeared to waver, glancing at the back door of the saloon. He pulled out his watch and popped the case open. "Harvey is probably wondering what happened to me. I've got to get back in there."

But he stood there irresolutely, as he closed his watch and slipped it back into his vest pocket. Thorne became aware of the sounds of wagon traffic on the nearby streets and the ever-present rumble of the stamp mills in the distance.

Finally Thorne said: "Oh, hell, I'll go down to the livery and get our horses and rent one for Rabbit. Let's go see what this is all about."

Burnett heaved a sigh as if relieved to have the decision made for him, and said: "OK. Let me go tell Harvey he'll have to cover for me until I get back . . . whenever that is."

Forty minutes later the three men were riding down Allen Street toward the westering sun, Thorne mounted on his sorrel, Rabbit leading the way on a dun, and Burnett bringing up the rear on a black Morgan. The big bartender wore a long duster over his town clothes consisting of a white shirt, black vest, and striped, gray pants. He had strapped on his .44 Remington which he always wore when not tending bar. Both white men had rolled a few items such as a razor, toothbrush, and clean shirts into a blanket and slicker and tied the rolls to their cantles. Full canteens were hooked over their saddle horns. Frying pan, salt, coffee, sugar, a slab of bacon, and a sack of beans, along with a small bag of flour and saleratus stuffed into their saddlebags comprised the larder. As they followed the Apache out of town into the desert, Thorne couldn't help comparing their preparations with those of the unencumbered Indian who had simply climbed aboard the rented horse and was ready to go. *More akin to the animals than we are,* Thorne thought. *White men can't do anything without all this impedimenta—the trappings and comforts of a softer existence. If I hadn't rented these horses, he would have led us on foot.*

They had been unable to coax from Rabbit any approximation of the distance they were to travel. "In the mountains."—was all he would say, waving his hand in a general southwesterly direction. A jaunt of at least a couple of days was Thorne's guess. So the two men had prepared accordingly.

They had ridden barely four miles, when Rabbit pulled his horse off the road into the desert and dismounted, indicating by signs and a few words that they would halt here and eat. The sun was just resting on the horizon.

Burnett, surprised by this early stop, looked his question at Thorne, but silently began unpacking the sparse foodstuff while Thorne gathered some dead brush and small sticks for a cooking fire. Rabbit took no part in the preparations. He squatted to one side, puffing on the remaining stub of his cigar he had lighted from a blazing twig.

When the meal was prepared, he accepted the tin plate Burnett handed him, and eagerly wolfed down the hot beans and bacon, helping himself to a second cup of coffee, with sugar.

The road they had followed from Tombstone led southwest through Pickemup toward Millville and Charleston.

By the time they had finished eating, scoured the utensils and plates with sand, and packed everything away, the blaze of red-gold in the western heavens was sliding down toward darkness. Thorne reflected that, when in town, he was hardly aware of this fantastic show of light and color that occurred nearly every evening.

Burnett was unstrapping his blanket roll from the saddle, when Rabbit stopped him. "No. We no camp here. We ride." He pointed toward Charleston.

"Hell, I was all ready to settle in for the night," Burnett grumbled, refastening the strap. "I wish you'd make up your mind. We could have eaten before we left town, and saved our grub for later."

They remounted and rode on into the twilight. Following the well-used, dusty road to Charleston was no problem, and they rode, loose-reined, letting the horses amble along. Rabbit set the pace, and he seemed to be in no hurry.

As they traveled toward the mining town of Charleston, a notorious hang-out for the rustlers, Thorne began to have second thoughts about encouraging Burnett to follow this Indian. The darkness of the desert night closed in around them, and he felt instinctively for the twin Colts he carried, one holstered and one in the leather pocket. He had taken the precaution of putting an extra box of .45 cartridges in his saddlebags. Whatever was waiting up ahead for them, he was determined to be ready.

CHAPTER ELEVEN

Thorne needn't have concerned himself about the town of Charleston. Some three miles farther, as they wound slowly past the wooden buildings and hoisting works of the Corbin Mill and Mining Company, Rabbit veered off the road and led them on a wide circle around Charleston. He seemed to know where he was headed, and Thorne and Burnett followed at his slow, steady pace. They stopped briefly at the shallow San Pedro River to water the horses, then splashed across and pushed on.

A nearly full moon appeared shortly after dark, paling the spangle of stars that were usually visible in the night sky. Thorne relaxed and even began to enjoy this night ride. The air was pleasantly warm, and there was no breeze. The silvered desert landscape took on an unreal quality of gray light contrasted with deep, black shadows. The low mountains seemed many miles away, but distances were impossible to judge.

The Apache rode with a straight back, as if he were proud of not having to travel afoot. Rabbit seemed to take things as they came to him, without thanks or question, as if it were all expected and preordained. If there were any surprises in life, he gave no indication of them. Yet it wasn't quite true that he gave no thanks. That's just what he was doing now, Thorne realized. What did his promise of "much gold" really amount to? There was no way Thorne believed this literally. But, obviously, Rabbit thought it was something good that he was giving Burnett in return for kind treatment, food, and whiskey. A doubt crept into Thorne's thoughts. This man was, after all, an Apache. Was he leading them into some sort of trap? Could he have been hired by some of the cowboy faction? Logic answered—"No."—to both of these questions. Rabbit was too simple and did not crave material things, aside from whiskey. If he had done something to be outlawed from his tribe, he wouldn't be inclined to help his people by taking revenge on the white interlopers. Thorne's hunch was that this Indian was just what he appeared to be—a simple savage who was addicted to alcohol and was attempting to show his gratitude to another human who helped provide for his needs.

Thorne put the whole issue out of his mind. In due time they would learn to what the Apache was leading them. There was no use speculating about it. He would just stay alert for any eventuality. But staying alert was one thing he was not able to do for long stretches at night. Thorne was basically a day person anyway, and he had been up and busy all day. Now, his body told him it was time to sleep. He found himself nodding as the easy motion of the walking horse lulled him into a state of relaxation.

Once his head jerked up at the howling of a coyote in the near distance. But the plaintive sound died away, and was not repeated. His head fell forward on his chest, and he dozed.

His horse stumbled, and then caught himself. The sudden sensation of falling brought him awake in an instant. The figure of the erect Indian on the plodding horse ahead of him was still there. Thorne twisted in the saddle and saw that Burnett was also fighting off sleep. He slouched in his saddle, and Thorne saw his bowler-hatted head jerk up as consciousness returned. The soporific effects of quiet moonlight, a long day, and a gently rocking saddle were beginning to show.

How long they rode this way across the desert toward the low mountain range he didn't know as he drifted in and out of wakefulness. He had tied the reins and looped them over the pommel of the McClellan saddle, and his horse plodded along in the cool night.

At last the world around them began to reappear in a gray light. Thorne roused up from a doze to sense the dawn creeping up from behind them. By the time the sun was hurling its eye-piercing rays over the eastern horizon, Rabbit was leading them down into a wash, near the foothills of the low mountain range. Large mesquite bushes that had reached down for some extra moisture were growing there, along with a palo verde tree, providing ample shade.

"Camp here," Rabbit said, dismounting.

Thorne dismounted stiffly. Burnett, unused to spending so many hours in the saddle, swung down with a groan and reached to loosen the saddle girth. The horses, before being hobbled, rolled gratefully in the soft sand, and then went to browse on the tender foliage around them. The white men poured some of the water from their two-quart canteens into their hats and gave the mounts a drink.

"Not as much as they need," Thorne said, "but it'll moisten their mouths until we can get to some real water."

"How far to the next water?" Burnett asked as the Indian came over to beg another cigar.

"Maybe tonight," he replied, accepting the smoke and the light. "We sleep now." He went to hunker near a mesquite bush where he could enjoy his cigar without confiding any more information to them.

"You want something to eat?" Thorne asked Burnett as the bartender sat down on the soft sand and tugged off his boots.

"Naw. I'm too tired. I just want to stretch out here in the shade and get some shut-eye." The big man was sagging badly.

"Wish I had thought to bring some hard bread to chew on," Thorne said. "Wouldn't have to cook all the time. Maybe some jerky, too." He took a couple of sips from his canteen before capping it. He sat down beside Burnett. "Where do you think he's leading us?"

Burnett shrugged. "Right now, I'm too tired to care." He stripped off the duster and rolled it up for a pillow. He placed his derby hat and gun belt within reach, and stretched out with a contented sigh. In less than two minutes his breathing became even and regular as he slept.

Thorne saw that Rabbit was still smoking, so he walked away and climbed up out of the wash to view carefully the surrounding countryside without revealing himself to anyone who might be in the vicinity. Some mesquite-studded hills rose just to the west of them, purpling to the range of low desert mountains some miles beyond. Rabbit was probably right—there was very likely water of some kind in those hills. The Apache had certainly been here before and knew the area. Rabbit didn't seem concerned about anything, a natural child of the desert, who could survive on whatever came to hand.

Thorne strolled about, keeping to the cover of the mesquite. No sign of human habitation was visible in any direction. If they had been traveling southwesterly all night, they had to be approaching Fort Huachuca, or maybe these were the hills south and east of the fort. He wasn't sure. He had neglected to bring a map. A serious oversight. Even though he had never traveled in this area before, he was good at orienting himself on a map, and he had studied a map of the region before coming to Tombstone. But the details had become sketchy in his memory.

He yawned mightily. He could feel weariness dragging at his limbs and eyelids. Time for some sleep. Scooping out a spot in the sandy soil beneath a mesquite bush a few yards from his companions, he settled down, using his rolled-up jacket for a pillow. His gun belt was close at hand. By the time the sun was well clear of the horizon, Thorne was sleeping soundly.

He awoke some hours later, drenched in sweat, his mouth dry. He crawled out from under the bush and brushed the dirt off. The sun was high overhead.

Burnett still slept, but was tossing and turning restlessly. The Indian was sound asleep on his back, one forearm lying across his face.

Thorne was itching in at least two dozen places from what he had determined, after examining his bed, were ant bites. He carefully removed all his clothes, turned them wrong side out, and shook them. He had never been a heavy sleeper. Unless he was exhausted, or had had several beers, any unusual noise or slight discomfort could wake him.

He was shaking and batting at his clothes, when a mounted Apache appeared. The rider jerked his pony up short at the lip of the wash, surprised at the sight of the naked white man standing a few yards from him.

Thorne was frozen for an instant as the two stared at each other. With a yelp of pent-up fear and surprise, Alex dove for his nearby gun belt. He rolled over once in the sand as he snatched the loaded gun from its holster and came up cocking the pistol. But the apparition was gone. His heart was pounding, as he scanned the edge of the dry wash, expecting to see mounted attackers charging down on him at any moment.

Burnett was scrambling up, aroused by the yell. "What the hell's the matter?" he sputtered, brushing the dirt and sand from his face and mouth.

"Apaches!" Thorne had no idea whether the man he had seen for a couple of seconds was, in fact, an Apache. But the image that was frozen in his mind's eye was one of a copper-colored torso, long black hair held in place by a headband. The only weapons he could remember seeing were a bow and a quiver slung over one shoulder, and a sheath knife at the waist.

"Where?" Burnett was scrabbling on the ground for his Remington, his pomaded hair in disarray.

Rabbit sat up, alert now, watching and listening.

"Just saw one, but there could be more," Thorne said. "Right there. He just rode off. I think we surprised him."

"Get your clothes on. I'll take a look," Burnett said, checking his weapon. "Rabbit, I may need your help," he said as he started cautiously up the slope toward the edge of the wash.

Thorne had never seen Rabbit move so quickly. One second he was sitting on the ground, and the next he was ahead of Burnett and creeping up behind a bush, near the spot where the horseman had appeared.

Heedless of his nakedness, Thorne sprang up the incline after them. Just as quickly he hotfooted it into the shade of a bush; his bare feet announced that the rocks were hot and sharp. He was just in time to catch a brief glimpse of the Indian rider before he disappeared behind a small hillock a hundred yards to the south.

"Whew!" Burnett let out his breath in a rush, as he lowered the hammer on his Remington. "Don't know who that was, but I hope none of his friends are around."

"Chiricahua," Rabbit said. "Hunting."

Thorne remembered the bow and the quiver of arrows. He wondered why the Indian wasn't using a rifle.

"It's quieter and saves ammunition," Burnett replied, when Thorne voiced his question. "Besides, most Apaches I've seen are pretty poor shots with firearms."

"Well, as long as we're all awake," Thorne said, still standing in the shade and scratching his bites, "why don't we have something to eat and then push on? I won't be getting back to sleep with all these little critters chewing on me."

"OK to travel by day, Rabbit?" Burnett asked, as he swung his gun belt around his waist and buckled it.

"We eat. We go," the Apache replied, pointing southwest.

"I like a man of few words." Thorne smiled as he picked up his clothes and shook them one last time before pulling them on.

"You don't get much fewer than that," Burnett said. He retrieved a frying pan from the saddlebags on the ground. "Gather up a little brush for a fire," he added. "Won't matter if anybody sees the smoke now. At least one Apache already knows we're here."

While the bacon was frying, Rabbit hunkered in the shade, entertaining thoughts of his own and staring into space. Again he took no part in the preparations, but accepted a tin plate of food and devoured it with relish—*as though he were royalty to be waited on,* Thorne thought.

It was about two o'clock by the sun, when they mounted and rode out, Rabbit leading.

Thorne was on edge and kept turning in the saddle to survey the terrain on all sides as they rode. But the desert was as harsh and dry and devoid of human life as he imagined the moon must be. Even the small desert animals had sought shelter in their burrows and nests from the baking mid-afternoon sun. Only a lone buzzard wheeled and soared high overhead on silent thermals.

Rabbit led them on what seemed to be an aimless, meandering route, dipping in and out of arroyos, skirting the base of the foothills. Finally, he halted and stared carefully around, as if searching for something. After several minutes, he kicked his horse into motion and headed to his right, into one of the many small cañons they had been passing. About fifty yards into the alluvial wash, he halted again and looked around.

"Ah!" he grunted with obvious satisfaction, as he pointed at a saguaro cactus some distance off. At first it appeared as if there were a bobcat perched atop the lightning-blasted cactus. But, as they rode farther along toward it, Thorne realized it was several flat planes of a pale green, prickly pear cactus growing out of the top of the blunted saguaro.

"Probably some seeds dropped by a bird nesting up there," Burnett said. "Strange-looking thing."

"Must be his landmark."

"I hope he knows where he is, 'cause I'm sure lost," Burnett replied. "All these little side cañons and foothills look alike."

Thorne uncapped his canteen and took two or three good swallows as he looked around at the foothills that were beginning to enclose them. Brush studded, with ledges of rock thrusting out boldly here and there, they were effectively cutting off any breeze, and the afternoon was growing very sultry. As he returned the strap of the canteen to the saddle horn, he experienced an uneasy feeling of closeness that wasn't related to the weather. He dismissed the feeling as a fear of not being able to see any distance around them. He preferred wide-open country, especially when there were hostile Indians about.

His gaze dropped down to the back of the Mescalero on the horse a short distance ahead. Then he twisted to look at Burnett, who brought up the rear. "I thought Apaches were supposed to be able to find their way without obvious landmarks like that cactus."

"I reckon this one's lost a little of his wilderness instinct. Too much demon rum and civilized living," he replied in a low voice. "Then, again, maybe he just hasn't traveled this area enough to know it."

The end of earthly life can come upon a man "like a thief in the night," Thorne thought. But much more often the grim reaper sends a messenger ahead to give notice of his coming. That warning, he knew, could take many forms, from a nagging ache in the chest to the blood-chilling *buzz* of a rattlesnake. He had the feeling that, for their small party, the appearance of one Apache hunter had alerted them to more lethal things to come.

Thorne rode with a tension in his muscles and a heightened wariness that hadn't been there before. He knew no Apache would be seen or heard until he wished to be, but he checked the loads in his Colt .45, acutely conscious of the narrowing defile.

Thorne knew that Burnett was also on edge. Just as he faced front once more, a shot cracked from the rocks above them, and a slug tore off part of his saddle pommel. Faster than an echo, several more shots racketed from the brush and pine-covered hillside. The next thing Thorne knew, he was leaning over his horse's neck, as their party of three pounded up the narrow cañon. Again several shots followed, but then suddenly ceased as they rounded a slight bend.

Rabbit slid out of the saddle and led his horse up a steepening incline, the two right behind him. Thorne had his Colt in hand as he cast a backward glance. No one in sight. Their attackers were probably changing positions, or pursuing along the cover of the rocky ridge above them. If they could only get up level with them and under some cover. He turned his attention to the incline, struggling up the loose dirt and shale and pulling his mount along.

The three men were strung out in single file, and no one had said a word since the shots were fired. Each instinctively knew they had to get out of the hole they were in and find shelter before the dry-gulchers could catch up.

Thorne's breath was coming in great, sobbing gasps, and sweat was stinging his eyes as he forced his aching legs up the last few steps to the top of the ridge.

Just as they stumbled into the shelter of trees, a shot boomed, and Rabbit's horse dropped. Then two shots cracked from behind, and the slugs clipped leaves from the trees over their heads.

Crouching and dodging through the scattered growth, Thorne and Burnett finally got their mounts tied behind a clump of stunted cedars. Then they flopped to the ground, pistols ready, to face their pursuers.

Rabbit, armed only with a knife, had made himself nearly invisible behind a small oak tree. His horse lay dead several yards back, blood oozing from a hole in the side of its head.

There was silence for several long seconds, broken only by the sounds of the shuffling of the two horses and the men's heavy breathing.

"Indians, you reckon?" Burnett panted the quick question.

Before Thorne could answer, two bronze figures with rifles appeared, moving silently across an open space some fifty yards away and disappearing into the heavier growth.

"Damn! Trapped like a gopher in a hole," Burnett hissed. "Don't know how many there are, but they can get around us in this cover and pick us off at leisure."

"Those two weren't mounted," Thorne replied in a whisper. "Let's mount up and ride like hell. If they've got horses, they're tethered back down the ridge a ways."

"Apaches fight better on foot," Burnett observed. "But what about Rabbit? He'll have to ride double with one of us."

A rifle cracked. Thorne's horse squealed and jerked backward, tearing off the small limb to which he was tethered. Thorne leapt to grab him, but the terrified animal plunged back, rolling his eyes, and galloped into the woods.

"Shit!" Thorne's frustration quickly turned to fear when another shot kicked up dirt three feet from his boots. He threw himself back to the ground at the base of the cedars near Burnett.

"Good thing most Indians are damned poor shots," Burnett observed coolly.

"Yeah, but now we're down to one horse," Thorne said. "Before they have a chance to circle us, get up on your Morgan and ride back into those hills like the devil was after you. Keep a straight course west as best you can. I'll cover you. Rabbit and I will follow on foot."

"Why me? I'm a good shot. I'll cover you. Or, if you don't want to do that, let's draw for it."

"Dammit, we haven't got time to argue! That's your horse. Besides, you're the biggest and slowest. Rabbit and I will catch up with you."

"Well, I guess that old knee injury *might* slow me down some. . . ."

Thorne rolled his eyes at the big bartender. "Get going. On the count of three. One . . . two. . . ."

Burnett holstered his gun and got to his hands and knees.

"Three!"

Thorne took aim at a slight movement of a mesquite bush and fired as Burnett jumped for his horse. He emptied his Colt as quickly as he could fire, aiming in the general direction of their attackers. The fusillade was almost one continuous roar. Then he rolled several feet to remove himself from the telltale cloud of blue-white smoke that hung in the air. He pulled his second Colt, and fired until it was empty. In the ringing echoes, he thumbed cartridges out of his belt loops and glanced around. Burnett and Rabbit were both gone. As he quickly punched out the empties and reloaded, he could see several flitting movements. The Apaches were gliding into position to flank him or cut him off from retreat. This bunch was either very careless or had nothing to fear, or they never would have allowed themselves to be seen, even briefly. They were masters of stalking.

He snapped the loading gate closed on each of his guns and held his breath, looking cautiously around. The ominous silence had returned. He heard nothing—not even the retreating hoofbeats of Burnett's horse. There was no answering gunfire. Maybe they knew he was now alone and were saving their ammunition while closing the noose on him.

He crawled away to the base of a nearby oak and sat with his back to the foot-thick trunk. The tawny grass, curing in the dry heat across the open spaces, was nearly knee-high. He didn't know where the Apaches were hiding, but he sat facing downslope, the way they had come.

Still, he saw it too late. A slight movement out of the

corner of his right eye. He jerked around to face it. The quick reflex probably saved his life as the iron-tipped arrow thumped into the tree, pinning him by his shirtsleeve to the oak. As one Apache drew back another arrow, a second Indian ran boldly into the open, stopped, and took aim with a rifle.

In the few seconds of life he had left, Thorne desperately tried to yank his gun arm free of the arrow. A yell of anguish escaped his lips. He knew his time was up.

CHAPTER TWELVE

But the rifle shot never came. The Apache's head was jerked backward as something landed at his back. He grunted wordlessly as the bloody point of a huge Bowie knife erupted from his naked belly. From behind, Rabbit kept hold on the falling body to shield himself as the bowman's aim was drawn away from Thorne and toward the friend of the white men.

With a desperate lunge, Thorne ripped his sleeve loose from the tree and took careful aim at the Apache who had swung his arrow toward Rabbit. The Colt roared, and the archer pitched sideways in a loose heap.

Two shots came almost simultaneously from the cover of the woods. One of them thudded into the body Rabbit still held upright. The other slug kicked dirt into Thorne's eyes where he lay on the ground in the tall, sparse grass. Through his blurred vision, he fired twice at the puffs of smoke, being rewarded by a yell of pain and then the crunching sounds of running feet.

Rabbit dropped the dead Indian, snatched the rifle off the ground, and pumped two quick shots after the fleeing attackers. Then he scrambled toward Thorne. Both men flattened themselves behind the small oak.

Thorne's heart was pounding, and he wiped a sleeve across his face to clear the sweat from his eyes. He didn't know how long they lay motionless. It seemed like a very long time. But, in reality, it was probably no more than a minute or two. They lay, facing in opposite directions, to watch the complete circle around them.

Finally, Rabbit pushed himself to one knee, then rose to his feet. "Gone."

"You sure about that?" Thorne asked, still looking warily around.

"Gone," he said again.

Just then Thorne jerked his Colt up at the click of an iron horseshoe against a rock.

Burnett ducked his head under a low-hanging branch and rode into view.

Thorne let out a breath of relief.

"Heard all the shootin', and thought I'd come back to see if you needed some help," he said, holding his Remington .44 in one massive fist. "Brought you this," Burnett continued, holding out the reins of Thorne's horse which he was leading. "Found him snagged in some catclaw about a half mile away. He got burned across the rump with a bullet, but he'll be OK."

Thorne walked to Burnett and took the reins. "Thanks. Rabbit says they're gone." He looked with renewed interest at the Apache. "He saved my life. I was a goner for sure, if he hadn't shown up when he did."

The man complimented never changed expression. "Chiricahua no good. Hide in rocks like coyote, then run away."

"There was a damn' sight more to it than that," Thorne said. "But I'll take his word on anything to do with Apaches from here on, even if he is of a different tribe." He pulled the horse around and handed the reins to Rabbit. "Here, you ride. You've earned it. I'll walk."

As the Mescalero flipped the reins into position and swung easily into the saddle, Thorne thought he detected the trace of a smile on the Indian's face.

Thorne looked toward the bodies of the two Indians. His knees were a little weak, and he sat down next to the oak tree and wiped his clammy face. A natural reaction to his own brush with death, he realized. He busied himself reloading his three spent cartridges. "What about those bodies?" he asked.

"Their friends will be back for 'em. And we'd better be long gone, when they come. Vengeance is one of their favorite pastimes."

Thorne heard the tension in Burnett's voice.

"Probably just a renegade bunch that jumped the reservation," Burnett continued, holstering his Remington and taking off his bowler to swab his face with a blue bandanna.

"I don't care where they're from," Thorne retorted, beginning to feel somewhat better. "If they're roaming these hills, killing and robbing, I'd as soon be safe in my hotel back in Tombstone. I'll take stage robbers any day over Apaches."

"You were the one who talked me into coming on this jaunt," Burnett reminded him, replacing his hat. His round, unshaven face, drooping mustache, and dirty vest and shirt looked oddly out of place with the dapper derby.

"Yeah, I know," Thorne conceded. "I guess when a man comes within an ace of losing the whole pot, he tends to have a change of viewpoint."

"Well, we've come this far," Burnett said, taking a deep breath. "Might as well go on. What else can happen?"

Thorne could think of a number of things, but said nothing. He'd had the same urge to push on, when he was out of water in the Sonoran desert. His crushed hat hung by its leather thong down his back. He pulled it up, punched it back into shape, and put it on his head. "I'm game, if you are. Let's go. What kind of rifle did you pick up, Rabbit?"

The Indian held out the weapon, and Burnett took it. "Damn! It's a Thirty-Eight. Won't match up with any ammunition we've got. We'll take it along, though, in case we need to fire off the rest of the rounds in it." He worked the lever of the Winchester, and an empty shell casing flipped out. He worked it again, prepared to catch the cartridge, but the weapon was empty. "Some luck. I guess they were short of ammunition. That's why they were using arrows. How much farther, Rabbit?" Burnett asked as the horses started off at a walk. Thorne was forced to jog to keep up.

Rabbit reined in. "We go quick." He looked at Thorne. "You ride here." He patted the horse's rump.

"He'll carry double for a while," Burnett agreed, glancing back at the silent woods. "If he says we need to make some distance in a hurry, I'm not gonna argue."

Rabbit gave Thorne a hand up behind, and they started at a trot deeper into the hills.

About an hour later, they seemed to have reached the crest of the range of hills. They rode along a broad ridge. The woods were not as thick as before, and nature seemed at rest, the birds chirping as they rode through the sun-dappled grass and bushes.

"Have any idea where we are?" Thorne asked, sliding off and stretching his legs, tired from gripping the flanks of the horse. They slowed the animals to a walk.

"Yeah, I think I do," Burnett nodded, looking carefully around at the rolling, wooded hills. "I think we're just a little east of the old, abandoned Mowry Mine.

"That doesn't tell me much."

"Several miles southwest of Fort Huachuca. This string of hills runs south a few more miles into Mexico."

Thorne nodded.

"I was over this way last year," Burnett continued. "If we keep riding this direction a few more miles, we'll come down into the Santa Cruz Valley, right near the little town of Patagonia."

"The Mowry Mine, you say?" Thorne mused. "Sounds vaguely familiar."

"Named for Sylvester Mowry. Former Army lieutenant who struck gold, silver, and lead here back before the war. He was accused of financing the Rebel forces, and the mine was confiscated by the government. Nothing was ever proven, but he spent some time in Yuma Prison. I think it was a ploy to get his mine, because it was rich then. It's since played out, and there's nothing left but a lot of empty shafts and tunnels."

"Wish I knew where he was leading us," Thorne said, talking about Rabbit as if he were not even present. If the Indian understood, he gave no sign, guiding his horse regally along the faint wagon trail they had struck. The trace was overgrown with weeds, showing long disuse, but it was still easier going than cutting cross-country.

"I don't know," Burnett replied. "But, if we don't arrive somewhere by tomorrow, I'm going back. I think I've humored him about as long as I can stand it."

Thorne knew by the way the big bartender was constantly looking around and appearing to sniff the air, he thought they were a long way from being out of Apache danger.

The oaks and junipers began to thin out as the road wound along the ridge. The serenity of the afternoon was such that it would have been difficult to convince an unsuspecting traveler there was a hostile Indian anywhere within a hundred miles.

"The little town of Harshaw should be somewhere down

this road a few more miles," Burnett remarked. "Another silver mining camp that went boom and bust within the last couple of years. Mines petered out quick, and then several flash floods washed most of the town away. Wrecked most of the place in a hurry."

Suddenly Rabbit halted his horse, kicked both feet out of the stirrups, and dropped to the ground. He trotted several yards to one side where the ridge dropped away in a steep slope. He was obviously looking for something, but the only unusual thing Thorne could see was the tall snag of a lightning-blasted oak on a promontory of rock about a hundred yards away.

Rabbit padded softly back to them. Instead of remounting, he took the reins just below the bit and led the animal back toward the edge. Burnett turned his mount to follow, and Thorne came along on foot.

In spite of the steepness of the slope, Rabbit found a way down, angling diagonally across the face of the hill.

Burnett dismounted and led his horse as the three of them dropped over the lip of the ridge and started down, single file. Before they had gone halfway to the floor of the brushy cañon, Rabbit stopped and tethered the horse to a scrub oak. Burnett silently did the same. Then the Indian glided on down the unseen trail.

Thorne's heart was beating faster. God only knew where they were going, but he had the feeling they were almost there.

Rabbit stopped so suddenly Burnett bumped into him. The Indian held up his hand, motioning them to stay put. Then he was gone, disappearing around a slight bend in the faint, overgrown footpath. A few seconds later, his head appeared briefly above the chaparral farther down. *Indians must have an instinct for stealth,* Thorne thought, observing

Rabbit's silent, ghostly movements. The Mescalero could glide with the effortless, cat-like grace of the natural athlete.

When Rabbit vanished, the peaceful woods and hills around them seemed to take on an ominous aspect. It was almost as if the presence of the Indian had provided them with a protective talisman in a hostile environment. As Thorne stood there, he reflected that his idea was not far off the mark, considering the athletic Apache had saved his life less than two hours before. He thumbed the rawhide safety loop off the hammer of his Colt.

The mid-afternoon sun appeared to be nailed to the sky. In the windless ravine, Thorne felt drops of perspiration trickling down his sides and from under his hat brim. The horses twitched and swished at the biting flies. Nature seemed to be holding her breath, waiting for something to happen. He and Burnett did not converse. It was as though some monastic vow of silence held their tongues.

After an indeterminate time, Thorne began to wonder if Rabbit had abandoned them. Was this some sort of trick? A practical joke, perhaps? Maybe he had led them all the way out here on a chase for some non-existent gold only to leave them to find their own way back to Tombstone, tired and hungry. Or, worse, yet, maybe he had led them here to be ambushed by other Apaches. He immediately rejected this thought. If that had been the case, Rabbit would have let the Apaches kill him earlier. So engrossed was he in these thoughts that he jumped, when Rabbit suddenly appeared beside them.

"You come. Horses stay," he said in a low voice.

They followed as the trail wound around the bank, then descended so steeply they had to squat to slide down on their feet, hands, and buttocks, scattering loose shale in their descent. To Thorne it seemed the clattering stones made excessive noise. However, except for any lurking Apaches, he had no idea why he was trying to be quiet.

The trail leveled out for about thirty yards as they were about three-quarters of the way to the bottom. Rabbit slowed and ducked behind a thick clump of mesquite. The two white men were on his heels, and they next found themselves standing in the well-concealed entrance to a cave. As they took a few cautious steps into the opening in the hillside, Thorne realized this was not just a natural cave in the rocky hill. Timbered shoring identified this as an old mine shaft.

"Gold here," Rabbit said, pointing inside. His voice sounded strangely hollow in the recesses of the tunnel.

Thorne peered at the rusty set of iron tracks, used for small ore cars, that led down into the tunnel at a slight angle. He was bursting with curiosity, but held his tongue for the moment.

Rabbit retrieved two lanterns from just inside the entrance. He handed one to Burnett. Coal oil sloshed, when Paddy shook it. Rabbit handed the other lantern to Thorne.

"You light. We go."

Burnett fished a match from his vest pocket and struck it against the rock wall. The two wicks caught and flamed up under the smoky glass. Before they were fairly burning, Rabbit snatched Burnett's lamp and was off, leading them into the drift.

In a few seconds the afternoon heat was a memory as the dark, stuffy mine enveloped them. The place had a dank smell of a closed-up fruit cellar. The tunnel was nearly seven feet high and about as wide, with some timbered shoring every dozen feet or so. Protected from the weather along with the dryness of the tunnel, the timbers showed no signs of rot or weakness.

"Part of the Mowry Mine?" Thorne whispered hoarsely at Burnett.

"Yeah. I think so. We're close. The place was well-developed with several shafts and tunnels. There was a lot of ore taken out of this area," he replied over his shoulder.

Thorne was talking mainly to distract the demon of claustrophobia that was beginning to crawl out of its cage deep inside his unconscious. He began to be aware of his own shallow breathing, as he watched the flickering lanterns for any sign that the flames were guttering due to lack of oxygen. He recalled the Tombstone miners discussing lethal pockets of underground gas that could kill with little or no warning.

Grotesque shadows chased them along the irregular walls. Once, Burnett's head thudded into a low beam. Along with a curse, a shower of dirt and small stones sifted down on them. Thorne's heart leapt, and he sprang back. But it was not the beginning of a cave-in, even though the ceiling and walls here were composed more of dirt and small stones than of massive slabs of rock.

"Made digging a lot easier, but dangerous as hell," Burnett muttered in response to Thorne's verbal observation.

It wasn't the answer Thorne wanted to hear. He forced his mind to ignore the suffocating tunnel that was leading them deeper and deeper into the earth. If other men had gone this way, he certainly could, he told himself. Instead, he focused on what might lie at the end of their odyssey.

They had gone more than fifty paces into the tunnel, stepping carefully around the rusty, ore car rails, when Thorne felt the floor leveling out. Before he could remark on this, the walls fell away on either side and they were several steps into a huge room. He paused and swung his lantern around. Even when he turned the wick up, the light barely reached the far walls of the circular cavern. The ceiling was at least twenty feet above them. Either the tunnel had broken through into a natural cave, or some earlier miners had removed many tons of rock and ore from this place. One thing for sure—the air was decidedly cooler and damper.

"I feel a draft," Burnett said.

The air fanning Thorne's cheeks confirmed the cross-ventilation.

"Must be somehow connected to the surface. I smell fresh air," Thorne remarked, gratefully drawing in a deep lungful. He wiped the clammy sweat from his forehead as he held the lantern high overhead. The light reflected off the trickles of water seeping down the seamed walls of gray rock. Several pools of unknown depth puddled the floor.

"Where in the hell are we, Rabbit?" Burnett's deep voice gave back an echo as if from walls of a chamber much bigger than they were able to see.

Thorne tried not to think of the millions of tons of earth pressing down over his head. This opening had been here for at least several years, he surmised. There was no reason to think it would collapse within the next hour. But logic was not on speaking terms with claustrophobia.

"No stop," Rabbit said, holding his lantern high and moving on.

"How much farther?"

"By and by."

"Shit!" Burnett was clearly losing patience and was also feeling the effects of the darkness and the closeness of the subterranean passage. He flung off his bowler, and shrugged out of his vest, dropping it to one side.

Rabbit crossed the large cavern and ducked into another opening in the wall. This time they went only about five paces before emerging into another room that appeared to be considerably smaller.

"Gold here," Rabbit announced, holding out his lantern.

There, stacked against the rocky face of the cave, were several boxes and canvas sacks. Even in the uncertain light of the smoke-darkened lantern glass, there was no mistaking the white block lettering on two of the dark boxes: **WELLS FARGO & CO.** Bold, black stencils on several canvas sacks nearby proclaimed, **U.S. GOVERNMENT.**

CHAPTER THIRTEEN

Thorne caught his breath at the sight. His mouth was dry and his heart pounding, as he set the lantern on an express box and went to one knee to examine the cache. There was no doubt it was part or all of the loot from months of stage and express wagon robberies.

Burnett, also stunned into silence, was squatting a few feet away, hefting a brick-size bar of gold bullion. The heavy metal gave off a rich, mellow gleam in the lantern light.

"See . . . I bring you to gold. You rich. No more work," Rabbit said, his face glowing nearly as much as the gold. It was more than Thorne had ever heard him say at one stretch. The Indian was very pleased with himself. His face nearly cracked into a grin as he awaited some approbation.

Burnett stood up with a grunt and looked at their guide. He started to say something, then stopped. Finally he said: "Rabbit, you are quite a man. I don't know what I was expecting, but it sure as the devil wasn't this."

Rabbit's grin revealed a set of even, white teeth in his dark face.

"This is one helluva stash. You have done us a *great* favor, but not the way you think," Burnett continued. His heartfelt thanks warmed his voice. "You've solved part of the mystery we've been working on for a long time. This gold was stolen from the stagecoaches. It belongs to the mines and to the Army. You understand?"

"You take?" Rabbit asked. "We load horses."

"We'll take it, all right," Thorne put in, "but it's not ours to keep. This belongs to many other people." As he spoke, he opened the unlocked boxes to find sacks of coins and stacks of greenbacks. He didn't know how much was here, but estimated between one and two million. There were even bank drafts and ornate certificates of mine stock and bundles of unopened mail.

Thorne stood up and let out a long breath. He and Burnett looked at each other with the same question.

"Do you know who put this gold here, Rabbit?" Thorne asked.

He shook his head. "No one here. I find cave. Good place to camp."

"You've never seen any white men around here?" Thorne persisted.

"No white man."

"I can't believe they don't have a guard on this," Thorne remarked.

"Would you bother?" Burnett said. "As well hidden as this is? Besides, these hills are crawling with Apaches. A natural guard."

"Well, it tells me one thing," Thorne said.

"What's that?"

"Whoever hid this . . . they're well organized. It's more than just a bunch of cowboys who're robbing a stage now and then to get a stake or to have some cash in their pockets for a big spree."

"Yeah. That's one thing I've found out," Burnett said. "No reports of anyone blowing a lot of money in the last few months . . . not in this area, anyway."

"Let me take another quick look, and then we'd better get out of here," Thorne said, kneeling once more to inspect the hoard. He took a few letters, a handful of double eagles, and a small packet of greenbacks and stuffed them into his pockets. Then he carefully folded a gilt-edged stock certificate and slipped it into his shirt pocket. "That oughta be enough evidence that we've found some of the booty," he said.

"Who're you going to convince? Behan? He'll just take it as evidence that you were in on the robberies." Burnett snorted in disgust. "It's great to get all this back, but it's only half the battle, unless we can link it with whoever stole it."

"Well, our first job is to get three or four pack mules and haul this stuff to town and have a full accounting made. Then we'll worry about who stole it," Thorne said.

"Why wouldn't one wagon do?" Burnett asked.

"Be tough getting it up here with those old mining roads all overgrown and washed out."

"You're right."

"Let's discuss it on the way back to town," Thorne said, standing up. "I've got to get out of here before I smother."

"Is there another entrance to this mine?" Burnett wondered. "Rabbit?"

There was no answer. Burnett swung his lantern around, but the Indian was not standing there.

"Rabbit! Where are you?" Burnett's voice rose slightly in alarm.

Fearing treachery, Thorne put a hand to his holstered Colt and backed away from the lantern, his eyes trying to probe the dark spaces beyond the feeble light. His heart began to pound.

"He was right here. Where'd he go?" Thorne fought to keep his voice steady.

"Rabbit!"

"Rabbit!"

Their voices echoed hollowly from the walls, as they took a few steps away from each other, moving their lanterns in slow arcs.

"Come on, Rabbit! This is no time for one of your jokes."

"Is he usually given to practical jokes?" Thorne asked.

"No. That's why I think something's happened to him."

"Be careful. He may have stepped into a crevasse or a shaft of some kind."

"We'd have heard something. He was standing right beside me," Burnett said. He stopped moving and held his lantern high overhead. The only sounds were his own harsh breathing and the distant trickling of water.

"Shall we make a search?"

"I think he took off on his own. He does that sometimes in town when he gets spooked. If he fell, or if someone grabbed him, we would have heard him holler."

"If he'd been hit with an arrow or a knife, he'd have dropped where he stood," Thorne said.

"What?" Burnett turned to look at him.

"Apaches could've followed us in here," Thorne replied, letting his imagination run to the least likely possibility.

They yelled for the vanished Indian once or twice more, their voices echoing away to be swallowed up by the enveloping darkness of the unseen chambers.

After several long seconds of oppressive silence, Burnett finally said: "I don't know where he got to, but I'm for getting out of here."

"You don't want to look for him?"

"I think he took off on his own. He's very resourceful. When we bring some men back to load this stuff, we'll bring some more lights and make a thorough search, if he hasn't turned up yet."

"Let's go."

"You remember the way out?"

"I think so." Thorne took his lantern and led the way back through the short tunnel to the large cavern. "The tunnel we came down should be almost directly across from this one." He proceeded confidently in what he thought was a straight line across the rocky floor.

Before he realized it, his boots were splashing into a pool of water. "I don't remember this." Not knowing how deep it was, he stopped and started to back up. Just at the edge of the pool, he stepped on a slick ledge of rock and one foot shot out from under him. He tried to catch himself, but fell backward into the water, snuffing his lantern.

"Damn!" Thorne sputtered, struggling to his feet.

Burnett grabbed his arm and helped him up.

"Lost my light!" he spat, disgusted by his carelessness.

They found the lantern unbroken, but Burnett was not able to relight it.

Taking Burnett's lantern, Thorne led on again, but the fall had thoroughly confused his sense of direction.

Suddenly he saw a wavering light, reflecting off the curving wall of a tunnel to his right. He knew it wasn't Rabbit, since the Indian had no light with him. Footsteps scuffed hollowly in the passageway.

"Quick. This way," he whispered hoarsely to Burnett. He didn't want to be caught in this mine. Shielding the lantern with his body, he veered to his left, looking for some place to hide. The sounds and the light were coming closer. Thorne was walking quickly, the shadows from the bobbing lantern leaping and retreating.

A gap showed in the rough wall. It was the entrance to another tunnel, and Thorne darted into it, with Burnett at his heels.

They went about twenty quick paces into the tunnel before they stopped to listen. Their harsh breathing was the only sound. Thorne turned down the wick of the lantern and shielded the remaining light. "I'm sure whoever it was must've heard us," he whispered. "See any light?"

"No."

They waited another minute. Then they heard water splashing and saw a quick reflection of light off the tunnel wall. Thorne's heart leapt, and he put his hand to the butt of his Colt. But then the noise ceased, and the faint glimmer of light did not reappear.

"Didn't the tunnel where we came in have ore car rails?" Burnett whispered.

"Sure did. All the way through."

"Then we're in the wrong passage. I thought this one had too much of an upward incline," he puffed as they started again.

Thorne also noticed the absence of any shoring. He turned up the wick of the remaining lantern. "Let's keep going this way. It's gotta lead to the outside . . . 'cause I can smell fresh air."

"Yeah. And at the angle we're climbing, we couldn't be too far from the surface," Burnett added.

At that moment, the lantern flickered briefly and went out, plunging them into a velvety blackness. "Oh, no!" Thorne began to panic. Without the light to hold it at bay, the blackness rushed in to smother him.

"Never mind," came Burnett's reassuring voice from behind. "It didn't go out for lack of oxygen. Out of fuel, I guess. But the matches were in my vest pocket, and I threw the vest aside on the way in." He nudged Thorne. "Let's go. We can make it."

The climb became ever steeper and the tunnel narrower, so that they finally reached a point where two men could not have passed each other. Thorne forged ahead in the darkness, leaning forward into the steep passage, panting heavily and trying to stay focused on each step, rather than the walls and ceiling pressing in on him.

He was finally forced to his hands and knees by the constricted space. The unlighted lantern clanked as he shoved it ahead of him.

"This was an air tunnel . . . ," Burnett panted behind him, also crawling. "It was never meant to haul out ore."

"If we ever get out of here, I'm not going underground again until I'm in a pine box. You and the Earps can go back in for that stash." The sweat of fear dripped from his nose.

The sweet smell of fresh air grew, and he finally saw a pinpoint of daylight ahead.

Less than five minutes later they struggled, one after the other, through a partially collapsed two-foot hole into a patch of mesquite on a hillside.

Thorne put the lantern down on the grass. Then he sat in grateful silence, gulping the fragrant air and feeling the dappled sunlight of the real world play over his head and shoulders through the foliage.

Burnett stood up and stretched mightily—a begrimed bear of a man, knees sticking out of his pants, minus his hat and vest, white shirt and face covered with soot and dirt.

Thorne knew he must look even worse, not only dirty, but wet. He didn't care. He was alive and unharmed, and that's what mattered. He pushed himself to his feet and wiped his hands on his wet pants. "Where are we?"

"*Ssshh!*" Burnett grabbed his arm and pulled him down. "There's somebody over there. . . ."

"Where?"

Burnett pointed. "About fifty yards away. Just around the bulge of this hill."

They worked their way carefully through the mesquite and crept up the hill.

When they finally reached the crest, Thorne realized they were somewhere above the tunnel where they had entered.

"There!" Burnett pointed.

Thorne heard a low murmur of voices, and then, looking in that direction, could see the tops of two felt hats on the path below him. He pulled his gun and checked the action to be sure it was free of dirt and water.

"Stay here," he hissed softly. "I'm going down."

Before the big man could object, Thorne was creeping through the undergrowth and across the face of the hill, as silent and supple as smoke. He slithered the last few yards, gun forward, until he was able, from beneath a low bush, to get a clear view. Two cowboys stood on the path, holding their horses and talking. Burnett's Morgan and Thorne's sorrel were still tied a few feet away.

A tall, lean man, wearing chaps, took a long drag on a cigarette and dropped it, grinding it out under his boot. "Damn! It's gettin' hot. How long you reckon they're gonna stay in there?"

"Dunno. Simon went in to find 'em over twenty minutes ago," the other replied, consulting his watch. "He oughta be marchin' them out here, any minute, at the point of his gun."

"Whoever it is, the boss ain't gonna like it," the tall man said. "And it can't be a couple o' Injuns, from the look of these rigs."

"No, it's white men all right. You recognize these horses?"

"Nope. One's a cavalry horse and rig. And there's nothin' in the saddlebags but some grub."

"I haven't heard any shootin'," the second man said. "Simon might just decide to plug 'em and drop 'em down a shaft in there, so they won't never be found."

"I don't reckon Simon's got the gumption to shoot anybody in cold blood," the tall cowboy opined. "Anyway, I reckon the boss might want to talk to 'em first."

Thorne lay still as a stone. The wet clothes clung to him and were beginning to itch, or else there were some ants crawling on him. But he dared not move. What should he do? He could jump these two and disarm them. But what of the man they called Simon who was in the mine looking for them? What if Simon came out with Rabbit? If Thorne were able to get the drop on all three, what could he do with them? He and Burnett would have to take them to Tombstone and charge them with something. Maybe possession of stolen property. They obviously knew what was hidden in the mine. What if they turned out to be working for the owners of the mine, and thought they were just guarding an inactive piece of mining property? Thorne dismissed this as a remote possibility. And who was this boss they referred to? The mine owner, or the one who had charge of all that stolen gold, silver, and cash? He had to know more. He lay still and waited, but the two men changed the subject and started talking about various women they had known in Tombstone.

The itching became worse, and it took all the will power he possessed to lie still.

Finally, a third man emerged from the mine tunnel. He wore no hat, and blinked at the sudden sunlight. "Couldn't find 'em," he said. "They took the two lanterns that was settin' just inside the entrance there, so all I had was the stub of a candle I had stashed on one of those beams."

"Hell, they gotta be in there," the tall cowboy said.

"Oh, I heard 'em hollerin' for somebody. And I saw their light from a distance. But when I got to the big cavern, they was gone. Don't know where. And they's at least six tunnels that run off that big room. I had to come out of there, when my candle burned down. I know that place like my own yard, but I ain't takin' the chance o' gettin' lost in the pitch black."

After a brief pause, the third man inquired: "What now?"

There was a pause as the men considered their alternatives.

"Let's take their horses into Tombstone," the tall man suggested. "We could say we found 'em wandering loose in the desert. Say we're lookin' for the owners. Maybe somebody will recognize who they belong to. Then we'll know who we're after."

"Good idea. In the meantime, who's gonna tell the boss about this?"

They looked at one another, none of them apparently relishing the task.

"He's not gonna be happy," the tall man said.

"Well, he can't blame us. Just lucky we came along and found 'em here."

"But we can't let 'em get away to tell anybody what they found."

"Do you know where all these tunnels come out?" the shorter of the three asked. "If not, how're we gonna catch 'em?"

"Unless they get lost and die in there, they're bound to come after their horses. All we gotta do is sit tight and wait."

The tall cowboy nodded. "We shouldn't have long. Reckon they'll be here afore sundown, if they're comin'."

"Did you get the money?" the third man asked Simon.

"No. I got t'chasin' their light, and my candle burned

down before I had a chance. I had to get out while I could still find my way."

The short man shook his head. "The boss ain't gonna like us not comin' back without our operatin' funds."

"Shut yer mouth about what the boss ain't gonna like!" Simon exploded. "All I hafta do is ride over to Patagonia and buy me a lantern. I'll have the cash, when we go back."

The smaller man grinned. "You go to ridin' around alone in these hills, you're liable to have an Apache arrow decoratin' your shirt."

"Where're the horses?" Simon wanted to know.

"Down the hill a piece."

"These horses act like they ain't been watered for a spell."

"Well, we ain't movin' 'em now. They're the bait for our trap."

He had hardly gotten the words out of his mouth, when several small stones came rattling down the hillside from behind Thorne. The three men jumped.

"That may be them now. Get out of sight!"

Thorne twisted around and saw Burnett's boots sliding down the steep slope toward him.

"Damn!" Thorne breathed. "Why didn't you stay put like I asked?" he muttered to himself. He looked back, and the three cowboys had vanished downhill into the brush. Thorne squirmed back out of his hiding place beneath the bushes, got to his feet, and dashed back up to intercept Burnett. "We can't go down there," he whispered urgently, pulling the big man down out of sight behind some scrub oaks. "They're waiting for us."

"They've got our horses?"

"Yeah. They heard you coming and ducked out of sight to grab us."

"What now?"

"We're afoot. We don't dare go for the horses. There are three of them, and they're armed and waiting."

They were silent for a few seconds. Burnett looked down the hill through breaks in the undergrowth where their horses stood patiently grazing.

"We're in one helluva fix. Rabbit gone . . . on foot in Apache country . . . and three men waiting to ambush us."

"Not so bad," Thorne said in a low voice. "We've still got our guns and full cartridge belts. We know where the stolen money is, and, if we just keep our heads about us, we can get back to Tombstone and get help. We'll have to travel at night, and it may take us a few days, but we can make it. We might be able to take those three, but it'd probably alert whoever they're working for."

"Right," Burnett said. "Those men will likely leave after dark."

"Yeah. They talked about taking our horses to Tombstone to see if someone could identify the owners."

"As soon as they leave, we'll head down to the water. There's a small stream in the bottom of this ravine. Wish we had our canteens so we could carry some of this water with us. I'm powerful thirsty." Burnett licked his dry lips. Sweat streaked the dust and soot on his broad forehead. "By the way, did you recognize any of those three men?"

"If I've ever seen them in town, I don't recall."

There was a scuffle in the brush just above them. Thorne jerked his head around and found himself staring into the black muzzle of a rifle.

"Then maybe you'll remember me," a familiar voice said.

With a sinking sensation in the pit of his stomach, Thorne raised his eyes and saw the grinning features of Frank Stilwell.

CHAPTER FOURTEEN

"Charley! Simon! Stump!" Stilwell yelled. "C'mon up here! I got 'em!" He turned back to the two captives. "Sling those gun belts over here at my feet."

A minute later, the crashing of brush heralded the approach of the three men.

"What the hell you doin' here, Frank?" the tall man inquired, when the three came up.

"I was sent to find out what was taking you so long. Spotted these two hiding in the brush from the trail up there. Knew it was close to the mine, so thought I'd better have a look."

"Hell, we'd have got 'em, if you hadn't come along," Simon said, obviously irritated that Stilwell had sprung the trap before he had.

"I doubt that. You'd have found yourselves in a gun fight, more'n likely," Stilwell said.

"Who sent you to look for us?" Simon demanded, changing his tack. "Doesn't the boss trust us?"

"Never you mind who sent me. The question now is what do we do with 'em?"

"You know these two?" the tall man asked Stilwell.

"Yeah. One's a bartender at The Occidental, and this one's named Thorne. He rode guard on the Bisbee stage a few days ago, when Sandy Bob was shot. They're both friends of the Earps," he added.

"Hell, that's reason enough to drop 'em down one of these shafts!" the short, stocky man called Stump snorted. "That damned Wyatt Earp pistol-whipped me last week, just because I was drinkin' and shot out a few windows."

"I don't want to hear about your troubles," Stilwell said. "We've all had problems with the Earps. But now's not the time to talk about them. What were these two doing here?"

"Best ask them. They were down in the mine," the tall man replied. "I don't know how they got out without us seein' them. Must've wandered out another entrance. Simon went in after 'em, but couldn't find 'em."

"What were you doing in there?" Stilwell demanded of Burnett and Thorne.

Neither man replied.

"I reckon, if you're not talking, then you know what's in there," Stilwell concluded.

Thorne wondered again about Rabbit. It was lucky they had wound up with only two horses. These men had no idea there had been three of them. But if Rabbit had been hurt or killed, or had simply run away, he could be no help to them now.

"I ain't takin' the responsibility of deciding what to do with them," Stilwell was saying. "Let's take them to the boss and let him decide. This is his operation."

"OK by me," the tall man assented.

The others nodded their agreement.

"Get their horses," Stilwell said. "We'll water them all and then get started."

Twenty minutes later Burnett and Thorne, hands tied to the forks of their saddles, were being led single file down the overgrown wagon road. Two of their captors rode ahead, and two behind. The road led past the abandoned adobe and wooden buildings of the Mowry Mine. No one was about. Scraps of iron workings and a rusty boiler were scattered here and there. *No hope for help from anyone here,* Thorne thought as they trotted past. The empty headquarters buildings disappeared into the trees behind them.

About three miles farther they passed an adobe cabin, its empty windows and door staring out at the road like a gaping skull. Another mile brought them to what a weathered signpost identified as the town of Harshaw. The wooden and adobe buildings, lining both sides of the dirt street, appeared to have suffered the devastation of both fire and flood. So this was the boom camp Burnett had described. From boom to bust in two years. From the number of buildings, most in various states of ruin, Thorne judged the place must have housed at least a thousand people or more. Two stone buildings, standing slightly higher than the rest, seemed to be in the best condition. But these things he noticed only at a quick glance. His mind was on their plight and on trying to work his hands loose from the cutting cords that bound them to the saddle. Yet, even if he got them free, he had no idea what he would do.

The lead riders reined up at the hitching rack of the largest stone building. A large, recently-painted sign above the door declared: **SANDERSON'S GENERAL MER-CHANDISE**. A general store in a ghost town—it didn't make any sense. Unless there were still a fair number of people living here.

The tall man untied their hands from the saddles, and they dismounted.

"Inside!" Stilwell ordered, glancing up and down the deserted street.

Burnett and Thorne, unarmed and outnumbered, had no choice but to obey.

A bell tinkled as the door swung open, and they all filed

in. The large room with a wooden counter, running the length of one side, was well stocked with everything Thorne would have expected to see in a store like this—from overalls and brogans to shovels and picks, canned food, coils of rope, leather work gloves, nails, pots and pans, bolts of cloth, even a couple of smoked hams that looked like old pieces of dry leather.

A clerk, lounging in a chair behind the counter, stood up. "What the hell is this?" he demanded, eyeing them.

"Caught 'em at the mine," Simon replied.

It was then Thorne realized this unshaven, well-armed man was no clerk. He was a guard. A shotgun lay on an empty shelf just behind the chair where he had been sitting. And, as Stilwell nudged them toward a doorway into a rear room, Thorne noticed the heavy layer of dust covering all the merchandise as well as the counter top. No business had been conducted in this store for a long time.

The back storeroom was nearly as dusty as the front of the store, but, strangely enough, the wooden plank floor was clean.

Stilwell reached into a narrow space between two tall shelves and pulled down on a long lever. An oblong trap door in the floor swung downward, revealing a set of stairs.

The tall man and Simon led the way down. Burnett and Thorne looked at each other. In spite of his resolve never to go underground again, Thorne could hardly ignore the rifle muzzle in his back. He took a deep breath and started down.

But, unlike the mine they had so recently escaped, this basement was well-lighted with lamps in wall sconces. In place of the odor of burning coal-oil, Thorne breathed a pleasantly fragrant perfume. When they reached the bottom of the twenty-odd steps, they paused as Stilwell swung the counterbalanced trap door back into place above them.

They went another ten paces down a corridor and then descended several more wooden steps. A few yards farther and they were standing in front of a plank door. Simon rapped sharply. A muffled reply came from within. Simon lifted the iron latch and swung the door inward, then stood aside as the rest of the group entered.

The room was large—at least thirty by forty feet, with a ceiling probably twenty feet high. And the light was different. Looking up, Thorne saw that the place was illuminated by some kind of natural skylight. He took this all in at a glance as his gaze swung to a man seated at a small, oak desk beneath the skylight.

"Well?" The imperious tone of the man seemed to strike fear into the four men who had brought in the captives. There was a long silence as the men glanced at one another. With the stare of the man in the chair boring into him, Stilwell finally cleared his throat and said: "Captain, we caught these men at the mine." Then Stilwell stepped forward, leaned closer, and spoke in an undertone to the man he had addressed as captain.

The man behind the desk stood up, focusing his attention on each of the prisoners in turn. Thorne thought he had never seen, or felt, a more penetrating gaze. The man was over six feet tall and lean. It would have been difficult to determine his age. The flat planes of his face were bronzed and clean-shaven with the exception of a sweeping trooper's mustache, tinged with gray. The hair was black, but a streak of snow-white hair about two inches wide ran from just left of a widow's peak straight back across his head. Standing only a few feet away, Thorne could see the gray eyes under the arch of black brows. Altogether, a striking, handsome man. In spite of being addressed as captain, he wore only a soft white shirt and black string tie, with gray pants. From the streak of hair, to the eyes, mustache, and trousers, there was a grayness about the man that reminded Thorne of the sharp leanness of a polished saber.

"Have they been thoroughly searched for weapons?"

Simon hastened to correct this oversight. In the process, he turned out their side pockets, discovering the gold coins, greenbacks, letters, and, in Thorne's shirt pocket, the mine stock certificate. He placed these items on the desk, along with a tiny penknife, handkerchief, and both men's billfolds.

"You men are dismissed," he said to the four. "I want to question them alone. Post a guard outside the door."

"Yes, sir," Stilwell said, and herded the others out the way they had entered, closing the door behind them.

The tall man came around the desk and stood in front of them, leaning his buttocks against the edge of the desk and crossing his booted feet. He regarded them curiously for a few seconds, and then said: "I forget my manners. Please be seated." He gestured at two wooden armchairs behind them.

Thorne suddenly felt very weary. The strain was beginning to tell.

The tall man folded his arms across his chest and gave them a tight smile, as if he were a parent about to have a chat with two miscreant sons.

"It's obvious from the contents of your pockets," he began, inclining his head toward the pile on his desk, "that what my men just said is true . . . you were, in fact, stealing from my mine."

Burnett opened his mouth to reply, but the man held up his hand. "You'll have your chance to talk. My men may not have mentioned it to you, but I take the greatest offense at *anyone* who steals from me. I can't abide a sneak thief. I would rather a man overpower me and take what I have by force than to pilfer it behind my back. Frank Stilwell tells me that you're a bartender in Tombstone, and you"— eyeing Thorne—"are a stagecoach guard and are associated with the Earp brothers. Is that correct?" he inquired with an oily unpleasantness.

Neither man responded.

"Well, well, you have nothing to say? Then, regardless of your occupations, let me ask what you were doing in my mine. No, let me guess. . . ." He spread his hands and tilted his head toward the ceiling as if concentrating. "You were out on a picnic and just stumbled across the mine and thought you'd go exploring, like two small boys. No? Then maybe a horse got away from you, and, while chasing it, you came across one of the tunnels and just went in. Still not right? Maybe one of the cowboys got drunk at your saloon in town and bragged about untold riches? Am I close?" He dropped his hands and stared directly at them. "It's obvious that *someone* told you or showed you. . . ."

"Hell, everybody in the Arizona Territory knows where the old, abandoned Mowry Mine is," Burnett interrupted him.

"Ah . . . you *can* speak. Yes, that is true. But you'll excuse me if I find it far beyond the realm of probability that you just stumbled across the gold, the cash, and the mail. And, having found it, you also saw the Wells Fargo chests, U.S. government bags, canvas sacks with bank markings, and things such as this stock certificate which even the simplest dullard could not fail to recognize as stolen property. . . ."

"You're a long-winded bastard!" Burnett butted in. "Why don't you just quit playing games and get to the point?"

A predatory gleam came into the man's gray eyes, and Thorne wished the impetuous bartender had kept his composure and let the man ramble on. The longer he talked, the more time it gave Thorne to figure some way out of their dilemma.

"All right," he replied smoothly, sliding up to sit on the corner of his desk, "if you are impatient, we'll get right to business. But it's such a shame. I get few visitors. And the art of civilized conversation has become so rare in the modern world. It makes me homesick for those long gone days before the war." He breathed a sigh and paused for a moment.

His words had flowed out with slightly rounded edges, suggesting perhaps a Mississippi origin.

"I am Brady Cox Brandau, former Captain in Mosby's Partisan Rangers in the War Between the States. Because I want no grandiose pretensions, I do not allow myself to be called general, which is the title my men wish me to have. You see no military trappings here."

"The soul of modesty," Burnett said dryly.

"You would do well to keep your sarcasm to yourself," Brandau replied sharply.

Indeed, the only adornment suggesting a military operation was a set of crossed sabers hanging on the wall behind his desk. In the upper V formed by the swords was the circular device enclosing the X and the four stars that, by now, Throne was very familiar with.

"Why are you telling us all this?" Thorne asked suddenly, unable to keep silent any longer.

"Because you are going to die very shortly," Brandau replied as matter-of-factly as if he were giving them the time of day.

Thorne's blood went suddenly cold.

"And I hate to see a man go to his death not knowing the reason for it. During the late war, even the lowliest private soldier knew that he was fighting to defend his homeland against the Northern invaders and to preserve a civilized way of life that was *brutally crushed!*" The last two words were almost shouted as he slammed his fist on the desk, making the brass inkwell jump. Thorne was startled at the ferocious outburst. But, in an instant, Captain Brandau was his suave self once more.

"Again, my hospitality is lacking. Too long among the excrement of society, I fear. May I offer you gentlemen some refreshment? A glass of wine, perhaps?"

Thorne was on the point of refusing, when he realized how parched his mouth and throat felt. A glass of wine—several glasses of wine—could hardly heighten the feeling of unreality this whole scene was giving him. He nodded his assent.

"Good!" He rubbed his hands together. "I could use an apéritif myself about this time of the afternoon. I have some excellent port I'd like you to try." He slid off the edge of the desk, went to a side door, and opened it. "I'd appreciate it, if you'd bring us some port," he said to someone in the next room. There was a muffled reply. "Thank you so much." Brandau closed the door and returned to sit in the desk chair, leaning back to cross his legs.

"Now, then, where were we? Ah, yes. I told you that you were going to die. It is a fate that will come to all of us, I fear. But you have been caught in the web of my grand plan, and your ultimate demise will occur a little sooner than the rest of ours." He gave a deep chuckle at his own humor. "But let us talk of other things while we enjoy our wine, shall we? Time is too fleeting for all of us, so we must enjoy each moment as we ride the slide toward eternity. There will be an opportunity over dinner this evening to tell you of my plans. You gentlemen will join me for dinner, won't you? I'd be crushed if you refused." The gray eyes receded to slits as he smiled.

Burnett and Thorne looked at each other, and silently reassured themselves that they were both actually hearing this strange monologue.

Just then the side door opened, and Thorne knew with certainty he was having a nightmare. A servant came in carrying a tray with four tumblers of wine. The servant was Julie Ann Martin.

CHAPTER FIFTEEN

"Thank you, my dear," Brandau said, getting up and taking the tray from her. He set it on the desk, and gave her an embrace, kissing her lightly on the lips.

Thorne knew his mouth was open and his eyes probably looked as big around as the wine glass. He swallowed hard a couple of times and tried to speak, but no words were forthcoming.

"Allow me to introduce my associate, gentlemen," Captain Brandau said, turning to them. "This is Ann Gilcrease. You know her as Julie Ann Martin. Among her many accomplishments, she was a most successful spy for the Southern cause." He chuckled at the thought. "Yes, many a Yankee officer was seduced by her charms into revealing military information that sent hundreds of their soldiers to be food for the worms." A grim smile of satisfaction etched his face. "She will be gracing our table at dinner this evening. I'm sure you will enjoy some of her stories. But, until then, what shall we toast?" He handed a glass to the woman, then one to each of the men, and took the last one for himself. "How about . . . to a healthy life, however long it may be, filled with all the pleasures the world can give?" He raised his glass.

Thorne numbly elevated his glass with the others and drank.

The aromatic wine seemed to clear a path down his

throat so he was able to speak again. But, by now, his head had caught up with his mouth, and he said nothing.

The initial shock began to wear off, and he could feel himself blushing with shame as the woman's eyes rested on him. What a fool he had been!—acting as her manly escort and protector, eagerly exchanging flirtations, falling before her seductions like some inexperienced cowhand. He consoled himself with the thought that many a smarter man than he had been duped by her in the past. Julie Ann Martin was really Ann Gilcrease, Confederate spy! The war had been over more than fifteen years. Her war-time episodes had to have occurred when she was no more than sixteen to eighteen years old. She had the looks and the figure for such an undertaking. But, more importantly, behind those blue eyes, also lurked cunning and an iron will. But what was she up to now? He glanced over at Burnett whose cheeks were red—either with embarrassment or anger. The Irishman didn't look Thorne's way.

"Gentlemen, we have an hour or so until dinner," Brandau said. "If you would like to freshen up, I'll have one of my men show you to your quarters. I'm sorry we have no bathing facilities and no clean clothes for you, but these flooded-out mine passages are only my temporary quarters. For you, they will be even more temporary. But, do the best you can. We will call you for dinner."

Captain Brandau went to the door at the front of his office and spoke to the guard just outside.

Thorne's head was in a whirl as the armed guard led them down a short corridor to another wooden door which he opened. He motioned for them to enter, then closed the door without a word. The sound of a bar falling into place was loud in the silence.

The room was about ten feet square, the items of furniture consisting of a rude, wooden bedstead, one chair, and a small wooden stand with a pitcher and bowl. A smoky lamp was burning in a wall sconce, the ventilation being provided by a roughly circular shaft that led up through the ceiling. Somewhere, probably thirty feet above, the late afternoon light was filtering down through the air shaft. Unlike Captain Brandau's office, this room was not lined with mortared rock.

"All the charms of a root cellar," Thorne commented, walking over and sitting on the hard bed.

Burnett poured out some water from the pitcher into the large, matching bowl, splashed some onto his face, and dried it and his mustache on his sleeve. "We gotta get out of here. But damned if I know how we're going to do it," he remarked, pacing around the small room, examining the dirt and rock walls. "If we had a long ladder, we might be able to squeeze up through that vent hole."

"And, if we had some tools and plenty of time, we could probably tunnel out, too," Thorne commented. "But we don't have either, so we might as well forget it."

"Do you get the feeling that Brandau is crazy?"

"He's definitely a little off plumb, but he's not stupid. It will be interesting to hear what this grand plan of his is all about."

"Yeah, something to divert our attention before he has us killed," Burnett remarked, his voice sinking.

In spite of the hopelessness of their situation, Thorne was calm and collected, his mind working clearly. "All we can do is go along with him, humor him, maybe give him a compliment or two to boost his pride, while we try to figure a way out. If we see there's no way out, I'm not going down without a fight," he concluded with tight-lipped resolve.

Thorne got up and followed Burnett's actions at the

wash bowl, sluicing away the dirt and sweat from his face and hands. He pulled out a pocket comb which had not been taken when the outlaws emptied his pockets, wet it, and ran it through his hair. "Might as well look as good as I can for dinner."

"You're still trying to impress that woman, aren't you?" Burnett said disgustedly, sitting down heavily in the one chair.

Thorne had to admit to himself that he probably was. He put the comb away. "Was she your mistress?"

Burnett nodded.

"Not that it matters now, but could she have been charming information about those treasure shipments out of you?"

Burnett heaved a long sigh. "Maybe one or two, now that I think back on it . . . in moments of weakness."

"Of course." There was no sarcasm in Thorne's voice, as he thought of the way she had begun to worm her way into his own affections—probably with a view to securing information about military shipments.

"How do you reckon she fits into this?" Burnett asked. "Is she only working for wages? I wonder if she had any real feelings for me at all."

"Beats me," Thorne replied. "You knew her better than I did . . . much better."

"Apparently, I didn't know her at all," Burnett said.

"Duplicity is the name of the game in the spy business," Thorne observed. "You had no reason to think she was anything but what she appeared to be—a beautiful, unattached woman who was in love with you."

"I still feel like a fool."

"No need to. Most men are fools when it comes to women. I was as taken with her as you were."

They fell silent for a few moments, and Thorne stared around at the room. "Looks like they just enlarged and furnished some old mine shafts and tunnels with wood salvaged from those ruined buildings up above."

"Yeah. Harshaw was honeycombed with tunnels . . . even under part of the town. Would you believe this town had three newspapers just over a year ago? Wonder if any of those people they served are still around?"

"I didn't see a soul on the street when we came in. And it looks like the general store upstairs is just a front in case somebody passes through the town."

Burnett nodded. "Whatever he's up to, this Brandau sure picked a good place to set up headquarters. Beats the Clanton Ranch all to hell. An old, abandoned mining town in the Patagonia hills. Mines worked out and half the town destroyed by several flash floods. Wonder how they deal with the bands of renegade Apaches roaming around here?"

"Probably stay forted up here most of the time, and travel in groups when they have to ride somewhere."

Burnett looked glum. "And to think I let you and that Indian talk me into coming on this jaunt after gold!" Even his elegant handlebar mustache was drooping.

"Too late for regrets now. We accomplished at least half our mission . . . we found the stolen cash. Or, rather, Rabbit found it and brought us to it, even though he figured it was anyone's for the taking."

"It's still a mystery what happened to him," Burnett said. "One second he was standing almost next to me, and the next he was gone without a trace."

"Let's just hope he's out there, running free some place."

"For his sake, I hope he is, but it won't help us none. I doubt he even knows we're here."

They fell silent again. Finally Thorne said: "I don't know

what the next few hours are going to bring, but, if we never see another sunrise, I want you to know it's been a real pleasure knowing you and working with you." He stuck out his hand.

Burnett gripped it, cleared his throat, and finally mumbled: "Thanks." He looked away quickly.

Then Thorne was all business again. "You got anything on you that could be used for a close-range weapon, if it comes to that?"

The bartender shook his head. "Nary a thing. They stripped me clean. Even me gold toothpick's gone."

"Then I guess we'll just go along to dinner in a few minutes and hope something presents itself, when the time comes."

"You know," Burnett said with a grin, "I'm hungry as a wolf. You'd think in a situation like this, I'd have lost my appetite. But, as you can see," he said, patting his ample midsection, "I can eat 'most any time."

"I'm hungry, too. Let's hope it's not the condemned men's last meal."

Shortly thereafter, one of the guards unbolted their door and escorted them down the corridor from the bedroom prison. Their path took a right turn, then a left, and ended up a flight of stairs where they entered a room on ground level. To Thorne's innate relief, they could see the trees and the early evening sky through the curtained windows that lined one side of the large dining room. As nearly as he could judge, they had come up somewhere behind the general store, on a wooded hilltop.

"Good evening again, gentlemen," Captain Brandau greeted them, turning from one of the windows and smiling broadly. He was dressed in a white shirt and tie and a black suit that set off his black and white hair and mustache. "Please be seated. Miss Gilcrease will join us shortly." He motioned toward the oblong dining room table that was set with a snowy linen tablecloth and sparkling china and silver.

Thorne wondered how such ornate furnishings and tableware could have come to be here, until he remembered that Harshaw, until recently, had been a wealthy, booming town whose residents could afford all the luxuries of any city.

"Mister Burnett, you will sit on my right. Mister Thorne, you will sit here, next to Miss Gilcrease."

The men quietly took their places. *This former Captain may not have retained his military trappings,* Thorne thought, *but he certainly has a taste for the finer things of life.*

Two lighted red candles made a glowing contrast to the white tablecloth. And between the two candles lay a beautifully-worked silver piece in the form of a circle about six inches in diameter with the familiar X and the four stars.

Hardly had they taken their seats, when the door opened and Julie Ann Martin/Ann Gilcrease entered the room. All three men automatically stood, and Captain Brandau held her chair as she seated herself on his left. Thorne was at her left, and, as he resumed sitting, he thought he had never seen her looking as lovely as she did now. Her dark hair was meticulously coifed, swept back and held in place by a diamond cluster pin on either side of her head. These pins matched a diamond necklace she wore, set off by the white expanse of skin above the low-cut silk dress of deep green.

"Gentlemen," she nodded to her left and right.

In spite of the artificiality of the entire situation, Thorne felt dirty and grubby in her presence and in this setting.

Captain Brandau picked up and tinkled a small bell on

the table. A door behind him opened, and a man in a clean white collarless shirt entered, carrying a large silver tray containing a smoking, sliced roast beef, garnished with potatoes, carrots, and parsley and set it in the middle of the table. He was followed by another man who delivered a bowl of asparagus and a loaf of fresh bread. The two men withdrew without a word through the open breezeway to the detached kitchen.

At the sight and aroma of the food and coffee, Thorne's stomach rumbled. He hadn't realized how hungry he was. He smiled to himself as he realized he had almost forgotten their peril for the moment. He planned to do the meal justice; he might need the strength it would provide. If all the food was being served from the same bowls and platters, he reasoned that it probably wasn't poisoned.

The plates were filled, and they began to eat. There was no talking. Only the clinking of silverware marred the formality of the situation. The beef was tender and well-seasoned. Obviously, Brandau had a supply of good food and someone who knew how to cook it. There was even sugar available for the coffee.

Well into the second helping, Brandau decided it was time to talk. He rose and filled his coffee cup from a silver service on the sideboard, and took it upon himself to fill the cups of the others. He resumed his seat at the head of the table.

"I promised to tell you something of my plans," he began, pushing back his chair and crossing his legs. "As you've no doubt already guessed, I am the mastermind behind most of the stage and bullion robberies in the southern part of the territory in recent months. However, I have not restricted my operations to this area. In fact, I've just gotten word that five of my men have taken one-hundred and twenty-five-thousand dollars in gold and silver ingots from a stage up north near Flagstaff. One of our larger hauls." He smiled as he sipped his coffee. "I'm particularly proud of this job because Wells Fargo was trying to hide the shipment in two whiskey kegs that were wrapped in brown paper and were being sent by the U.S. Mail."

"Inside information, I suppose," Burnett commented.

"Of course," Brandau said. "We have contacts inside Wells Fargo . . . agent Rufus Williams in Tombstone, for one. And you, Paddy Burnett, are another, thanks to the lovely Miss Gilcrease, er . . . Miss Martin, here. In fact, you, Alexander Thorne, as a Secret Service agent, representing the Yankee government, are fortuante to be alive. I had given orders to have you shot that night, just to get one more operative out of the way." He smiled at Thorne. It was a smug smile of superiority. "But, as luck would have it, we got the wrong man, and the driver was hit, instead, when the coach got past my men. Too bad."

His off-handed attitude at the shooting of Sandy Bob Crouch seemed to enrage Burnett whose face reddened noticeably. But Thorne was glad the big man held himself in check.

"How did you know I worked for the Secret Service?" Thorne couldn't resist asking.

"I told him," Julie Ann replied, speaking up for the first time since the meal had started.

Thorne turned to look at her, amazed. "How did *you* know?"

"Oh, Alex, you are too modest. I've followed your career for several years. I have been working as an undercover operative, in one capacity or another, since the war. I know all about you." She smiled.

In spite of her response, her voice and smile and the familiar use of his given name revived a twinge of feeling for her.

"I doubt you could find a better spy, informant, undercover agent, or whatever you choose to label her calling," Brandau put in. "It's really a natural gift, you know, honed by many years of experience. I'm most fortunate to have her on my side."

"And just what is it you get out of all this?" Thorne asked, looking directly into her blue eyes next to him.

"She will be . . . ," Brandau began.

"I want to hear it from her," Thorne cut him off, keeping his gaze directly on her.

She met his eyes steadily as she replied. "I will marry the handsomest, bravest, smartest man I have ever met," she replied. "And I will be a co-ruler with him."

"What are you talking about . . . co-ruler?" Burnett sneered.

"We will preside over a small new country of our own," Brandau said. "But, I'm getting ahead of my story," he said, pushing his dishes aside and ringing the small hand bell. "If everyone is finished, we'll have some brandy."

The two waiters came in and poured each of the four diners a small glass of brandy in glittering cut-glass tumblers. They left the decanter on the table, along with one of red wine, and withdrew.

Captain Brandau leaned back in his tall armchair, sipping the brandy. His gray, icy eyes took on a faraway look as he smoothed his sweeping mustache with a linen napkin.

"I will not bore you with a recitation of all the evils the Yankee politicians have visited upon the Confederacy. Besides, both of you were probably too young to have fought in that conflict. Suffice it to say our way of life was destroyed forever. And my beautiful plantation home in Mississippi was ruined, the land confiscated, and my family murdered. As you can imagine, all this left me with an abiding hate . . . and hate is hardly a strong enough word . . . for those who did this, and for their way of life. Many of my fellow Confederates groveled and pledged allegiance to the Union. But I have never forgotten, and certainly never forgiven, what those voracious destroyers have done to me and my homeland." He paused to take a couple of sips of the brandy, his face clouding with the memory.

"There have been those since Appomatox who have stolen Army rifles, tried to capture portions of the Southwest or Mexico to set up their own personal versions of the lost Confederacy. All have failed. The government of the Union destroyers was too powerful. They were crushed by the United States Army like small remaining embers of a fire that had been put out. I had the urge to join one or two of these movements, but I did not. I could see their plans were flawed. They were obsessed more with pride and power, than with good sense. Even the Mexicans, who are forever fighting among themselves, kept the filibusterers from setting up feifdoms in the state of Sonora."

He stood and strode to the sideboard where he removed the lid from a circular humidor and selected a tapered cigar. He sniffed it with obvious pleasure. "Perfectly made Havana Royales," he said. "The finest cured leaf. Would you gentlemen care for one?" He brought the humidor to the table and held it out. Thorne shook his head, but Burnett helped himself, bit off the tip, spat it into his hand, and then lighted the cigar from one of the red candles. "Ahh. . . . Excellent!" the big man enthused as he blew a cloud of fragrant smoke toward the ceiling.

To Thorne's immense surprise, Julie Ann also helped herself to one of the Havanas, allowing Brandau to snip off the end with a penknife he carried on his watch chain, then hold a candle for her to puff the cigar to life. Then he lighted his own.

"One of the good things of life I was mentioning earlier," he said. "Now, then, to continue. . . ." He sipped his brandy. "My desire for revenge against the Yankees was no less powerful than that of thousands of other Southern men and women. But I formulated my own plan. My plan would succeed because of its simplicity. No grandiose schemes for power and glory. I would hit the United States government and the Yankee capitalists where it hurt the most . . . in their pocketbooks. I would take any and all money and gold that I wanted. A million dollars, or even several million might not cripple the U.S. government, even though the loss of that much might crumple a few private companies or banks. But it would make me a very rich man. At least I would be more than compensated for my war-time losses."

"What good is all that money, if you're on the run and can't enjoy it?" Thorne asked, sipping the brandy and beginning to feel a little more relaxed.

"Just the point I was getting to," Brandau replied, puffing on his cigar. "I needed a safe place . . . a haven where I would be in complete control and able to use the money any way I wished. Any of the land the Yankee aggressors claimed as their own would be out of the question. Even land that I would buy for myself in the remotest mountains would not be inviolate. The monstrous federal government has shown its true face by sending its Army into every corner of the continent to ferret out the wild Indian tribes, and to put a stop to the private practice of Mormon polygamy, even though it was a legitimate part of their religion." His tanned face was becoming darker with anger. Nervous energy forced him out of his chair, and he paced back and forth near the sideboard, puffing his cigar and raking his fingers through his black and silver hair.

"I asked myself where I could find such a place. Has anybody ever found such a place before? Then it came to me . . . the mutineers of her majesty's ship, *Bounty*. Pitcairn Island. They were not found there until nearly thirty years after their mutiny. Of course, by then, most of them had destroyed each other over the native women they had brought from Tahiti.

"But, by diligent searching, we have found such an island. I will not divulge its location, except to say it's in one of the chains of islands in the South Pacific. It is not presently on any nautical chart I have seen. It is well out of the shipping lanes, is about ten miles long by four wide, rich in vegetation, soil, and clean water, with a good anchorage and a forested mountain. In short, ideal for a secret, small, defensible country where I and my bride would rule absolutely."

"A Pacific plantation where you would once again be lord and master," Thorne commented dryly.

"Exactly, except that we will own no slaves. With the gold and the greenbacks converted to gold through banks of other countries, we will fortify this island with cannon and small arms. We will have complete control over who comes and goes, the population the island will support. We will have the finest material goods brought in by schooner. . . ."

"How are you going to keep a place like that secret?" Burnett interrupted.

"After a few years we won't have to. But it would take the ships of several navies to blast us out of there, or a large invasion force. And, as long as no one can prove where our gold came from, why would they bother to make war on a small island country that is minding its own business?"

"It's happened before," Thorne commented. But he had to admit that what Brandau said made sense. "And who is going to inhabit this island kingdom besides you and your cigar-puffing bride?" He glanced at Ann Gilcrease who did not change expression as she tapped the ash from her smoke onto her plate.

Brandau smiled beneath the mustache. "Jealousy is an ugly thing, Mister Thorne. I doubt that we will have children," he continued pointedly, "and I have no dreams of starting any dynasties. Frankly, I don't care what happens after the two of us are dead. The few primitive natives we evicted to take that island can come back and claim it for all I care.

"But, to answer your question . . . it will be the men I have recruited, the cowboys who have helped me gather the gold and hide it, the men who have been such a burr under the saddle of Wells Fargo and the Yankee mine owners from Ohio and elsewhere. These men and their wives or girl-friends are the ones who will share this kingdom. After all, most of these boys are from the South . . . Texas, Mississippi, Alabama. Their feelings are the same as mine."

"I have never seen an operation of this size that didn't have its leaks or its turncoats," Burnett said, leaning back in his chair and eyeing the former cavalry officer.

"Oh, I have no illusions about that. In fact, we've had a few already. The dead man that Billy Clanton brought into Tombstone recently and tried to claim a reward for . . . he was one of ours. He got greedy and was caught filching some of the gold . . . more than his small allowance, so I ordered him shot as an example. Billy Clanton did the job and then got the idea of claiming he found the body. I agreed, since it had the effect of throwing suspicion off the Clantons."

170

"That was the fella who had the watch fob that looked like this," Thorne said, pointing at the circular silver device with the X and the four stars that was resting in the center of the table between the two candles.

"Precisely. I thought Billy would have taken the man's watch, but he didn't. That symbol is the insignia of our organization. As I said before, I am not a man who goes in for much show or ceremony. The Knights of the Golden Circle with members divided into castles, and all the other secret societies of the Confederacy were just so much folderol. But the men who joined me wanted something like a blood oath, or a secret symbol to identify members, like some fraternal organization. So I finally agreed to adopt the stars and bars of the Confederate battle flag rearranged into the simple, circular pattern you see there. A nicely done ring of solid silver. . . ."

"Representing a ring of robbers," Thorne interrupted.

Brandau continued as if he had not heard. "The boys voted to call themselves The Rebel Legion. It's all rather silly and childish . . . like playing pirates . . . but, if it will serve the purpose of binding allegiance from my followers, then I'm all for it. Most of my men are of a rather simple turn of mind. As long as they have someone to do their thinking and planning for them, they perform marvelously." His gray eyes became as hard as diamonds. "Of course, discipline must be maintained. Punishment for infractions is swift and harsh. They understand that."

"That's the symbol I saw burned into Bill Heard's belt," Thorne said.

"Ah, yes, poor Bill. Got himself shot, holding up that Bisbee stage," Brandau said, squinting through the cigar smoke. "In fact, I believe it was your bullet that did him in," he said, looking at Thorne.

171

"He's still at Doc Goodfellow's. They'll be able to make him talk, when he comes around."

"I'm afraid he won't be coming around, as you put it. My men tell me he died two days ago." He smiled and finished his brandy at a gulp. "See? You were a better shot than you realized."

Thorne's heart sank. With Bill Heard probably went the Earps only hope of breaking the silence of this secret society. The other cowboys had certainly proven to be a close-mouthed group so far. Probably the threat of instant death, coupled with a steady supply of expense money and the promise of much more, kept them in line, even when they were drinking.

Thorne looked at Ann Gilcrease who was quietly sipping her brandy and looking as beautiful as ever. The woman had perfect control of her emotions, and Thorne knew it was a useless endeavor to try to make her suspicious of the motives of her mentor and future husband. She had too much experience to be taken in by that. Even if Captain Brady Cox Brandau did drop her, it would be much too late to help him and Burnett. So the next thing out of his mouth was said mostly in desperation. "So I presume your lady love is also your executioner, when it comes to disposing of traitorous or disobedient followers?"

"No. Stilwell, the Clanton boys, or Frank McLaury usually take care of that. Curly Bill Brocius was just not quite stable enough to be depended upon. I will say that Ann has a most exquisite taste, when it comes to torture. I've seen a lot of suffering, but what she can do with a flaying knife makes even my skin crawl."

Ann smiled and inclined her head at the compliment as she helped herself to another full glass of brandy from the decanter. None of the men offered to pour for her. Thorne could feel his face blanch at the thought.

"She claims an Apache squaw taught her their secrets of slowly removing the skin, one strip at a time, exposing millions of outraged nerve ends."

Thorne swallowed hard as he glanced at the emotionless creature sitting next to him. Then he took a deep breath and looked across at Burnett, who shook his head the slightest bit to indicate his incredulity at this entire scene.

Dusk had settled outside the curtained windows, the only light in the room provided by the soft glow of the flickering red candles. The dull gleam of silverware, the rich color of the brandy, and the sparkling cut-glass against the white linen gave the room an elegance that could equate to the finest dinners Thorne had ever attended. It took little imagination to place himself in the dining room of Brandau's ante-bellum Mississippi mansion—an effect the captain had taken considerable pains to recreate.

"Well, gentlemen," Brandau said, slipping out his gold watch from a vest pocket and popping it open. "We've lingered long over our meal, and, as much as I've enjoyed this, it is, regrettably, almost time to say good bye, since I still have much to do this night." He closed the watch carefully and slid it back into his vest pocket. "As I've mentioned before, the pleasures of life are brief. Briefer for some than others. I hope you gentlemen enjoyed your dinner. I'm sorry there was no dessert, but my cook did the best he could on short notice." He smiled that icy gray smile of his that Thorne had come to detest.

Captain Brady Cox Brandau stood and pushed his chair back. "It is time for you to leave. But don't worry. As Marcus Aurelius once wrote . . . 'He who dies in extreme old age will be brought to the same condition with him who died prematurely.' You're just going on ahead of the rest of us." His hand came out of his side coat pocket with a nickel-plated Derringer.

Thorne caught his breath as the twin barrels of the .44 were aimed at his head.

CHAPTER SIXTEEN

Ann Gilcrease stood up quickly and placed a hand on his arm. "Brand, not at the table," she said softly.

The steely eyes flickered to her, and he wavered. "Perhaps you're right, my dear," he said. "It would make a terrible mess. I suppose I was just in too much of a hurry since we're moving out this evening."

"Let me deal with them," she purred, snuggling next to him and looking directly at Thorne. "They represent the rich Yankee capitalists and the United States government. We'll make an example of them."

Brandau's eyes were snapping with excitement as he lowered the Derringer. "Their screams won't be heard, will they?"

"No, darling. But scream they will."

Thorne thought she seemed slightly drunk.

"Take a couple of the men to help you. They could prove unpleasantly athletic," Brandau said.

"I'll meet you in about two hours," she said, sliding away from him and going toward the door.

"Don't be late, my dear," he smiled after her. "Remember, we'll begin the move before midnight."

She nodded.

"I'll send Stilwell and McReynolds with you," he added. "They're both getting restless. It will be good to give them a diversion. I only wish I could spare the time to come along and watch." He licked his lips, and his gray eyes glowed with an intensity that reminded Thorne of a hunting puma.

Thorne's hand slid over the table knife beside his plate. As soon as the woman left the room, he was tensing his muscles to lunge at Captain Brandau who had slipped the Derringer back into his side coat pocket. Thorne moved his chair back slightly from the table, casually, head down, as if resigned to his fate.

The door closed softly behind Ann, and Brandau's hand reached for the small bell on the table he used to summon the waiters.

Thorne gathered his legs under him and sprang. Brandau was caught off guard and staggered back, the bell jangling as it flew into the air. Thorne's knee hit the edge of the table, and it took some of the force out of his rush. The round-bladed table knife struck Brandau's coat lapel and skidded off. But, before the tall man could recover, Thorne was on him like a cat, bearing him to the floor. He pinned the man's arms to keep him from reaching in his pocket for the Derringer. The captain was at least ten years older than Thorne, but his limbs were as strong as piano wire. He twisted and heaved, breaking Thorne's grip and throwing him off.

Out of the corner of his eye, Thorne saw the door open and the two waiters enter. He was vaguely aware of a chair smashing one of them as Burnett intercepted the pair, evening the odds.

Brandau was scrambling away, his hand going to his coat pocket. Thorne jumped for him again, and the two, locked together, crashed into the sideboard, upsetting the silver service.

In one quick motion, Brandau spun Thorne around, whipped out the Derringer, cocked, and fired. His aim was hurried, and the bullet shattered a window. Before he could cock again, Thorne knocked his arm upward and aimed a vicious kick at the tall man's groin. The toe of his boot caught Brandau dead center, and the captain went down with a cry of anguish.

But the shot had sounded the alarm. Burnett was just putting the finishing touches on the second waiter, when Stilwell and another man rushed through the open doorway, guns drawn.

A shot blasted. All struggling stopped. Burnett and Thorne backed away slowly from the two men, hands at shoulder level.

Brandau was bent double on the floor, groaning.

"Are you shot, Captain?" Stilwell asked anxiously. "If they've shot you, I'll kill 'em where they stand!"

"No," gasped Brandau. "I'll be all right in a minute."

"It's his lovemaking that'll be affected for a while," Thorne grated with a grim smile.

Coffee from the overturned silver service was dribbling from the sideboard onto the floor when Brandau pushed himself painfully to his feet. There was a look of pure hate in his eyes. He steadied himself, still partially bent over. "I'm going to enjoy seeing what Ann will do to you. I will laugh while you scream for mercy, while you beg to be shot. Before she's through, you'll even wish the Apaches had gotten hold of you!"

The two waiters, somewhat the worse for their clubbing by Burnett, were slowly getting to their feet. One of them had an eye that was rapidly swelling shut. The other was holding a handkerchief to a nose that was streaming blood all over his white shirt.

"Take them down to the second level and chain them in the vault. Then stay there while Miss Gilcrease works them over," Brandau said to Stilwell and the cowboy with him.

"Yes, sir."

Stilwell motioned with his gun. "That door."

Burnett and Thorne were herded back out the door through which they had entered. The way led down the stairs into the first level of tunnels below ground. Then they were taken down another flight of wooden steps to a level probably twenty feet below and into a chamber roughly circular, about thirty feet across, that still bore the marks of mining activity.

"Back up to those rings!" Stilwell ordered. "Put the shackles on 'em," he added to the man with him.

Burnett and Thorne were handcuffed, hands behind them, to two iron rings fastened to the wall about waist level.

"Where's Miss Gilcrease?" one of the men asked.

"Right here," a feminine voice answered, entering from a side tunnel, holding a lamp. The light shone on the diamonds and the low-cut green dress she still wore. "Are they well secured?"

"Chained to the wall," Stilwell assured her. "They won't be going anywhere until you're done with them."

She set the lamp on the floor, and then went to each of four coal-oil lamps burning in wall sconces and turned up the wicks until the room brightened noticeably.

"I'll need plenty of light to work by," she said, pleasantly enough, looking at the two chained men.

But there was something about the look in those blue eyes that was not right, Thorne thought. She was either drunk, or she had slipped a mental cog, was his quick assessment.

From among the pleats of her full dress, she produced a small box and opened it to reveal a folded, pearl-handled straight razor on a red velvet lining.

An involuntary shudder ran over Thorne, and he could feel the blood draining from his face.

"You can go," she said peremptorily to Stilwell.

"The captain told us to stay," the cowboy answered.

"Well, I'm telling you to leave. I'll deal with the captain later. I work better alone."

Stilwell hesitated, still holding his Colt. "What are you going to do?"

"I said, get out!" she shouted at them.

"But. . . ."

"What can they do? They're chained. And I have a gun." She pulled a Derringer out of her pocket.

"OK. We'll wait at the top of the stairs."

"Close the door after you."

The two men reluctantly retreated up the stairway, and Thorne heard a door bang.

"I think I'll start with the handsome one," she purred, gliding toward Thorne. "You know, I was very much attracted to you," she said. "For that very reason, I was hoping not to see you again. I have a weakness for rugged, virile men. I was hoping you would be eliminated, because I knew you would just make trouble for us. That's why I asked Brand to have you shot off the box that night."

"Too bad your plans didn't work out," Thorne managed to say, grasping at any stalling tactic. He had trouble keeping his voice steady. He looked sideways at Burnett. The bartender's eyes were wide as he stared at the woman.

She opened the pearl-handled razor and regarded it. "This belonged to my second husband. A beautiful instrument, don't you think?" She held it up, and the lamplight glinted from its honed edge.

Thorne held his breath as she came close to him. Slowly,

deliberately she sliced the buttons from his shirt. He heard them hitting the hard floor, one by one. She spread his shirt apart, and he felt the blade cutting the hairs from his chest.

Then she stopped and stepped back. Thorne let out his breath in a long sigh. She regarded him with her head cocked to one side and that strange look in her eyes. Then she slipped up close to him again, sliding her hands over his chest without touching him with the blade. He was acutely aware of her as she pressed herself against him, the warmth, the scent of jasmine. She raised her face to him, and her lips sought his. He tasted cigar and brandy.

Thorne did not return the kiss.

After a few seconds she stepped back. "I thought you have been wanting me ever since we made love that night."

Thorne licked his lips and swallowed with difficulty. "Under different circumstances, maybe. . . ." His mind was in a whirl. He feared her unpredictability, her instability, and tried to think of something to say that would not antagonize her.

"Ah, what a shame. . . ." She again ran her hands over his bare chest.

Should he play up to her? Maybe gain her sympathy? "Julie Ann . . . ," he began.

But she had already turned her back on him and moved to Burnett. She cut off his buttons with a few deft flicks of the razor. Then the blade began in earnest.

"*Aagghhh!*" Burnett jerked back against the wall. "She cut me!" he yelled as though he couldn't believe she would really do it. Blood glistened red against the matted chest chair.

Again she applied the blade, and he went rigid, throwing his head back and gritting his teeth. Sweat popped out on his forehead.

In desperation, Thorne gripped the ring behind him that secured his handcuffs, pushing himself up with his arms. He lifted his knees and slammed both boot heels into the woman's head, knocking her several feet away from Burnett. She lay on the floor, unmoving.

"Damn!" Burnett gasped. He looked at her inert form, then back at Thorne. "What now?"

"I think I just ruined any chance I had with her," Thorne replied, completely at a loss for anything serious to say.

They were mute for several seconds.

"You reckon you broke her neck? You hit her pretty hard."

"I hope not."

"She's going to be as mad as a riled-up rattler when she comes to."

The door opened at the top of the stairs. "Everything under control down there?" Stilwell's voice called.

Before Thorne could caution him to stay quiet, Burnett yelled back. "She passed out. Must be drunk."

There was a muffled expletive as boots thudded on the wooden steps.

When Stilwell reached the bottom, he was alone. He went straight to the fallen woman. "She's still breathing." He retrieved the lamp she had set on the floor, when she first came in. He brought it closer and examined her as the two chained men looked on. "Her ear's bleeding, and she's got a lump on the side of her head."

"Guess she hit it, when she fell," Burnett said.

"Somehow you hit her," Stilwell said, ignoring the lie. "*Of course!* Your feet are free. I knew I should have stayed."

"Then I hope you've got a strong stomach," Thorne said. "Have you ever seen anyone flayed alive before?"

"Flayed?"

"Yeah. Having the skin stripped, piece by piece, exposing millions of nerve endings. The Apaches sometimes do it. In fact, that's what she was doing to him," Thorne said. "Look at his chest."

Stilwell looked, with obvious distaste. His broad, smooth face, with wavy hair falling over his forehead, looked even more youthful in the soft yellow light of the coal-oil lamps. The cowboy hesitated, looking from Burnett to Ann Gilcrease's still form.

"I reckon she'll come around in a few minutes," Thorne said. "She'll probably have a headache. You gonna help her peel us out of our skin?"

Stilwell seemed to hesitate. His nostrils flared as if the odor of this dank cavern, the stale air, coal-oil smoke, and blood was repugnant to him.

"Horse shit!" he finally blurted. "I signed on with this outfit to share in the gold . . . not to torture chained prisoners. I'm no damned Apache!" He yanked his Colt and moved toward them, thumbing back the hammer. Thorne gritted his teeth, waiting for the bullet that would send him into eternity.

But, instead, Stilwell's free hand went to his vest pocket, and he pulled out a key. He reached around behind Thorne, inserted the key, and clicked open one of the shackles. Leaving the key in the lock, Stilwell backed away, still covering them with his gun. "Turn your partner loose," he ordered.

"What about our guns?" Thorne asked, as he unlocked Burnett's handcuffs.

"Just be glad you're gettin' away with your lives."

On a sudden impulse, Thorne crouched by Julie Ann and fumbled his way into the pocket of her voluminous dress. He withdrew her Derringer.

"Leave that hide-out gun!" Stilwell snapped, thrusting his Colt forward.

Thorne shoved the weapon into the side pocket of his jeans and held up both hands. "Don't worry. It's only for protection later." He lifted one of the lamps from its wall bracket, and paused to look at Julie Ann.

"C'mon!" Burnett snapped. "You gonna wait till she comes around enough to give the alarm?"

Julie Ann stirred and groggily pushed herself to a sitting position, her dark hair falling over her face where the diamond hair clasps had been knocked loose. She put a hand to the side of her head without looking up.

"Julie, I'm sorry I had to do that. It's just that. . . ."

"*Let's go!*" Burnett commanded.

Abruptly, Thorne turned away and led the way into the tunnel at which Stilwell was pointing. The passage was about a hundred feet long and then dead-ended in a crossway.

"To the left," Stilwell said from behind.

They turned left and went another fifty feet or so.

Thorne instinctively cringed at the sight of two or three rats skittering away from the edges of the light along the wet floor. This part of the mine was apparently little used.

"Hold it!" Stilwell ordered, and Thorne stopped by a log that had been notched to form a narrow ladder.

"That'll take you outside. Comes out behind the buildings on the south side of the street. You're on your own."

"How do we know there's not somebody waiting to gun us down as soon as we climb out of this hole?" Burnett asked.

"If that was the case, I wouldn't have bothered to unlock you. I could have shot you in there, or let some of the other men do it. Worse yet, I could've let that witch finish carving you up."

"Are our horses up there?"

"Give 'em a damn' inch and they want a furlong!" Stilwell exploded. "Hell, I don't know where your horses are. I want you on foot so you won't be gettin' back to town any too soon, 'cause I'm riding outta here with a saddlebag full of cash. I ain't spending the rest o' my life on some damned island with a couple o' crazy people telling me what do do."

"You know they'll kill you," Thorne said.

"They'll have to catch me. I can give as good as I get."

"Why'd you turn us loose?" Thorne asked.

"This ain't no time to be examining the teeth of a gift horse," Burnett muttered under his breath, wiping his sweaty face in the lamplight. "Let's get outta here."

"I've never murdered a man in cold blood in my life," Stilwell said. "Shot a few in self-defense and one or two that needed killin', but I'm not a murderer. I'll take any loose cash I can find. And I figure I've earned what I'm takin' outta here. This territory's seen the last of me."

"If you help us bust up this organization, we'll do all we can to get you off in court," Thorne said.

Stilwell laughed bitterly. "You better get outta here before I change my mind," he said, again drawing his gun.

Without another word, Thorne reached for the ladder and started climbing.

CHAPTER SEVENTEEN

The notched log led to a wooden ladder on the next level. Thorne inadvertently kicked over a lantern, set near the ladder, which he righted before starting up. The ladder brought them through a small hole into the black of the night woods.

Thorne wormed his way out into the fresh-smelling air. "Where are we?"

"Beats me," Burnett answered in a whisper. "Stilwell said this would bring us out behind the buildings on the south side of the street."

They both hesitated, waiting for their eyes to adjust to the darkness. When they did, Thorne could still see almost nothing.

"We've got to get out of here," Burnett said in a stage whisper.

"Where do you reckon they stashed our horses?"

"Could be 'most anywhere . . . even underground," Burnett replied.

Thorne looked up. But it was so black, he couldn't tell if the sky was blocked by a canopy of trees, or there was an overcast. He took a few cautious steps, with his arms outstretched. "We could go north to see if we can find the main street, but I have no idea which direction is which."

"I don't see a light anywhere. You reckon this whole outfit stays underground?" Burnett wondered aloud.

Thorne selected a direction at random, and they crept forward cautiously. Suddenly he put his weight down, and his ankle turned on a steep drop-off. He tucked his shoulder and rolled down several feet, slamming onto his back.

"Alex! Where are you?" came the urgent whisper.

"I'm OK," he gasped. "Just stay still. I stepped into some kind of a gully." He rolled to his hands and knees and felt around. "A dry wash. Probably an eroded ditch from those flash floods."

As he climbed back up the bank, a blink of light caught his eye. He paused and looked again. He moved his head to one side, and the lights of two windows appeared. There was a black structure in the way that had blocked his seeing them earlier. "C'mon, this way."

He scrambled out of the gully and led the way toward the light. If nothing else, it might get them oriented. They stumbled over some loose boards and burned timbers of a ruined building. Finally feeling, more than seeing, their way past it, they found themselves in the rutted, overgrown main street of Harshaw.

Thorne stopped Burnett with one hand. "Those windows. See the white curtains inside? Isn't that the dining room where we just had supper?"

"I dunno. Looks kinda like it," the big man whispered. "You're not thinkin' of goin' back in there, are you? Thanks to some glimmer of conscience in Stilwell, we just got loose."

"Didn't Brandau say they were moving out tonight?"

"Yeah. I think he said something about leaving before midnight. Maybe if we can get our hands on a couple of horses, we can get back to town and round up some help."

"No time," Thorne countered. "We've got to do what we

can to stop him, or at least put a crimp in their operation."

"You can't be serious!" Burnett whispered hoarsely. "We need to get out of here. That woman is probably already spreading the alarm. They'll be combing the area for us. Brandau can't afford to let us get away, knowing what we know."

"Exactly. It'll be a distraction. Something they'll have to think about. We'll be the burr under their saddle. We'll use the Apache tactic of hit-and-run."

Burnett took Thorne's arm and guided him back off the vacant street behind a tumbled down adobe wall. "That's crazy," he whispered, looking around apprehensively. "We're afoot and, except for that two-shot Derringer, unarmed. Let's hoof it down the road as fast as we can and then take to the woods and hide out until they're gone and have quit hunting us. If they don't leave tonight, we'll just keep going and hope we can dodge any pursuit."

"The best defense is a good offense," Thorne quoted quietly. "Brandau won't be expecting us to come after him."

"What are you going to do?"

"I wish I had questioned him a little more about what he meant when he said they were going to move out tonight. But I think I was in shock during that entire dinner. Wasn't thinking too clear."

"He must have meant they were going to collect all that stolen loot in the mine and leave."

"Right. Time to close up shop in Arizona Territory and establish his new kingdom in the Pacific," Thorne said. "In fact, it's a long way between that Mowry Mine and that island. How are they going to transport it without being seen? It'll take an ore wagon or a string of pack mules to get it to the West Coast or the Sea of Cortés. We'll figure out a way to disrupt that or slow them up. Let me think about it a minute. There's got to be something we can do and still stay out of sight." He was having trouble concentrating. "You know, I feel like I'm going to wake up any minute and find out this is all just a nightmare."

"Yeah, I know what you mean," Burnett agreed. "But I know it's real, 'cause my chest stings like the devil's own pitchfork's been at it where our girlfriend tried to peel off my hide." He put a hand to this chest where his buttonless shirt hung open. "At least it's almost stopped bleeding." He stood up from behind the crumbling adobe wall where they crouched, raised his head, and sniffed several times.

"What's wrong?"

"Hell, I don't even smell any horses or mules. Wonder where they've got 'em corralled?"

"You know, we've been led to believe that this is a big organization. But I'd bet there aren't more than eight or ten people here, counting Brandau and Julie Ann. Brandau mentioned a robbery up by Flagstaff, so there must be others, but I don't think we're outnumbered as badly as I first thought."

"We have to get our hands on some weapons, if we're going to do them some damage," Burnett said with some reluctance in his voice.

"Have you got any matches?" Thorne asked.

"No. They were in the vest I left in the mine. What'd you have in mind?"

"Setting the town on fire."

"What?"

"There's enough dry wood left in these ruined buildings to make a nice blaze. And there's a wind coming up, too," he added, noting a flicker of lightning through the trees to the west.

"What good will that do?"

188

"Maybe create some confusion and slow them down from whatever they're planning to do. It'll give us some light to see what's going on, and, if it's big enough, somebody might see the flames and come to investigate."

"Sounds like a good start to me. All we need is something to start the fire with."

"There was the lamp I kicked over," Thorne said.

"We still need a match," Burnett said.

"Come on. I've got an idea."

With some effort and several wasted minutes, Thorne was able to retrieve the lamp. It sloshed heavy with coal oil.

"Now for some buildings that'll burn. . . ."

They felt and stumbled their way along behind the vacant shops and houses parallel to the street. Thorne thought they were making a lot of noise, but it couldn't be helped. He stopped on the windward side of a row of four or five wooden buildings. He unscrewed the cap from the lamp and splashed the coal oil here and there on the walls and the piles of fallen boards. Then he pulled the Derringer he had taken from Julie Ann, broke it open and extracted one of the cartridges. Gripping the lead bullet between his back teeth, he carefully twisted the brass casing until he pulled the lead slug loose. He spat it out and then sprinkled the small amount of black powder on a saturated board. He snapped the Derringer closed and felt around on the ground for a rock. He gripped one the size of his fist.

"OK, stand back." He hit the rock a glancing blow with the steel barrel of the gun. He held it close to the board and struck it twice more. Sparks jumped, the powder flashed, and the coal oil ignited and blazed. The flames ran along the board and quickly followed the fuel to more tinder-dry wood.

The rising wind did the rest. In less than thirty seconds,

the flames were crackling and licking eagerly up the side of the wall at the sagging roof.

"Let's get out of sight. That oughta bring 'em out of their burrows like a bunch of termites out of a rotten log."

They retreated into the cover of the woods and waited. They didn't have long to wait. A muffled shout from somewhere, then another, and the sound of a door slamming. Black figures could be seen running in the glare of the roaring flames that had quickly jumped to the second house in a shower of sparks.

After several minutes, Thorne realized no attempt was being made to put it out. Of course. There was no water. Or, at least not enough. Nothing below ground would burn, unless the fire somehow got to the wooden stairways and ladders.

Thorne grabbed Burnett's arm, and the two of them went dodging and darting between the trees and over the washouts and piles of spoil in the flickering light toward the eastern end of the main street.

"The general store!" Thorne shouted above the roar of the flames and the falling timbers. Window glass was shattering in the intense heat. The roof of the stone general store across the street was ablaze. There was no activity in or around the place. It seemed to be deserted.

The wooden building where they had eaten dinner that evening stood behind the general store and was still untouched by the flames. Even though lamps or candles still lighted the windows, it, too, appeared deserted.

Just as they passed the last burning building, a shot blasted from across the street, and Burnett stumbled and went rolling, headfirst, into the weeds of the dusty street.

"Paddy!" Thorne yelled.

A figure moved out of the darkness beside the general

store and aimed carefully for a second, closer shot.

Thorne didn't remember drawing the Derringer from his pocket, but it was suddenly in his hand and cocked. He knew he had only one shot, so he forced himself to wait a fraction of a second longer as he aimed at the man who was no more than thirty feet away. The man saw him at the last moment, and swung his six-gun. The two weapons roared at once, and Thorne felt the bullet burn past his left cheek. But his assailant dropped in a heap.

In one jump he was at Burnett's side in the foot-tall weeds, gripping his friend by the belt.

"Hell, quit tryin' to drag me!" the big man sputtered, scrambling to his feet. "Let's get out of the light!"

"You OK?" Thorne cried, as they dove out of sight behind a collapsed porch roof that was still beyond the flames.

"Just shot off my boot heel," the bartender panted. "That's why I went down. Numbed my foot for a few seconds."

"Can you walk?"

"Yeah. But I won't be running too fast. Feel like I've got a wooden leg."

"You never were a sprinter."

"Thanks for the help. But that was your only bullet."

"If I can get over there to the body, I'll take his gun and belt."

"Too late," Burnett said. "There's more of 'em coming."

They flattened out as the hoofbeats of several horses came toward them. But the horses were coming from the east, right down main street. There were four cowboys, riding two abreast, and behind them came a team of four stout Morgans, pulling what appeared to be an enclosed prison wagon. The wagon and its escort pulled up just beyond the general store whose interior was being rapidly engulfed in flames. The man at the reins was wearing a hat that shaded his face, but the instant he jumped down and spoke, Thorne recognized the form and voice of Captain Brady Cox Brandau.

"Check that man," Brandau ordered, and one of the mounted cowboys instantly dismounted to attend the man who lay crumpled at the edge of the street.

"He's dead. Shot in the neck," came the quick assessment.

"Then they're still around here, and they're armed," Brandau's deep voice said. "No matter. Bring Miss Gilcrease and let's move out."

Thorne squirmed to a better vantage point where the gap between two boards was wider. He heard a door slam, and a few seconds later Julie Ann came around the corner of the general store, dressed in a divided, leather riding skirt, white blouse, boots, and carrying a flat-crowned hat.

Brandau said something to her, then gave her a hand up onto the wagon seat. He climbed up beside her, took the reins, and popped them over the backs of the team. The sleek animals lunged into their collars, and the wagon started forward, the four-man escort riding ahead. The wagon rumbled down the street, and the men hardly looked at the leaping flames that were consuming the remains of the wooden structures on the south side of the street. But their horses shied with instinctive fear.

In the intense light from the sheets of flame, Thorne took a good look at the wagon. It was painted dark gray and appeared to be reinforced, with high, wide, heavily spoked wheels. It had no ornamentation, and the roof jutted out over the driver's seat. There were no windows in the sides, but the padlocked, double door in the rear was fitted with two barred windows. As the wagon rumbled down the sloping street and curved to the left out of sight, Thorne thought he saw a face appear at one of the barred windows in the back of the wagon.

Just after the wagon disappeared, the intense heat of the advancing flames drove them out of their hiding place. They crept around the building and ran across the street toward the flaming general store. Thorne slid alongside the warm stones of the outer wall to the rear and looked around. The dining room where they had eaten earlier in the evening was still untouched, the lamplight spilling out an open doorway.

"Stay here," he said to Burnett, and ran back around front to the body of the man he had shot. The man's gun belt had been taken. "Damn!" he breathed. He returned to Burnett who was still watching the dining room from the back corner of the general store.

A flash and a sudden boom startled both of them, and they jumped away from the wall. Then they realized it was the approaching storm they had been too busy to notice. Thorne motioned, and the two of them ran to the wall of the dining room and looked in a window. The place was empty; the table appeared just as they had left it. The silver service lay overturned on the sideboard, and the red candles guttered low in their candelabra. The dirty dishes and the wine decanter were untouched.

They went inside and passed through the breezeway at the back and checked the detached kitchen. No one was around.

"They've all skedaddled," Burnett said.

"Yeah, unless there's still somebody below ground."

"You feel like going down to see?"

"Not with this fire going and me unarmed," Thorne retorted.

They retreated to the dining room and helped themselves to a drink of water from a pewter pitcher on the sideboard. The brandy had disappeared, but they finished the remainder of the wine. Burnett filled a glass and dribbled a little of it over his chest, cringing as the alcohol contacted the raw flesh.

"For the pain in my heel," Burnett said, holding up the crystal glass to the candlelight and squinting through the rich, ruby color.

"How is your foot?" Thorne inquired, stabbing a chunk of roast beef and sprinkling it with salt.

"Throbbing. Probably so swollen, I couldn't get my boot off. But I'll make it."

"Well, that rules out following them on foot. I'll scour the area to see if they left any horses." He popped the roast beef into his mouth. "Let's get outside . . . in the dark we'll make a harder target for anybody who might still be prowling around here."

The ceiling of the general store collapsed with a roar and a shower of sparks as they left the dining room.

The opposite side of the street was still burning fiercely, and had even set the grass and some of the closer trees afire. The wind was gusting now, and the fire was a hungry demon, devouring everything to leeward of its fiery maw.

But it was not to last. The remaining shadows were erased by a brilliant white lightning flash for a heartbeat, then thunder cannonaded as the storm broke over the Patagonia hills. A sheet of rain swept up the street from the west. Thorne and Burnett stood in the partial protection of the breezeway behind the dining room as the rain began to snuff out what was left of Harshaw.

CHAPTER EIGHTEEN

They took turns standing guard and sleeping the rest of the night under the tin roof of a collapsed adobe cabin. The deluge had reduced the fire to hissing billows of steam within the first thirty minutes, and then it had rained steadily another two hours before moving on to the east.

Thorne awakened from an uneasy dream of being chased into a smoke-filled room from which there was no escape. He opened his eyes a slit to see the gray sky through an angle of broken wall. He rolled over and pushed himself to a sitting position, rubbing his gritty eyes. Burnett sat in a corner of the adobe hut, head resting on his knees, asleep.

"No wonder he didn't wake me for my watch," he muttered. He shook the bartender gently by the shoulder.

"Oh!" The big man awoke quickly, but took considerably more time to break his frame loose to a standing position. "Oh, I feel awful! Stiff and sore in every joint and muscle. Why don't you just shoot me and put me out of this misery."

"If I had another bullet, I might," Thorne replied dryly. "You fell asleep on watch."

"Sorry."

Thorne waved it off. "We both needed the rest. And it seems they didn't leave anyone around to bother us."

They stepped out into the street and took a look at Harshaw. It was a forlorn sight. Tendrils of smoke still curled up here and there from heaps of stinking, blackened rubble.

"What next?" Burnett asked.

"I haven't the slightest idea."

They stood for several minutes, not yet fully awake to face the new day and new problems.

Finally Thorne said: "I'll take a look around for some horses."

He was back in fifteen minutes. "If they left any livestock, they're not anywhere within walking distance. Let's see if we can scrounge up some food and then walk back up the road toward the Mowry Mine. Much as I detest going back in there, I'd like to see if they left any of their stash."

In the small kitchen, they found a half a slab of bacon and some bread and a partially empty jar of honey.

"Nice of them to leave us a little food," Burnett commented, as he lifted one of the stove lids to start up a fire from a stack of kindling. The small kitchen across the breezeway from the unburned dining room held several shelves of canned goods, sacks of flour, beans, and other staples. Stick matches were conveniently set in a holder on the upper side of the stove. They even found a sack of coffee beans, crushed some, and brewed themselves a fresh pot. Water was apparently carried from a creek to supplement the rain water that was caught and stored in wooden barrels.

"Feel up to a little walk?" Thorne asked after they had fortified themselves with a hearty breakfast.

"I hope you're not going to ask me to walk back to the Mowry Mine," Burnett groaned.

"Sure. It'll do you good. Knock the heel off your other boot and even up your legs. You won't have any trouble."

Thorne had said it in jest, but Burnett, using the stove poker, did just that.

"You remember how far it is?" Burnett asked as they walked along the faint wagon tracks in the bright morning sunshine.

"About three miles . . . maybe four."

"Without my boot heels, I feel like I'm walking uphill," Burnett commented, leaning forward and trying to get into a comfortable walking rhythm.

It was nearly two hours later, when they finally reached the point where they had been captured, and Burnett sank to the ground on the grassy slope, looking dirty, unshaven, and disheveled. "Whew! I hope this was worth it."

"Better be glad we didn't run into any Apaches," Thorne said, descending the slope to the narrow trail that led to the mine tunnel.

"We may be unarmed, but I feel a little safer with this," Burnett said. He indicated a wide-bladed butcher knife he had thrust through his belt.

Thorne was back up the hill in a few minutes. "I forgot there were no lanterns at the tunnel entrance. We left them where we climbed out of that air shaft at the top of the hill. Hope I can find them. They're probably full of rainwater by now."

"No matter," Burnett said. "The coal oil is lighter. It'll float on top. We should be able to get one of them to burn." He patted his shirt pocket where he had thought to stash a fistful of matches from the kitchen.

They had no trouble locating the lanterns under the mesquite bush where they had emerged from the mine. After several tries, they were able to get one of them to burn. While Burnett stood watch behind a bush, Thorne swallowed his instinctive fear and started down the tunnel.

Twenty minutes later he was back, setting the lantern on the ground. "Cleaned out. Nothing left but a few letters scattered around. All the cash, all the bullion . . . gone."

"They were probably loading up, while we were having that dinner with Brandau," Burnett said. "While you were in there, I found the remains of a lot of scuff marks and boot tracks out here. That prison wagon we saw must have been parked right up the hill there. The rain washed out most of the tracks, but it was heavy enough that it cut into the dry soil, here and there, where the wheels turned."

Thorne sat down heavily on the grassy slope. His mind went back to the prison wagon Brandau had driven away. "Do you reckon they had all that bullion in that wagon?" he asked.

"From the amount of gold and silver I saw in that mine, it would have to be a pretty stout wagon."

"I took a good look at it," Thorne said. "It'd been reinforced, and had heavier axles and wheels."

"There were only four horses pulling it," Burnett pointed out. "Depending on how many hills they were going to pull, or how far they were going, it couldn't have been too heavy."

Thorne turned this over. "You're right. But that team had four of the finest-looking Morgans I've ever seen."

"They're not draft horses, but they're damned good in harness," Burnett agreed. "They've got a lot of bottom. Sure wish I could get *my* Morgan back."

"I would guess that bullion weighed more than a ton," Thorne went on. "But there were also a lot of greenbacks."

"Well, if they didn't carry it all away in that wagon, they must have stashed the rest of it close by . . . probably in that mine. They didn't have time to move it very far, if it was all there to start with."

Thorne shook his head. "I think they took it all. Brandau wouldn't have gone to all the trouble of stealing that stuff to leave any of it behind, unless he was forced to. And that load of rifles I found in Mexico has probably already been moved on down to the gulf by now. Then aboard some schooner bound for the South Pacific."

Sitting on the grassy hillside in the morning sunshine, they pondered the situation in silence for a couple of minutes. Thorne thought of Julie Ann as he had last seen her in her riding outfit, sitting beside Brandau on the wagon seat as they rode out of town in the flickering blaze of the burning buildings. She must have been aching from that kick in the head that had knocked her unconscious. She was certainly tough and resilient. Why should he be surprised at that? She had survived in the dangerous, shadowy world of spies and intrigue since she was in a teen-ager.

"Where do you reckon they headed?" Burnett interrupted his musings.

"When they reached the end of the street, they turned south."

"The other fork goes toward Patagonia," Burnett said.

"They must be over the Mexican border by now."

"*If* they were headed for the border," Burnett said. "We've just assumed that's the way they were going."

"That heavy wagon must have cut some deep tracks into the road during and after the rain."

"As hard and long as it rained, they might have bogged down in the mud, or slid off the road," Burnett said. "The roads in these Patagonia hills aren't much. Just some overgrown tracks, and fairly steep in places."

"We could probably follow them pretty easily," Thorne said.

"On foot? And unarmed? Huh! First of all, we'd never catch up with 'em. If somehow we got lucky and did come up on 'em, what could we do?" He grunted as he tugged off one boot and began to massage his foot with both hands. "Our best bet is to start back toward Tombstone and pray we don't run into any more Apaches. With a good turn of the cards, we'll make Charleston in a couple o' days, where we can get some horses."

Thorne knew he was right. It was the only logical choice. But he couldn't give up the idea of pursuing them while the trail was hot. He had the empty feeling that Brandau and Julie Ann and the whole outlaw operation was going to slip away while they went for help. In fact, it might be too late already. In the ten- or twelve-hour head start they already had, the wagon and its escort could already be safely across the border and well on its way toward the Sierra Madre Mountains, where they could hide out until any pursuit had given up. Then they could proceed with getting to the gulf and out to their Pacific island, if that was really their ultimate destination. Or, they could be taking the same route as the stolen guns—across the *Gran Desierto*. In any case, by the time he and Burnett returned to Tombstone for help, and the authorities got permission to enter Mexico, this ring of robbers and their leaders would be long gone.

"You didn't see anything of Rabbit in there, did you?" Burnett asked, breaking the silence.

"Nope."

They rested a few more minutes. Finally, Thorne pushed himself to his feet. "You're right. We might as well start back. How long do you think you can walk in those boots?"

"Don't rightly know. Maybe an hour or so," Burnett said, and pulled his boots back on with some difficulty. "We're not getting any closer to home sitting here." He struggled up and began stumping down the road that wound along the top of the ridge to the east.

A slow mile passed under their feet. The road began to

slant downward, then broke out from under the trees. A vista of rolling wooded hills was opened up to them. Thorne tried not to think of how many miles lay before them.

They paused. Thorne had the distinct feeling they were not alone. But the feeling, he realized as he looked around, was caused by the fact that the terrain was familiar. It was near here that they had fought it out with the Apaches.

"Seems like weeks ago," Burnett said, when Thorne mentioned the fight. He sat down on a fallen log.

"Wish I had a weapon," Thorne said. "I have a crawly feeling they may be watching us right now."

"Not likely. They've moved on. Raiding Apaches don't stay in one place long."

And then it happened. Thorne saw the dust before he heard the hoofbeats. "Quick! Back into the trees!" He grabbed Burnett's arm and pulled him out of sight. Thorne's heart was pounding as they crouched, listening to the drumming of several horses coming up the trail.

The sound grew louder, and then the riders came into view around a bend some fifty yards away. The first two men looked familiar, the way they sat their mounts. Then Thorne saw the third, and he let out a shout, leaping out into the road.

"Rabbit! Virgil!" he yelled, waving his arms.

The three horsemen reined up, two of them reaching for their holstered guns.

"Alex Thorne!" Virgil Earp cried. "By God, you're a sight!" He swung down from his horse and handed the reins to his brother, Morgan. They gripped hands. "Burnett! You OK? Both of you look like you've been through it."

"We'll tell you all about it," Thorne said, relief washing over him. He felt energized again. "Have you got a couple of spare horses? Ours were taken."

"Didn't bring any," Virgil answered.

"Rabbit!" Burnett went over to the still-mounted Indian and gripped his hand with obvious emotion. "Rabbit, where the hell did you go when we were in that mine?"

"Hear noise. I go see," he answered with no expression.

"Why didn't you say something, or come back and lead us out of there?" Burnett asked, with some exasperation.

"No time. See men take you. I go to town." No details, no apologies. Thorne had the feeling that, even if the Indian had a better command of English, he would not have made a better explanation. The man was an enigma. On the one hand he seemed totally self-serving, yet he had led them to the gold stash, and he had saved Thorne's life during the Apache attack. And now he had run many miles to Tombstone to bring back help. Apparently, his aboriginal mind saw no reason to justify his actions; it was results that counted. And, Thorne had to admit, the results so far had been good.

"You have cigar?" Rabbit asked.

Burnett shook his head. "No."

Virgil turned to Burnett. "Let's get some place where we can talk."

"Climb up behind me," Morgan said to Burnett.

Virgil reached down to give Thorne a hand up to ride double.

"The Mowry Mine. About a mile up the road," Thorne directed.

"Good. That'll give us a chance to stop and let the horses rest," Virgil said, mounting up again.

There was no more talk until the party of five men dismounted and unsaddled their horses hear the Mowry Mine.

"You're lucky we finally decided to follow this Indian,"

Virgil said, hitching up his gun belt and hunkering down on the grass.

"Yeah," Morgan agreed. "Rabbit came to me with some wild tale about you two being trapped in a mine in the hills. He has trouble with English, and I didn't really understand at first. Then I remembered I hadn't seen you two around in a few days. And Rabbit . . . well, he looked even more ragged than usual, like he had run all the way back to town. I would have gotten rid of him, but he was cold sober. The clincher came, when he pulled out a stack of greenbacks and said there was much more in the mine."

"We have a list of serial numbers of all the stolen bills from those robberies," Virgil added. "And these matched."

"We got some extra horses and headed out," Morgan continued. "Rode like hell until our horses wore out, then dropped them at Wilson's ranch, switched mounts, and kept riding all night."

"Where's Behan?" Burnett inquired.

"He was down at Fairbank, when we left, so I didn't have to worry about telling him."

"Didn't leave any word, either," Morgan chuckled.

Thorne glanced down toward the bottom of the ravine where Rabbit had led the horses to water them in a small stream that was flowing full with run-off from the rain. "This is the second time that Apache has saved my life."

"What's the story?" Virgil asked.

With Burnett adding comments, now and then, Thorne briefly related their tale, from the time Rabbit had talked them into going to find the gold and bringing it up to date.

"Incredible!" Virgil breathed, shaking his head. If I'd heard this from anybody other than you two, I don't think I'd believe it. It's just too fantastic! A madman and a crazy female Confederate spy, heading up some secret society that is robbing to get a fortune to start an island kingdom?"

"If we hadn't gone through it, I wouldn't believe it, either," Burnett said. "But here's part of the proof." He flipped back his buttonless shirt to reveal the scabbing raw spot where his skin had been peeled off.

"You say they headed south last night, sometime before midnight?" Virgil asked thoughtfully, chewing on a long stem of grass.

"Right."

"So they've got about a twelve- or fourteen-hour head start." He took a deep breath. "And our horses are tired."

"Let's take a look at their underground headquarters first," Morgan suggested. "Where's the nearest telegraph?"

"Fort Huachuca," Burnett said. "Roughly twenty-five miles across the hills, northeast of here."

"Not much help," Virgil said. "If they headed straight south, they probably crossed the border hours ago."

"That's what we thought."

"We'll follow, but we'll have to take it easy until we can get some fresh horses at a ranch over in the Santa Cruz Valley," Virgil decided. "And we're gonna have to rest. Haven't had any sleep in about forty hours." The dark circles under his eyes told of his fatigue.

Morgan stood up. "Let's get on with it. We'll take a look at where the stuff was stashed, and then ride on down to Harshaw."

CHAPTER NINETEEN

Since the general store was only a ruined shell of stone walls filled with burned débris, the Earps descended into the converted mine by way of the escape route Thorne showed them.

The two brothers emerged thirty minutes later, amazed at the underground headquarters.

"Looks like they were holed up here for months. All gone now. Nothing but a little furniture left behind," Virgil said to Burnett and Thorne who, with Rabbit, had stayed above ground. "Appears some records were burned, but not as a result of the fire up here."

Virgil and Morgan rode down the road and scouted the area around the town. When they returned, they reported they had found a stone corral about a half-mile from town.

"Three horses in it," Morgan said, dismounting. "All dead. Their throats were cut. Two of them were still saddled. I imagine they were yours."

"One of them a big, black Morgan?" Burnett asked.

Morgan nodded.

"Damn! That was the best horse I ever owned. And the most expensive."

Morgan rubbed a hand wearily over his unshaven face. "I don't know about all of you, but I'm about done in. Maybe a little food will revive me." He reached for his saddlebags.

"There's food in the kitchen back there," Thorne said. "Come on."

The men stoked up the fire in the iron cookstove and feasted on smoked ham, beans, onions, and canned tomatoes. Afterward, the Earps stretched out on their bedrolls in the shade of the building and slept. The tireless Rabbit was on some jaunt of his own. The horses were picketed in a grassy area to rest and graze, while Thorne and Burnett stood guard with Virgil's Winchester and Colt.

They had found the body of the man Thorne had shot the night before. Virgil had recognized him as Conrad Doyle, a cowboy who sometimes worked on ranches in western New Mexico. He had been suspected of doing some rustling. Except for some personal items, the dead man's pockets contained $300 in untraceable gold eagles and double eagles.

"Probably his weekly allowance," Thorne had guessed as Virgil confiscated the money. "They were in such a hurry last night, they forgot to clean out his pockets. Just took his gun belt. He must have had a lot of faith in Captain Brandau to take all the risks of the robberies for this amount, when he could have had thousands."

"Maybe it was the idea of never having to be on the dodge again, when he got to that island," Virgil had said. "Then again, some men are just born leaders and naturally draw the allegiance of others."

"Well, Stilwell told us he was having no more of it," Thorne had remarked. "Said he was packing off all the loot his saddlebags could carry. Wonder where he headed?"

They had no tools to bury the body, so Virgil and Morgan had dropped it down the shaft into the mine.

"Maybe it'll keep the wolves and coyotes from getting him," Burnett said. Buzzards had already worked over so much of the face that Virgil had had trouble identifying him at first.

An hour before sunset, the men were up, somewhat refreshed, and ready to ride. Rabbit and Morgan took Burnett and Thorne on behind to ride double.

They took the west fork of the road out of Harshaw toward the small town of Patagonia, a few miles away. Since they were the only ones in the party somewhat familiar with these hills, Rabbit and Burnett were leading. They had ridden less than two miles, when the setting sun showed a flash of blue moving up the road toward them. There was no place to hide and no time to run, so the lawmen reined up alongside each other, guns drawn, blocking the road.

Thorne was relieved to see that it was a column of cavalry consisting of about two dozen black troopers and a white officer. The soldiers pulled rein, and the officer rode forward a few yards to meet them, introducing himself as Lieutenant John Gillespie of the Tenth Cavalry. The Earps showed their badges and gave their names.

"Oh, yes, I've heard of you," the young lieutenant said, giving them a frank look of appraisal. "The newspapers, when I get a chance to see them, are full of your doings in Tombstone. Aren't these hills a little out of your jurisdiction?" He cast a curious glance at Rabbit and Burnett, then at Thorne.

"You might say we're a posse on the trail of some stage robbers," Virgil said, without going into a long explanation. "You don't have a couple of spare horses or mules we could buy, do you?"

" 'Fraid not. In fact, one of our horses cast a shoe back down the trail. Lucky I have a farrier along. And the pack mules are loaded down with supplies. I'm under orders to set up camp near the Mowry Mine, and to use it as a base of operations to scout for Apaches in the surrounding area."

"I wish you had come along a few weeks earlier, Lieutenant," Virgil said. "The Mowry Mine was where all the stolen gold and cash was hidden. The gang had a temporary headquarters at Harshaw, just up the road. As it is, they got clean away last night."

"Which way were they headed?" Lieutenant Gillespie asked.

"Not sure. All we know is they turned south out of Harshaw."

"You're going the wrong way, then."

"We need to get to a ranch in the Santa Cruz Valley where we can get a couple of mounts for these two men," Virgil said, indicating Burnett and Thorne.

Gillespie removed his hat and wiped a sleeve across his forehead. "The hostiles have run out a lot of the ranchers in the valley, but Jim Meeks is still there, about ten miles west of Patagonia. He might have some horses you could buy, since he sometimes supplies remounts for the Army."

"Many thanks, Lieutenant. We'll keep traveling tonight, until we get there. Safer that way." He gathered the reins to move his horse out of the way.

"The road down to Patagonia's fairly easy from here," the officer said. "Hope you catch them."

"I'm confident we will. They're traveling in a heavy wagon, hauling a lot of heavy gold and silver bullion."

Some of the nearby troopers heard this remark and looked at each other, nodding, wide grins breaking out on their faces.

"What kind of wagon?" Gillespie wanted to know.

Burnett spoke up for the first time. "An enclosed, dark gray prison wagon with bars on the back doors. Four men riding horseback escort."

"What?" The officer's eyes opened wide in surprise. "We just stopped that wagon this morning about thirty miles southwest of here."

"You didn't hold them?" Thorne was incredulous.

"There was no reason to. I checked their papers. The credentials of the man driving looked authentic. He even showed me his badge. Claimed his name was Deputy U.S. Marshal Milton Patterson. He had written orders to deliver three prisoners to the Yuma Territorial Prison."

"Forgeries!" Thorne spat.

"Apparently they were, but I'm no expert in such matters," Gillespie said. "And I had no reason to suspect they were anything but who they said they were. I did think it a bit odd that a woman was riding on the wagon with him, though."

"Julie Ann . . . ," Thorne muttered under his breath.

"Which way were they headed, Lieutenant?" Virgil asked.

"West. On the road toward Arivaca."

"Then they were headed for Yuma, all right," Burnett said. "But, that way, they'd have to cross about the loneliest stretch of desert on the continent."

"*El Camino del Diablo* . . . the Devil's Highway," Thorne finished. "But it has to be better than the Sonoran desert."

"Thanks for your help, Lieutenant," Virgil said, reining aside so the column could pass. "You've given us a place to start without going many miles out of the way."

The officer gave him a half salute and motioned for his column to proceed.

After they had passed, the five men continued on down the road toward Patagonia, facing a beautiful red and gold sunset through the breaks in the trees.

"Why Yuma?" Burnett wondered aloud.

"Brandau probably has his own steamer on the Colorado River to take the gold down to a ship in the gulf," Thorne said.

"Why not just go southwest overland to the gulf?" Morgan asked. "Save at least a hundred and fifty miles. If I can read a map, so can they. And they'd be safer across the border."

"Because, even if the Devil's Highway is a mighty rugged way to go, there are at least several water tanks along the route. If that heavy wagon doesn't break down or get stuck in the sand, they can make it," Thorne said. "Five summers ago, one of my assignments took me down to a Mexican village on the northern gulf." He shook his head. "I almost didn't make it. No surface water for man or beast, unless you happen to go during the rainy season."

"Well, you oughta know," Burnett said.

"Besides, Mexican *bandidos* would love to get their hands on that gold and silver," Thorne said. "No, their safest route would be the Devil's Highway. They've got their forged papers, and practically no chance of running into any other travelers."

"And there are no towns along that route I can send a telegraph message to," Virgil said. "Pretty smart. They just disappear into the desert along that old Spanish trail, and, the next thing you know, the money is aboard a riverboat, down the Colorado and out of the country."

"I said Brandau was unbalanced, not stupid," Burnett reminded him.

When they reached the small town of Patagonia shortly after dark, they automatically gravitated toward the one saloon. Rabbit judiciously stayed outside with the horses as the other four trooped inside.

While they ordered beer and helped themselves to the free lunch, Virgil flashed his badge at the barkeep, a lean, balding individual with deep set, ferret-like eyes.

The bartender told him there was no livery in town. He consulted the half-dozen patrons in the place, and they all agreed there were no spare horses for sale in Patagonia. They confirmed Lieutenant Gillespie's guess that the nearest place to obtain mounts was at the Meeks Ranch, ten miles west of town.

"We also need to buy a couple of guns and ammunition," Virgil said.

"Dean Crampton owns the hardware," the barkeep said. "Store's closed, though."

"We need those guns. And we've got the cash."

"That's Crampton, sitting right over there. He don't take kindly to doin' business after hours."

But the sight of gold coin quickly persuaded the hardware owner to interrupt his poker game and reopen his store.

Thorne and Burnett selected two .45 Colts and five boxes of cartridges.

They returned to the saloon, where Burnett tipped the bartender, picked up a slice of bread, a hunk of cheese, and a pickled egg for Rabbit, and they left.

"If you're ridin' out to the Meeks Ranch, be careful," the barkeep called after them. "He keeps an armed guard on duty after dark."

To give the horses some relief, Burnett and Thorne switched mounts to ride double with Morgan and Virgil the last ten miles. The ride was uneventful, and, about 8:30, they came in sight of a rambling adobe structure with a flat roof. Yellow lamplight illuminated the two front windows beneath the porch roof. Bright moonlight silvered the house, the surrounding outbuildings, and the corral.

An unseen dog set up a deep-throated barking from somewhere.

"Hullo, the house!" Virgil called in a loud voice.

Thorne noted a slight movement above the parapet formed by the wall where it jutted above the roof.

"We're lawmen from Tombstone. Want to buy some horses!"

It was several seconds before the reply came. "Step down and come up on the porch, one at a time, so we can get a look at you." The voice came from inside the house. Then Thorne saw a sliver of light as the door was opened a crack.

They did as they were ordered, Virgil and Morgan showing their badges.

"What brings you to these parts, Marshal?" Jim Meeks inquired, when they were all comfortably seated in his plain, but cozy, living room, with the door barred behind them.

Meeks was a burly man with abundant coarse black hair and a black beard.

"Just needing to see if you've got two good saddle horses we can buy," Virgil answered. He volunteered no other information. "The barkeep in town said you might have some."

"Could have. How much you payin'?"

"Depends."

"We'd just as soon have a couple o' mules, if you've got 'em," Burnett said.

"I'm keepin' my mules. Need 'em in harness." He glanced toward Rabbit who sat off to one side. "He your prisoner?"

"No," Virgil answered quickly. "Our tracker."

"You boys want a drink? Or do you want to take a look at my horses now?"

"I'd like to select them in the daylight," Virgil said.

"You'll be wantin' to spend the night, then. I'll get Luis to put your horses up."

"No need. We'll throw our bedrolls out by the corral, and take care of ourselves and the horses."

"OK, but don't sleep too soundly. I've got a guard on the roof, and there's a bright moon, but I've lost a lot of stock to Apaches the last few months."

Meeks brought out a crock jug and poured each of them a generous slug of his store-bought whiskey before they said good night.

They unsaddled and turned their mounts in with the rancher's stock and slept with their guns ready in hand in the deep, black shadows next to the outer wall of the adobe corral. They were all so tired they left the guarding to the sentry on the roof, and slept soundly.

All but one. They awoke just after dawn to find that Rabbit had somehow appropriated Meeks's jug of whiskey and was thoroughly drunk.

CHAPTER TWENTY

"Damn! What a time for Rabbit to fall off the wagon!" Burnett fumed, when he had extricated the nearly empty crock jug from the Apache who was unable to stand up.

"Well, what do we do now?" Virgil asked. "He can't sit a horse in that condition."

"Worse than useless," Morgan agreed.

"And I was just getting used to him being sober," Thorne said.

"We'll lose most of a day, if we wait around here for him to sober up," Virgil said.

"Do you think he's valuable enough as a tracker to wait?" Morgan asked the assembly, as they stood by the corral wall, breathing in the cool morning air and looking at one another for a solution.

"I don't think this is going to be so much tracking, as it is guessing where they're going, and then trying to head them off," Thorne said. "They've already got about a day and a half head start on us, even if they are pulling a heavy wagon."

"With that ruse of escorting prisoners to Yuma Prison, they could travel the main roads, and we wouldn't be able to track them," Burnett said.

"I think they'll avoid the main roads as much as they can," Thorne said. "Brandau knows we got loose and that somebody will be after them, sooner or later, asking if anyone has seen a wagon like theirs pass. So he'll avoid being seen, if he can."

"We need to move out as fast as we can," Burnett said, looking down at the unconscious Indian who was flat on his back in the dust. A horse fly was buzzing around his open mouth. "We owe him a great debt for breaking this case for us. But all we can do now is buy him a horse, so, when he sobers up, he can ride out to wherever he's of a mind to go."

Jim Meeks clumped down off his porch and came toward them, stuffing in his shirt tail. "Well, gents, have you had time to look over my stock? Luis will have breakfast ready shortly. Soon as you make your selections, we'll close the deal over some beef and biscuits."

Burnett told him about Rabbit, apologized, and paid him for the jug. "Can we lug him some place safe, where he can sleep it off?" he asked. "When he comes around, I want you to give him the horse and saddle I'll buy from you, and send him on his way. But I want no harm to come to him, you hear?"

"Sure," Meeks said, looking curiously at the drunken Apache and back at Burnett. "You just gonna ride off and leave him here?"

"We have to go. He'll understand," Thorne said. He noticed a slight smile on the rancher's face. "When we ride back through here, we'd better not find out that you've put him on some spavined old nag with nothing but a saddle blanket. You got that?"

"I'm a fair man. I wouldn't even cheat an Indian," Meeks protested.

An hour later, with the sun just poking up over the Patagonia hills, the four men rode away from the ranch, leaving Rabbit to sleep off the whiskey in the musty hay of the barn. They rode steadily, west by south. With only a brief stop to rest the horses, they arrived at the old town of Arivaca by late afternoon.

"By God, we hit it right, boys," Virgil said, after questioning the livery stable operator. "That lieutenant was correct. They came through here yesterday. But the main thing is, they traded four horses to the livery and bought six mules."

"*Six* mules?" Burnett arched his eyebrows.

They looked at each other.

"They didn't sell the Morgans," Virgil said.

"Then they kept the best and strongest horses to pull the wagon," Thorne said. "They replaced the four horses the escort were riding."

"And the extra two?" Burnett asked.

"I figure they want a couple of extras in case any of the others give out," Virgil said. "Liveryman said they wanted eight mules, but he only had six."

"If they're making for the *Camino del Diablo*, they may be going to use the mules to pull the wagon or to pack the gold in case the wagon bogs down on that hellish road," Thorne suggested.

Virgil took a deep breath. "The only way we're gonna know is if we get after them. They have more than a day's head start on us. If we're all game, we'll rest two or three hours, grain the horses, and keep on."

Three long days later they reached the cottonwoods that marked the pond at Quitobaquito Springs, close to the Mexican border. It was mid-afternoon, and the September heat was unrelenting. Two long-legged herons flapped away from the shallows as they rode up and dismounted.

Thorne was so tired he didn't even feel surprised when

he saw the lead-colored prison wagon, sitting abandoned along the shore. They had known they were on the right track because they had picked up the deep tracks of the heavily laden wagon two days earlier. It had not taken an expert tracker to follow them. But here the trail ended. Or, at least, the trail of the prison wagon ended.

"Looks like they camped here and probably transferred the load to the mules," Virgil remarked, studying the ground.

Thorne squatted to stretch his back and tired legs. "Well, this is the last dependable water. There's Papago Wells, and the Tule Well, and finally the tanks at Tinajas Altas, if they aren't dry."

They all knew it was at the end of the brief annual rainy season in the southern territory, and rainfall along the *Camino del Diablo* was chancy at any time.

"If we camp here, cook some food, and rest until about ten tonight, we can start out in the cool of the night," Thorne said. "They're probably hauling a couple thousand pounds of bullion and coin. Can't travel very fast with that kind of a load. We should be able to make up a lot of distance."

"Sounds good to me," Morgan said, starting to unsaddle his horse.

"Tell us some more about this Captain Brandau," Virgil said, squatting by the fire an hour later with a tin cup of steaming coffee. "Is he desert-wise and tough enough to make a wasteland crossing like this?"

Thorne nodded, thinking of the dreamer and ruthless schemer. "Yes, I think so. I don't know how much experience he's had in desert travel, but he has the toughness and, of course, he has the cowboys with him. And the fact that he had the sense to abandon this heavy wagon and travel on by mule and horse tells me he's got this escape well planned. I'm sure he's carrying kegs of water."

Virgil sipped his coffee thoughtfully. "We probably don't have enough containers for water ourselves," he said. "We can fill the coffee pot . . . that'll give us an extra half-gallon . . . but it's not enough with just one two-quart canteen apiece."

"When we stopped in Arivaca, Burnett and I each bought an extra canteen," Thorne said. "I've done this before."

"I'm mainly concerned about the horses," Virgil said.

"If we travel at night, that'll help considerably," Thorne said. "We should be able to make it to the next two wells OK. If we have to go as far as Tinajas Altas or beyond, we may be in trouble."

"Look what I found," Morgan Earp interrupted, walking up to the fire and dropping a stout, wooden Wells Fargo express box at their feet. "Found it over in the willows by the edge of the pond, when I was filling my canteen. There are two or three more over there. Looks like they tried to sink 'em out of sight."

"Just as I figured," Thorne said. "They transferred everything to the pack mules. Discarded these boxes as useless weight." He turned to Virgil. "Did the liveryman, who sold them those mules say whether or not he included riding saddles or pack saddles?"

"Never thought to ask, and he didn't mention it."

"They must've had *aparejos* already prepared and in the prison wagon," Thorne said. "Just like the men who took the rifles. Good planning."

"Well, let's see how it adds up," Burnett said, setting down his coffee cup and beginning to count on his fingers. "There were four men on horseback, two riding the wagon seat, and you saw at least one face in the back window of the wagon. Lieutenant Gillespie indicated there were prisoners inside, so there must have been at least two inside. That's a total of eight. They traded four horses for six mules. And they kept the four Morgans that were pulling the wagon. So they have ten animals for eight people and about a ton of gold, silver, and currency. The normal load for a pack mule is about two hundred and fifty pounds, so we can assume they are mighty heavily loaded . . . especially for a trip across the Devil's Highway."

"That's assuming they didn't pick up another animal or two since Arivaca that we don't know about," Thorne added.

"I think we've got a good chance of catchin' them, if they stay on this road . . . such as it is," Burnett said. "I don't think they'll strike cross-country to the gulf. It's just too risky. And Brandau didn't seem like a man to leave a lot to chance."

"You're right," Thorne agreed, standing up and pitching the dregs of his coffee cup away. "I'm gonna catch a nap. We'll be pushing hard tonight, and I want to be fresh."

As soon as the moon was high enough to give good light, the four men were in the saddle and trotting at a steady clip. Trot for thirty minutes, walk for ten minutes, dismount, and lead the horses for ten minutes, then repeat the process. Now and then, to be sure they were still on the right track, Virgil would get down and strike a match to examine the faint, seldom used road. The hoofprints were still fresh and clear—the only tracks that had been made since the last rain.

"It's almost as if they want us to find them," Virgil said, swinging back into the saddle.

"Yeah, Brandau's smart enough to know that somebody will be on his trail," Thorne said.

"Maybe he thinks he's got several days' head start," Burnett said. "Figured it'd take us two or three days to walk some place where we could get some horses. He couldn't know Rabbit would bring the law so quick."

"You're right. Brandau would have all this planned out. He didn't figure on having to deal with us. But even after Stilwell turned us loose, I don't believe Brandau thought we'd be any threat," Thorne said.

"Wonder where Stilwell went?" Morgan said after a considerable silence.

"From the way he talked, he was hightailin' outta the territory with as much gold as he could stuff into his saddlebags," Thorne answered.

"And it's good riddance to him," Virgil said.

"I'd like to recover the several thousand in bullion he's probably carrying," Burnett said.

"Huh! Just consider that money as a ransom Wells Fargo paid for your lives," Virgil said philosophically.

"I reckon you're right. If we can catch up to Brandau, he'll have the bulk of it."

As the night wore on, their conversations dwindled. They rode and walked in silence until an hour after the moon waned, when they lost the road completely. Then they halted and unsaddled, pouring enough water into their hats to moisten the horses' mouths. Then they tied their mounts to nearby bushes and lay down to rest.

As the gray light of dawn came stealing up from the east, they were saddled and on the road once more. They ate up the miles toward Papago Wells, where they arrived by midmorning.

The horses drank their fill and grazed, while the men

built a fire, cooked some food, and rested. The sign of their quarry was so plain in the sandy earth that they could hardly wait to be on the trail again. So, barely four hours later, they saddled up and started again. It was a mistake. The mid-afternoon heat smothered them like a heavy blanket. Their pace slowed as they shed as much clothing as possible, tying jackets and vests behind their saddles, tipping their hat brims against the fiery tormentor that slid ahead of them down the western sky. The land around them was a profusion of desert growth, from the flaring tendrils of the ocotillo to the giant saguaro whose stately, uplifted arms were silhouetted against the reddening sky.

The sun finally flamed out below the level horizon ahead of them. The clear sky gradually lost its rosy hue, and stars began to blink in the darkening heavens. The men plodded on, leading their horses, legs stiff and tired, fighting fatigue.

Virgil Earp struck a match to find the trail, then another match to check his watch.

"It's a half after midnight. Why don't we camp here till dawn? I'm beat, and I know the horses are tired."

There was no disagreement. The adrenaline surge of the chase had given way to a slogging test of endurance.

By the time the sun was up, they had drunk coffee, smothered their tiny fire, and were starting across the baked, flat, powdery, dry surface of *Las Playas,* the dry lake beds that were totally devoid of any vegetation.

"*Whew!*" Morgan gasped, pulling his horse out of line to avoid the fine dust being churned up by the horses ahead of him.

"This must lead straight to the gates of hell," Burnett remarked.

Thorne was busy pulling his bandanna up over his nose and mouth.

CHAPTER TWENTY-ONE

Thorne's worst fears were realized. They rode up and dismounted, disturbing several of the buzzards from their feast.

"Damnation!" Burnett breathed, surveying the carnage. The Apaches had done their grim work well. Six bodies lay scattered about a dead campfire, four of them with arrows still protruding from them. All had been partially stripped of their clothing. Except for slashing open the arms, legs, and torso to disable the victims in the afterlife, the Apaches did not appear to have tortured them. Blankets were twisted around two of the bodies as if they had been caught asleep.

Only one animal—a dead mule—remained. Some meat had been hacked from its hindquarter before the buzzards had begun to rip it apart.

Thorne looked quickly for Julie Ann. But all the bodies were males. He carefully examined the faces of the dead and also failed to see Captain Brandau. Two of the men he recognized as guards he had seen in Harshaw. Three others were Simon, Charley, and the man referred to as Stump, who had accosted them at the Mowry Mine. The last one was one of their waiters at the dinner.

As the shock began to wear off, Thorne became aware of the *aparejos* that had been ripped open with knives and their contents strewn around. Flour and corn meal powdered the crusty dirt of the lake bed. Torn sacks of dry beans were spilled. But what caught Thorne's eyes under the mess of foodstuffs were packets of greenbacks and small bars of gold and silver bullion that had been cast aside with everything else. Several gilt-edge stock certificates fluttered past their feet and flew upward in a gust of dry wind as if to emphasize their worthlessness in the aboriginal mind.

The two Earps walked among the leavings of the raid. No one spoke for several minutes.

"Looks like this is the end of the trail," Virgil finally said. "The Apaches have done our work for us."

Thorne shook his head. "Not quite the end. Captain Brandau and Julie Ann are not here, and possibly one of their men. We don't know exactly how many of them there were to start with."

"They probably took her captive, most likely for trade or ransom. And they might have taken him along, too . . . maybe to practice a little torture on later."

"Something must have scared 'em off before they could use any of their usual tortures on these men," Virgil said.

"They took all the horses and mules," Morgan added. "Except this mule that they cut up for meat."

"How long ago, do you reckon?" Burnett asked, squinting up at the vultures that were impatiently circling overhead.

"A few hours maybe. Not long," Thorne replied. "The buzzards haven't had time to gather and really get to their work." He reached down and moved the arm of one of the victims. It was rigid. "*Rigor mortis* is still present, and the bodies haven't yet started to bloat."

"You thinking Brandau and the woman might've gotten away?" Burnett asked softly, studying Thorne's face.

"I'd like to think so, but it's not likely. If these six couldn't stand 'em off, she and Brandau wouldn't have had a chance." Yet, as he spoke, he was examining the tracks in the scuffed earth.

"Knowing the two of them, they could've put the Apaches up to this, so they could take off with a mule load of gold and nobody would come looking for them," Burnett surmised.

"Some other tribe, maybe," Thorne said. "Not the Apaches."

"Wonder why the Indians didn't take the gold at least, if not the paper money. They've learned the value of gold, when it comes to buying white man's goods. Think of what they could've bought with that in Mexico," Burnett said. "Food, guns, horses."

"Don't know," Thorne said. "Apaches have a traditional hate for the Mexicans from centuries past. They'd rather steal from them than buy. Maybe they were in a hurry, and the gold was just too heavy to carry. They left the food, too. Besides, we're assuming these were renegade Apaches. Who really knows?"

"I pulled out one of those arrows and took a good look. Chiricahua."

Thorne nodded, squatting and examining the tracks. The two Earps joined him.

"The raiders came in from the north," he said, pointing at the well-defined moccasin tracks. Probably left their ponies somewhere off the *playa* and crept in on foot. See, there's where it looks like a couple of them bellied along."

"Looks like there was one helluva fight," Burnett commented. "There are traces of blood all over the ground. If the Apaches had any dead or wounded, they carried them away. All the tracks of the animals head toward the Sierra Pinta Mountains."

They stood and looked at the plain trail that led up out

of the baked *playa* and disappeared into the desert vegetation in the direction of the low, ragged peaks jutting up northwest of them.

"Well, it's clear to me what we have to do now," Virgil said. "Clean up this mess, and see if we can identify any of those bodies before we bury them. Then we carry all the paper money we can stuff into our saddlebags, hide the gold and silver until we can come back with a wagon and retrieve it." He hitched up his belt. "And the sooner we get to it, the better, 'cause it'll take us the rest of the day."

"What're we gonna use for shovels?" Morgan wanted to know.

"We'll have to improvise. Might have to wind up using picket pins, knives, and frying pans."

"Damn!" Morgan said, appalled. "That's a lot of work to bury six men. Why don't we just leave 'em for the buzzards?"

"They may be outlaws, but they're white men and deserve to be put below ground, and not have their bones stripped by vultures and coyotes," Virgil replied sharply.

Morgan swallowed and looked away without responding.

As they set to work gathering up the scattered treasure, Thorne found his eyes constantly drawn to the rugged gray bulk of the Sierra Pinta etched against the blue, cloudless sky.

"I know what you're thinking," Burnett said, following Thorne's distracted gaze. "You can't bring yourself to believe the Apaches have got the woman and Captain Brandau."

"Yeah. I can see them taking her for a slave or for trading material. But why him? It just doesn't make sense." Thorne made a sudden decision. "Boys, I'm going to take a rifle and follow that trail a ways to see which way they went."

Virgil arched his brows in surprise. "Think that's really a good idea? What do you hope to find? You could very well wind up like these poor devils."

"Brandau and Julie Ann Martin are missing. I need to satisfy myself that the Apaches actually took them. They could have been wounded and later crawled off into the mesquite to die."

"That's damned unlikely," Virgil snapped, frowning.

"Nonetheless, I'm going," Thorne said, stepping up to his ground-reined horse. "Can I borrow your carbine, Morg?"

"Sure," the young man replied, reaching for his scabbard.

"I won't go farther than the base of those mountains," Thorne said, accepting the loaded carbine and putting his foot into the stirrup. "Be back in two or three hours."

"Let me ride with you," Morgan said.

"Not on your life," Virgil said. "I need you here to help bury these men."

"Well, I'm going to keep you out of trouble," Burnett said, pulling his Colt out of his belt and checking the loads.

Both men mounted and turned their horses away from the grisly scene. They trotted up out of the *playa* into the familiar desert shrubbery once more, then slowed to a walk as Thorne kept an eye on the hoof marks that joined up and mingled with those of several unshod ponies and then led as straight as a macadam road toward the low mountains. They spurred their mounts to a trot again, eyes automatically sweeping from side to side, scanning the clumps of mesquite, yucca, and saguaro for any signs of ambush. Thorne knew that if even a dozen Apaches didn't want to be seen in this terrain, they wouldn't be seen. He prayed they hadn't left a rear guard to cut down any pursuit. The death scene and the trail were both fresh, probably made since dawn. And it was not even midday yet, he calculated with a quick glance at the sun.

They rode another four miles without seeing anything but a few birds and the quick movement of small lizards darting away from their horses' hoofs. The low mountains began to take on a wrinkled, gray-green texture as they gradually approached.

"Whoa! Look here!" Thorne pulled up short and guided his horse carefully around as he stared hard at the ground, reading the sign.

"What is it?"

"Tracks of two shod horses veer off up toward that cañon." He rode slowly along. "The rest of the animals went down to the left this way for another thirty or forty yards and stopped. Then it looks like a couple of unshod ponies turned and followed up that cañon." He looked at Burnett. The hoofprints in the sandy soil plainly showed that the bulk of the horses or mules had paused, milled around, then gone on southwestward along the base of the mountains.

"Let's go," Thorne said, reining his dun back toward the alluvial wash that sloped up into a rocky cañon.

Thorne carried the carbine across his saddle, and Burnett gripped the Colt in one hand as they rode at a walk. He tensed when he saw the two sets of tracks converge and continue straight up the cañon.

They rode another fifty yards. With a start, Thorne jerked up his horse at the sight of an Indian pony that ambled out of the chaparral some forty yards away, casually browsing on some mesquite leaves. A red saddle blanket was askew on the pinto's back, and a rope hackamore trailed from its muzzle.

"Hang onto my horse. I've gotta see what's up ahead," he whispered hoarsely to Burnett. Thorne hit the ground running, carbine in hand.

The floor of the cañon was screened off from their sight by the profusion of desert growth. Thorne knew that no lizard ever crept as cautiously or silently as he did for the next ten minutes while he worked his way forward. Finally the shrubs and cactus thinned, and he slipped up behind a big saguaro to get a better view of the sloping cañon floor.

At first he saw nothing other than the trees at the head of the cañon, more than a half mile away. Then his eyes, in the glaring sunlight, picked out the bodies of two nearly-naked Indians. They were lying sprawled and unmoving on the brownish slope in the open, about twenty yards apart. From the positions of their limbs he knew they were unconscious or dead. He looked uphill beyond the bodies. The slope ended at the base of a vertical wall of gray rock that jutted up about three hundred feet. His gaze moved farther upward to the inevitable vultures, black wings spread and soaring above the mountain. These creatures sensed death. He trusted them to tell him he had nothing to fear from the two Indians on the slope. Were there any others? No. The tracks of the unshod ponies had been only two in number. And the two riders were lying out there in front of him, stone dead. What or who had killed them? He carefully scanned both sides of the narrow cañon. There was no movement, no sign of anything human or animal. The sun was almost overhead, making shadows nearly non-existent. Was there a break in the cañon wall on the left? He moved his head back and forth, and realized an optical illusion had prevented him from distinguishing the cañon wall from a jagged slab of rock that had split off from it. The huge, seamed rock was tilted out from the wall far enough to conceal at least several horses and men at its base.

Even as he studied the rock, he caught a brief flash of sun glinting off metal or glass. His heart leapt. Someone was concealed behind that gigantic rock slab.

He wormed his way backward until he was again in the thick brush, then crouched, and ran back down to where Burnett was impatiently waiting with the horses, his gun drawn.

"Someone's hiding in the rocks up there . . . has ambushed two Apaches," he panted quietly, taking his horse and tying him to a mesquite bush. "And I'd bet my next month's pay that it's Brandau." He couldn't keep his voice from rising with excitement.

"You're not thinking of going up there after him are you?" Burnett's tone expressed incredulity.

"You don't think I've come this far to let him go, do you?"

Burnett shook his head. "The Apaches will come back, looking for their friends, and they'll take care of him. Either that, or the desert will do the job."

"No. I'm going up there to see if I can talk him out."

"If you want to see another birthday, I wouldn't advise it."

"I don't think the Apaches will be back for many more hours. They've got the horses and mules. They're putting some distance between themselves and those killings back on the *playa*. They won't realize these two are overdue until late tonight. Even if they do come back, we've got plenty of time. You can stay here and guard the horses, if you want . . . I'm going up. Tie up your horse and see if you can catch that Indian pony, before he decides to follow up the other band." He checked the carbine to be sure it was fully loaded. Then he dug into his saddlebags and put a double handful of cartridges into his side pockets for the Colt he had thrust through his belt. "If you hear any shooting, come running."

"I'm not standing around here waiting for any Apaches to come back. I'm going to ride down and bring the Earps."

Thorne thought a moment. "Good idea."

"Just promise me one thing," Burnett said, heaving himself into the saddle. "Don't get yourself killed. We've come through all this and about used up our share of luck."

"You've got my word on it." Thorne turned and started away before any more could be said.

When he reached the point where the chaparral thinned out, he worked his way to his left as far as he could go toward the cañon wall whose base still lay at least a hundred feet above and three hundred feet in front of him. But, from there, he was able to get a much better view of the cleft in the wall. From below, it had been almost impossible to see. It was no wonder the Apaches had been ambushed. A man with a rifle and a good eye could have done it from that concealed position before they knew anyone was near.

Shielded behind a thick saguaro, he cupped his hands to his mouth, took a deep breath, and yelled: "Brandau! This is Alex Thorne! Come on out!"

The last of his words reverberated back in a mocking echo from the rock walls, then faded into silence.

There was no response. "I know you're up there, Brandau! I've got three more men coming. You won't get away!" Again the echo bounced back and died.

"Sing out, if you're hurt!" Thorne shouted. The echo shouted back, and then all was silence.

"I'll give you thirty seconds to answer!" he yelled, then began to count slowly to himself. At the end of a minute, he worked the lever of the Winchester, rested his elbows on the ground, bracing the weapon, and sighted on the crack at a point about thirty feet above the base of the wall. He fired. The blast of the shot ripped the peaceful silence, slamming back and forth from the rock walls.

The echo had hardly faded when a shout came from above. "Stop shooting, you fool! You almost hit Ann!"

Thorne felt the blood draining from his face. Julie Ann was in there with him! He felt a tightness in his chest. "Come on out and let's talk!"

Several long seconds of silence dragged by.

"Give it up, Brandau! You can't take us all, like you ambushed those two careless Indians."

A white cloth was thrust into sight on the end of a rifle barrel. "I'm coming out under a flag of truce, but I'm keeping my guns!" Brandau yelled. "I'll meet you halfway."

"Bring . . . Ann with you!" Thorne shouted back, the name sticking in his throat. He wanted both of them where he could see them.

The flag of truce was withdrawn, and several seconds later two figures appeared, walking along the treacherous top of the steep slope.

Thorne got to his feet and started out to meet them. The pair stopped some distance from their sheltering rock, but made no move to descend the slope. Thorne toiled upward, digging the edges of his boot soles into the soft soil. Would Brandau's idea of Southern honor desert him now? The captain could get an easy shot at him as he climbed at an angle, leaning into the hill. He was having a hard time keeping his eyes and his rifle on the couple as he struggled up the steep slope.

Finally, reaching the base of the rock wall, he paused, breathless, before he started gravely toward them. Both men were holding a rifle at their side. Brandau was in shirt-sleeves and hatless. The noon sun shone brightly on the white streak in his hair.

Thorne stopped about six feet from them. Being careful to make no sudden moves, he used his left hand to tip his hat to Julie Ann. "Ma'am."

"You used to call me Julie," she replied, looking directly at him with those disconcerting eyes.

"That was before I knew you as Ann Gilcrease . . . torturer," he replied coldly. His heart was pounding. And it couldn't be entirely attributed to the climb he had just made.

He shifted his gaze to the tall, ex-Confederate officer. "Well, Captain, thanks to the Chiricahuas, your trip to that Pacific plantation took a wrong turn."

"You have a way of kicking a man below the belt, sir, both literally and figuratively. If it's gloating you want to do, go right ahead, since you appear to have the upper hand at the moment."

"It's over, Captain. The two of you are coming back to stand trial for robbery, conspiracy, murder, and whatever else you've been up to," Thorne snapped, suddenly out of patience. "I don't know how you got away from that Apache raid, but all your friends were killed. It's over."

"Sensitivity."

"What?"

"That's how I . . . we . . . got away."

"What are you talking about?"

"My men were all tired and didn't think it necessary to post a sentry last night. Fortunately, I couldn't sleep and heard a horse whinny off in the distance about an hour before dawn. I roused up Ann, and we led two mules off a safe distance in the dark, just in case. We were nearly two miles away by the time it began to get light and we heard some shooting." He paused reflectively. "They paid the price for their laziness."

"Your concern overwhelms me," Thorne said with sarcasm. "And the gold you worked so hard for is scattered all over the *playa*."

The tall man shrugged. "As the Roman emperor, Marcus Aurelius once wrote . . . 'Receive wealth or property without arrogance and be ready to let it go.' We've got enough in our saddlebags to see us out and away until we can start again."

"You're talking like you have a future. You ran up into this cañon and left a trail a blind man could follow. Two Apaches broke off from the main band and followed you, and so did I."

"Too bad for them. We left the mules tethered in those trees at the head of the cañon and climbed up here. You can see what happened, when they tracked the mules." An icy smile. "I can lay an ambush with the best of 'em."

Thorne looked down at the distant bodies. "Long, downhill shots. Damn' good shooting," he said with genuine admiration.

"Thank you, sir." Brandau inclined his head slightly. "I've always been a dead shot with a long arm. It saved me many times during the war."

Thorne's glance took in the pistol that was belted around Julie Ann's slim waist. She was dusty and trail-worn, but her hair had been pulled back out of the way and fastened at the nape of her neck. Just a hint of dark circles under her eyes indicated the several days of stressful flight she had endured.

Then Thorne's eyes returned to Brandau, who cradled a Winchester in the crook of his left arm. He realized with a start that the brace of pistols the captain wore in shoulder holsters were Thorne's own ivory-gripped, nickel-plated

Colts that had been taken from him by Stilwell at the Mowry Mine.

"Figured you'd have been gone from here by now," Thorne said.

"In this country, water is life. We've been filling our canteens from a slow seepage back in the rocks."

Thorne's eyes again sought Julie Ann who was regarding him with that intense, personal interest he remembered so well. The crazed, glassy look in her eyes was gone; she was tired and sober now. He found himself wondering what would have happened if he had met her five or ten years ago. After all, she said she had known of *him* and had followed his career as a Secret Service operative.

"As much as I enjoy a good conversation, I know you're only stalling until your friends arrive," Brandau said. "So, once again, I'll have to say good bye."

"You talk as if you plan to just ride out of this cañon. What makes you think you can get past me?"

Brandau shrugged. "Well, the only thing I can think of . . . is *this!*"

Thorne never saw him move. Swifter than a striking rattlesnake, the captain's right hand came up. A knife blade flashed. Thorne looked down at the stag handle that was protruding from his right arm, just below the elbow. A partially bent arm was the only thing that had saved his abdomen. He gasped at the horrible, sickening pain as his arm went limp, and he dropped the carbine. It was only the space of about two heartbeats, but it seemed much slower as Thorne watched the captain swing down the rifle from the crook of his arm, working the lever and aiming at his belly. It was strictly a survival instinct. Thorne's foot lashed out, kicking the rifle barrel up and sideways. The shot exploded, striking the rock wall at an angle, and the tall man staggered.

Ignoring the pain in his useless right arm, Thorne lunged for his assailant, knocking him into the woman and tangling his arms to keep him from bringing the rifle into play or reaching the guns in his shoulder holsters. There was a searing pain in his elbow as the knife was knocked loose.

But Thorne was fighting for his life, and he sprang behind the taller man before he could twist away, crooking his left arm around the captain's throat. Brandau got his feet under him and gave a mighty backward shove. Both men went off the narrow ledge. Locked together, they tumbled and rolled over and over down the steep slope, loose dirt flinging into Thorne's eyes and mouth. The pain in his elbow was like a hot iron, but he hardly felt it now as he forced himself to keep his left arm locked around the other's neck. He had to prevent Brandau from reaching those shoulder holsters. His head hit a rock, and his senses were reeling even as they slid to a stop.

Thorne threw his legs around Brandau's long torso in a scissors lock. But Brandau slammed his elbow back in a vicious jab, knocking the wind out of Thorne and loosening his grip for a second. In that second, he twisted away. Thorne saw him drawing one of his Colts from the shoulder holster. Brandau was uphill from him. In one awful moment, he realized the captain was out of his reach. The nickeled barrel caught the sunlight as it was brought to bear. The Colt roared, jetting smoke. A slug slammed into Thorne's left thigh, and he went down, groping with his good left hand for the pistol in his own belt. But it was gone, lost in the fall.

Then something big fell on him, nearly crushing him. It was Brandau.

Thorne's pain-fogged brain couldn't comprehend what

was happening. He struggled with a fading feeling. One arm and one leg were not usable. Why didn't Brandau finish him? His assailant was just lying across him, not moving. Thorne forced his mind to focus. He pushed Brandau partially away with his good left arm and saw a red stain spreading across the middle of the captain's white shirt. He had been shot.

Thorne looked back up the hill. Julie Ann stood looking down at them, holding the rifle. Had she shot him? He couldn't see her clearly.

The nauseating pain in his arm and leg reared up to overwhelm him. He felt light-headed, and the high rock wall tilted crazily in his sight. Then he knew nothing more.

CHAPTER TWENTY-TWO

"More bacon?"

"Yeah, thanks." Thorne handed his tin plate to Burnett with his good hand. His throbbing right arm was in a make-shift sling, and he sat on the ground, his wounded left leg straight out in front of him, bound in a torn shirt.

He looked across the campfire at Julie Ann who was eating under the watchful eye of Morgan Earp.

He shifted his weight slightly and leaned back against a saddle to ease the pain in his thigh. The bullet had not hit an artery, but Doc Goodfellow would have to probe for the slug. Thorne hoped the wound wouldn't begin to mortify before they reached Tombstone.

Virgil Earp came over and squatted beside him. "You gonna make it?"

"Sure." He managed a wan smile.

"We should be back in two more days, maybe three, if we go easy. We'll get some whiskey in Arivaca tomorrow to clean those wounds."

"What about the gold?" Thorne's memory of the past two days was intermittent and somewhat hazy.

"We buried it and marked the spot. I'll lead someone back with a team and wagon to get it. I think we'll recover at least three-quarters of what was stolen."

"Thank God that ring of robbers is broken," Thorne said. "We may never recover the guns in Mexico, though."

"Fortunes of war," Burnett said. "General Crook should be glad you got to the bottom of it."

Virgil nodded. "We won't have to reckon with that so-called Rebel Legion any more. Maybe just a scattered hold-up now and then. Nothing organized. But we can deal with that."

"You know, Brady Cox Brandau was quite a man. But I don't think he could quite decide what he wanted to be . . . hedonist, stoic, fatalist, or outraged Southern gentleman."

"He was a little of all those," Burnett remarked, returning with a tin plate of bacon and beans. "Eat hearty. You'll need your strength." He sat down on the ground, picking up his own plate. "No telling what Brandau might have been, if he had funneled all that talent and energy into something legitimate."

"He was a natural leader of men, all right," Thorne agreed.

Because of his wounded elbow, Thorne couldn't wear the shoulder harness, but he put his hand down to touch the rig containing his recovered Colts that lay on the ground beside him. He was trying to think of a way to thank the burly bartender. Finally, he spoke around a mouthful of food. "Damn' good thing you got back there when you did."

"We heard the shooting," Burnett said. "It was all over by the time we arrived." He looked toward Julie Ann. "She gave us no trouble. Didn't try to hide or run. Just surrendered her guns. You knew she shot Brandau, didn't you? We buried him in the cañon."

Thorne nodded. "But was she aiming at *me?*"

"I don't know, but I'd bet she'll claim in court she was trying to save your life. It might get her neck out of a noose."

Thorne's eyes were again drawn to Julie Ann. The firelight was playing over her animated features as she smiled up at the handsome Morgan Earp. Thorne noted that the youngest brother had apparently taken the time and care to comb his hair and was sweeping his mustache with one hand as he laughed at something she said. Had he not known better, Thorne would have seen nothing more than a coquettish young woman being courted by an admiring young man.

But he knew better. He simply could not imagine her hooded figure jerking spasmodically at the end of a hangman's rope. He wondered if prison life would age her or break her spirit.

It turned out to be idle speculation. Before they reached Tombstone, Julie Ann Martin/Ann Gilcrease, the woman of many faces and unknown motives, was gone. She disappeared the next night with a horse, a gun, and a canteen, leaving Morgan Earp with a sore head and a red face to confront the outrage of his older brother.

Wells Fargo and the U.S. government would issue a Wanted flyer for her, of course, but a former spy would have no trouble altering her identity and fading from the stage, Thorne thought. What would happen to her now? Would she change her life style? Maybe somewhere down the months or years he would see her again. Perhaps as a face in a crowded San Francisco restaurant, or on the streets of St. Louis. Would he recognize her? Not likely. Only by some lucky chance would he ever know the end of her story.

As they rode slowly into Tombstone the following afternoon, Thorne smiled to himself at the crestfallen look on Morgan's face. Morgan had just been overmatched. But Alex Thorne, for one, was casting no blame. He knew what it was like. He had been there.